NOWHERE NEAR MILKWOOD

NOWHERE NEAR MILKWOOD

RHYS HUGHES

PRIME BOOKS
Canton, Ohio

NOWHERE NEAR MILKWOOD

———•◆•———

Prime Books, Inc.
P.O. Box 36503, Canton, Ohio 44735
www.primebooks.net

Trade paperback ISBN: 1-894815-11-4
Hardback ISBN: 1-894815-59-9

to Shaswati Ghose

my only friend
in that vast country known as India

(with equally vast respect)

vidyabhilasakupitam nijabalasakhya
tandrya kathamcid anuniya samipanitam
cetoharam pranayinim akhilendriyestam
nidram prasadayitum adya namaskaromi

(She who forsook me, when I fondly burned the midnight
   oil at Fame's false shrine, has now by her young sister
   Sloth—I know not how—been pacified, and home to
   me returned. My yearning heart, I swear, henceforth
   I'll keep constant in worship of my first love, Sleep.)

— Attributed to Laksmidasa

TABLE OF CONTENTS

MARTYR TO MUSIC

IN THE MOONLESS GUTTER

I was walking down Habershon Street, heading towards a party. I had my banjo in its battered case, a real happy instrument, untuned but as sexy as a suspender belt snap. There was power in my right hand. I was hoping to perform for the guests in return for something, I don't know what, a bowl of peanuts maybe. Darren was waiting for me there with his fringe. He was a generous, mutant host.

My band, Disability Bill & the Cussmothers, had revolutionised the local music scene. Everyone knew where it was at now. Except me, who forgot to look when it changed. I could taste the anger in the air. The fumes of this lovely lowly city slapped me in the face. Cars roared sly mockery as they sped past. I offered a wave in return, kissed them all, cast my lips like wedges of cheese.

People always ask me where I get my ideas from. They say: "Bill, where exactly do you get your ideas from?" And I just evasively hunch my multiple shoulders. But at last I'm willing to let you know the answer. Why friends, I get my best ideas from the moonless gutter. It must be a moonless one, or the idea will fool nobody and appear as it is: like the torn ear of an old teddy in a box.

In the moonless gutter, if you are lucky, you too might be able to find some ideas. This is how you go about it. Leave your cares behind, on the mantelpiece if you like, and stroll out with a bottle of arrack. The tongue will burn like a flag in some Iraqi city during a time of suitable crisis. As you walk, don't bother to look where you're going.

Take regular sips from the bottle.

When you've finished and reality is not quite the place it was, sit on the pavement and let the cars flow past like wavelets on a stinking beach. Roll the bottle under the wheels of a vehicle. The driver might stop and greet you directly. He may, or may not, strike you over the head with a bat. If he does, then rejoice, for the gutter will seem moonless whatever the time of day.

This is the method I choose for my inspiration. In the centre of the city, somebody is guaranteed to strike you over the head. The ideas become songs. For example, a song came to me while I was lying all but unconscious after being clubbed and left to choke in my own blood in a particularly moonless, almost starless, gutter last week. It was the song I planned to play at the party.

But I wasn't there yet. I was still walking down Habershon Street, which is a street where the houses look all the same. Suddenly this girl came up to me. She was pretty: about twenty, tall, slim with long black hair cascading over her shoulders, and she wore black satin trousers and a dark top exposing a bare golden midriff. She asked if I was interested in business. That's what she asked.

"Why yes," I replied, "actually I'm thinking about opening a small ironmongery or maybe a shipyard."

She burst into tears and sat down, with the drops cascading down her sculpted cheeks. I tried to cheer her up. I sat right next to her, in the moonless gutter, and I took out my instrument and I struck a dim chord. I played 'Gallows Pole' and one half of 'Duelling Banjos', which was an easy win for me. But she wasn't cheered. It was probably beyond her appreciation. Youngsters know nothing about music. So I finished and wiped my snotty talent on my sleeve.

"What's your name?" I asked.

"Selene," she sobbed.

"Well, come to the party," I urged.

What do you know, she did.

*

Darren wasn't at the door to greet us, but thankfully his wife was, and she kissed my cheek and I said: "Thank you." She looked bewildered and answered: "Nobody has ever thanked me for a kiss before." Her name was June, but she was a bit late for the season, which was winter. In a low voice, I introduced my new friend as my girlfriend. I don't believe she was deceived. There were fifty people in the house, most in the kitchen. Only one in the lounge. Just dandy.

"Where's your band, Bill?" I was asked.

"I lost them getting here," I said, "but it doesn't matter because I want to try out a new solo set."

The fridge was full of beer and the chairs were loaded with cats. That's the way I like it, especially when I don't have a choice. Darren turned up soon enough, with a pet monkey balanced on his shoulder, but when I mentioned it, he denied it. I stroked it anyway. He looked just a bit uncomfortable. I wondered where the people were going to dance. The rooms were too narrow for strutting your stuff, unless you did it partly up the stairs, which can be tiring.

Darren had this amazing way of moving, a sort of glide. Then I saw he was balanced on rollerskates and that the carpets had been removed to facilitate his locomotion. The trundle of his wheels on the floorboards was real bluesy. I imagined myself back in the delta, though I've never been there, on a lonely night at a station, waiting for a train to come and chug me to where the *southern cross the dog*, whatever that means. I feel rather than know things.

"What does his monkey play?" I asked June.

"His organ, do you mean?"

"That sounds about right," I agreed.

She went off to deal with some other guests who were lonely. There were a few faces I recognised. Brian was there, and Woody, and Mike from Pink Towers, who everyone said was gay, but who never tried it on with me during my entire stay. I guess I have too many knees for his hands. Or perhaps he just didn't fancy me.

I briefly spoke to Ros, who was an artist for book covers. She was insistent that I serve as a model for some appallingly bad novel. I was tingling with a peculiar passion as she prodded me over, calculating the angles of my monstrous contours.

"How many shoulders do you have, Bill?"

"More than several," I responded.

She smiled. "Don't shrug. I might lose count."

"I have a larger share of other things too," I said. "Sometimes my disability has many advantages."

"But I don't need those for the book."

I think she had an eye on my new girlfriend. Ros is like that. She is an equal and opposite reaction to Mike. That's fine by me, for I'm a bohemian type. I really enjoy my gay friends, because having them makes me look tolerant and progressive, whereas the mirror just makes me look hideous. I even prefer cleaning my teeth in front of a gay friend. But I was fully accepted here. Darren was a mutant too. He hid it well. It was all in the fringe. His hair had a life of its own, like tentacles, like worms, like little licks of despair.

When I reached the centre of the kitchen, on my way to the fridge for a beer, I found myself teetering on the edge of a deep circular pit. Nobody held me back, so I saved myself. I must have sweated in anguish for a full minute, as I tottered on the rim. But I pulled back at last and wiped a cuff across my brow.

"A bottomless hole," explained June.

"How did that happen?" I cried.

"It's a sculpture of one of Ros's paintings. She usually paints a picture from a model, but she didn't have a model of a bottomless hole, so she did the painting first and then made the hole. Just for the sake of consistency, you understand."

I peered once again over the lip. The circular pit was shaped like a funnel, unless that was a trick of perspective. The opening was like a new moon, a non-moon, or maybe a lunar eclipse without a gutter to loom over. That was disturbing. There couldn't be anything at the bottom, because it didn't have one, but my mind loaned a brooding presence to the base of this deep nothingness.

"What was the painting for?" I wondered.

June answered: "A book about the pitfalls of the publishing world. We had no room for the model anywhere else. We want to buy a new carpet anyway, so it's fine right there."

"A book about the music business would need an even deeper pit," I joked, but nobody cared to giggle.

"Where do you get your ideas from?" asked Brian.

"From the flat field?" prompted Woody.

I let my guard down. "Never. In the flat field I could get bored. I find them in the moonless gutter."

"How reliable is that?" they chimed.

"You'll see," I promised.

The girl I came in with had wandered into a dark corner, attracted by the relative emptiness like a magnet to an iron eyebrow. I decided to play there, for romantic reasons.

I knew there was something wrong as soon as I plucked the first note. It wasn't the one I was expecting. And the first step of my dance bore very little resemblance to the routine I'd worked out. I was confused but the solution was simple enough. The idea I got from the moonless gutter the previous week had been superseded by another. Then I realised I had sat in another gutter to comfort Selene when she commenced weeping. The idea from *that* moonless gutter must have replaced the other one. This wasn't too bad, certainly not a disaster. It just meant I was unprepared for my own set. Frequently that can be an improvement. I might impress myself as much as the audience. I hoped that would be the case now, so I went with my destiny and continued playing.

As if through a fog, I saw Darren's monkey clapping its hands. Then I wondered if ideas aren't the only things which can be deliberately or accidentally picked up in moonless gutters. And maybe gutters aren't the only places to pick up such things. What if types of jungle beast can be acquired while, say, balancing on rollerskates? Maybe Darren didn't even know he had a monkey living on him. That's a terrible thought, isn't it? But it helps to explain all manner of apes and their locations. Climbing flights of steps while weighed down with gibbons, making an extra pot of tea for perched chimps, showering under the shadow of a gorilla: all of them unfruitful responsibilities.

I continued to pluck notes and dance. I did this faster and faster. Each step of my dance followed a note. I know that's not original, but I think it sometimes still works.

Then it was done. I bowed politely.

"What the heck was that?" spluttered June.

"Was it a crate?" asked Ros.

"Was it a rusting crane?" suggested Brian.

"I thought it was a bag of nails," offered Woody.

"Or a capstan," sniffed Mike.

"No, it was an adjustable spanner."

"Surely it was a porthole?"

"A mast without a sail."

"A saw with seventy-three teeth."

"A frayed orange hammock."

I was shocked. "It was a song, wasn't it?"

"Whatever it was," said Darren slowly, "it wasn't a song. It looked like all the items and objects one might find in an ironmongers or maybe a shipyard. Tools, cables, rails."

"You mean the notes were solid?"

"Yes, and they had definite practical shapes."

I stamped my feet. There was minor thunder in the house. I shouted with joy: "This is marvellous! I have all the stock I need to set up in business! The music world can go hang itself. I'm tired of the headaches involved in the creative life. Exhausted with all the worries and little insecurities, the relentless doubts, the struggles. This is much better. And I'll set up my ironmongery *inside* the radius of a shipyard. With all those items, that's what I can do."

"That's incorrect," said June.

"Why?" I almost screamed.

"Because those objects no longer exist."

"How?" I nearly shrieked.

"Your dance kicked them down the pit," she said.

"A funky dance," added Darren.

I believed him, but it was small consolation. I took it anyway, but I had to give it back. He wasn't referring to my performance. No, he was looking into the future. He was making a prediction about himself. For suddenly, he skated directly into the mouth of the bottomless pit. I ran forward and peered over the edge. He had plunged in at a tangent and was now skating on the sides of the hole, round and round, down and down, in a tight spiral. Like dishwater.

His speed increased rapidly and his fringe awakened. Abortive style kept the hair fastened to the man, and centrifugal force kept the man fastened to the circular wall. His monkey glanced up and our eyes met. I saw a touch of madness in its look and a pinch of infinite sadness. Then it turned its head away and started spanking Darren with one of its very long arms. Enough monkeys have been spanked by enough men in history to justify one getting its own back.

This spanking had a slow calculated rhythm. Darren waved his arms, swung his hips, wobbled his knees.

"That's the funky dance," I said bitterly.

"He won't stop until he gets to the bottom," murmured June. "He's done this before. It's a habit."

"Impossible. If the pit goes down forever, he can only skate into it once. You contradict yourself."

"It's just a model," she hissed.

"Will he set up in business down there?"

"He might," she snorted.

I licked my lips and asked: "What did you think of my performance? Be honest. What was it *like*?"

June remained silent, so I turned and appealed to the gathering as a whole. There was a brief pause. "What was it like?" they echoed. "What was it like?" Then they all leaned forward together and whispered their verdict. It was the same verdict from every mouth. It was very honest. Because they whispered it at the same time, the result was a deafening wind that knocked me back. I fell and crushed my banjo. Then I regained my feet and ran out of the house.

It was the worst verdict I'd ever been given.

What had I done to deserve it? As I pounded the slabs of Habershon Street, I realised my mistake. The girl I'd taken to the party was named Selene. That's the word in an old language for *moon*. And I had sat with her in the gutter. So the gutter hadn't been entirely moonless! The idea which controlled my song was false. These revelations shuddered me right into town. I felt awful. I wandered aimlessly, peering in at the windows of clubs and cafés, not with envy but with shame. I wanted to be just a dark shape outside bright glass.

At one window, the window of a restaurant, I stopped. I recognised the people who were seated around a table. The table was laden with food but they weren't eating. It was the Cussmothers, the band entire, devoid only of me, who was a nullity. Without me, they seemed to have increased in number. They made strange gestures with their hands, never smiling. I realised two things at the same instant. The first was that they had won a recording contract and were celebrating. The second was that all bands who win recording contracts are inducted into a secret society which may one day control the whole world.

They were learning how to shrug, wave and point like members of the Illuminati. I didn't resent this. I left them to it and resumed my walk. Having dozens, maybe hundreds, of feet makes even the loneliest walk too fast to be anything other than comical. That's my punishment. But I felt sick for a different reason. My last performance had been rated with the worst of all possible metaphors.

So what *was* it like?

The torn ear of an old teddy in a box.

ADVENTURES IN THE GRIN TRADE

Here's one regular bill you weren't expecting. It's me, Disability Bill, fresh from the Cussmothers, that crew of stale traitors and secret agents. I'd just started my solo career, not strictly through choice, and I was looking for gigs in various places. Trouble is, the Cardiff scene is largely sewn up, like old pajamas worn by a lusty girl over a very long history of loving. Talking of such women, I met one eventually, but not just yet. That's later. I worked for her in one sense; waited for her in another, a more foreboding type of sense. That isn't my favourite type, but I'll take what I can. Senseless not to.

Tramping the Cardiff streets was demoralising business, all in all, not to mention none in none, which is the number of gigs I secured in my selected venues. I shuffled down to the Docks, but they didn't want me in the *TALL STORY*. It was an Open Mike Night, the first he'd played since his botched operation. Lengths of intestine like real organ pipes. Back along City Road, the *INDIGO CASBAH* was throbbing to its own booked bands, several hundred of them by the din of it, all playing unconnected things in different sections of the enormously complex interior. I didn't bother to lose myself in that maze.

I tried the *BIG BIRD GULP*, but found it exceedingly seedy. Nor did the *COGITO & DOUBT* fill me with confidence. They had a tubthumping band and the subsequent leaks were serious. I hunched far past. Get the picture? Something was happening in the *HERMETIC TRADITION*, but I never learned what, because that venue has no win-

19

dows or doors and the people inside are forever sealed, and maybe by now they've regressed into a species which doesn't want to come out, and I had no pressing need to go in once I thought about what I've just said, though I won't denigrate all cannibals, because I knew one who lived under a bridge, played a mean sax and gave me good advice.

What he told me came into my memory now. There was a place where anyone could find a gig, but it wasn't a pub. It was a completely different city, some fifty miles west of Cardiff as the crow flies, gibbon swings, puppet dreams (stiff not sweet). A brutal place with monstrous citizens who dwelled in houses erected on the slopes of hills. They ate seaweed, not frequently, but often enough for it to be a smell as well as a rumour. The waters which lapped the shores gave up its plants reluctantly and the tension on the beach was unbearable. So almost nobody ever went there. But gigs really were abundant.

It was my last chance. I was broke and had lots of little mouths to feed, all my own. I couldn't even afford to travel to this other city. I had to hitch a ride. Think it easy to hitch when you have extra thumbs? It's not. Cars don't stop for you. Even when the drivers aren't scared of my shape, they're overwhelmed by the number of parallel requests for a lift, and so unconfident of carrying such an apparently immense number of passengers at once, they forget to brake. It almost made amputation seem profitable. On the other hand, I'm squeamish about blades, so cancel that thought. Don't mind chopping and changing my mind on this subject, but not my thumbs. I needed a plan.

I soon had one. I walked out of the centre of Cardiff, through the outer suburbs of the north, and stood on the side of the motorway sliproad. In a pocket I keep a sentimental stocking. It wasn't given to me by a girlfriend but by a shop mannequin. In fact, I'd taken it without permission, but the expression in the dummy's eyes seemed to say, 'Go ahead, I just want you to be happy,' and I obliged. I was chased out by security. Now at last it would serve a useful purpose. I rolled up one trouser leg and drew the silk thing on. It tickled. Then I secured it with a garter I'd snatched from the same shop. It sure looked pretty.

All my other legs took one step backward into the bushes. I was inside the bushes, but my alluring leg, just the one, remained outside on view. So I hid and waited for results. Now the motorists sounded their horns as they passed. The wind whipped the top of my thigh, which was creamy and exposed. I lacked the high-heeled shoe for a perfect display, but it turned out mine was good enough, for a car pulled up and waited for me to get in. I rushed out and yanked the door before the driver could lock it. Then I jumped into the seat beside him. His disappointment was vast, but it was too late to speed away.

"Where to?" he grumbled.

"Swansea," I replied. "It's my destination."

He glanced at my abundance of legs. "Why not run there? I reckon you could make it in about an hour."

"That would use up my spare energy."

"So what's in the case?"

"My banjo," I said, and I lifted it out and played him a few bars of an obscure Kentucky number, 'I Feel Like Turkey Dressed Up As Chicken Tonight', from the oven archives.

He whistled low. "Bluegrass?"

"Yes, but what images does it evoke?"

"An old pigdog walking round and round on an unmown lawn, prior to curling up to sleep," he answered.

"What manner of pigdog?"

He pondered carefully. "Doomed."

"Does he flatten the vegetation under his body?"

"Of necessity, he does."

I smirked. "That's because my banjo has been crushed. I sat on it. The song was supposed to be a straight scratch-'n'-peck tune, but the stalks of the crotchets have been trampled flat. Those notes should wave above the rhythm majestically. Doggone it!"

"No, he's still there," he said.

And that's how the rest of the journey proceeded. Puns, innuendoes, all meaningless, but anything to stave off the subject which drivers and hitchers always talk about, or rather which drivers lecture on and hitchers are forced to listen to, namely how they (the drivers) used to be hitchers in their youth *before they became businessmen* and how great it is to be free on the road, but let them reveal how successful they are at business, they're *THIS* successful, made their first million just before they were a millionaire, made their second after, but have nothing to show for it, due to a mysterious force called exaggeration, which always gets in the way, but observe the suit and dental work!

Outside, there was nothing much to look at . . .

In a field to our right we passed a mansion which my driver claimed was an asylum for people who believed they could change into animals. It was run by a German inventor.

"I bet he has a name," I asserted.

"Don't know, don't care neither, just making small talk, trying to help you avoid certain other themes."

"It might be Karl," I suggested.

He nodded. The mansion receded behind us. He didn't like my game, so we reverted to facile banter.

But as we turned off the motorway and wove through the outskirts of Swansea, he grinned at me.

"Why do you want to be here?"

I said, "I'm looking for gigs. I'm a professional. I need to find work or else I'm finished. I'm starving."

His grin became a laugh. Air passed between it in both directions and sounds of mirth arose, which my ears drank, but I have too many for all to be properly satisfied. The ones on my head sipped the most; those on my hips the least. He explained:

"I'm a music reviewer and I'm going to review music."

"Is that a tautology?" I wondered.

"No, but I know of a place, the place I'm driving to, which has a big gap in its lineup for tonight."

"I'd love to play there!" I cried.

"Then come all the way with me," he said.

I mumbled: "So you're not a businessman after all? Our avoidance of commercial talk was wasted effort."

"Yes, because we could have ignored the topic without trying. But it's pointless to fret about that. Worry instead about the frets on your spoiled banjo. Do they still operate?"

"After a fashion," I admitted.

"Which one precisely?"

"Pigdog," I said, and clarified the point when he frowned: "Everything I play will be a grunting howler."

"Can you inflate the object?"

"It's an instrument, not an ego," I pointed out.

"Don't fiddle with it, then."

"Can't. I have an oily curtsey, but no waxed bow. I won't scrape along. I'll pick it like a boxer's nose."

Yes, that's what it was, flattened eternally, unlike my ambitions which still yearned to swell, to rise and parade and demand a single pat on each one of my shoulders, which is equivalent to the greatest praise accorded to anyone in the whole of reality. As we drove through the streets of this city which wasn't Cardiff, I saw that the scene here could never be sewn up. It should have flapped open like a worn curtain, thin and agitated, in bluster and sigh, but rusting things weighed it down. These stood on the horizon, metal tanks and towers which sprouted pipes. A place of ancient industry, but I felt a curious elation. I didn't yet appreciate the difference between sewn and stitched.

My driver, the music reviewer, told me his name was Goodbut, a name which had destined him for that job from his birth, for reviews always contained his name somewhere in their text, even if written by someone else, as in ' . . . this tune is very good, but . . . ' It was essential, he revealed, to keep a tight rein on his enthusiasm, in case he was proved wrong later by the opinion of posterity. I believed him, nearly. We rattled down many streets and more streets, and the complicated layout of Swansea wasn't shy. It demonstrated itself openly, behind closed terraces, and the cobbles hurt my buttocks. But something's always doing that somewhere, I have such a surplus, and I don't mind.

We stopped in a region of the city called The Uplands, where the local bohemians like to cavort, and Goodbut indicated the venue which had a gap, the *UPLANDS TAVERN*, and I agreed to examine it more carefully. I got out and he followed me through the entranceway. It was dark inside, cold, muted, matted and rough, with a circular bar in the centre of the big main room around which one could stroll or prance at varying speeds, if one had the inclination, and a few recesses and little rooms and booths on the edges which were bare but strangely smelled of carpets. I think it was the breath of drunkards passing over hairy tongues. The stage wasn't very spacious, but it would serve.

The publican stepped forward and greeted my companion. He tickled me under a random chin.

"Is this your pet monster?"

"No," said Goodbut. "He's an act."

"Used to front the Cussmothers," I confirmed.

"Well, I'm sorry for you," the publican said, and he seemed at a loss, not knowing whether or how to comfort me, and the ensuing silence was awkward, so I broke it fast:

"I need a gig. Bottom of the bill will suit me."

They both rolled their eyes. "That's impossible! There's only one space left and it's at the very top."

I blinked twenty eyelids. "What?"

"The support acts have already been arranged. It's a great lineup down there, each one leaning on the one directly below, the base one hoping to curve right round and lean on the top one, which hasn't been secured yet, though we hope it'll be you."

"That's an unusual setup," I said.

"Sure it is, but we're not in Cardiff now. Take a look at this poster for the evening. Read the names. There's a space above Toni Trumpet, isn't there? That's what you have to fill."

I studied the sheet. It was laminated and printed in a nice selection of coloured inks, a different hue for each name. Beneath Toni Trumpet was an act called The Rag Foundation; below them Grampa Chaff; under him Satori, a bunch of progressive rockers; beneath them a singer-songwriter by the name of Bridget Wells. Including me, five acts, one for each finger of a standard hand, or for each one of other things with five elements, the cool minutes of a *take*, west coast, difficult timings, or the outer moons of Uranus, or strained similes in a single too clever sentence like this one, or the lovers you deserve tonight, no more nor less, and the regrets which just happen at weekday noons.

The publican was talking to Goodbut behind my back, or behind one of my backs, unaware that another section of me was directly facing them and in a position to hear everything they said. It wasn't polite. It wasn't uncommon. The publican asked my driver why he had given me a lift in the first place, bearing in mind the extreme foulness of my shape, its lack of redeeming qualities, its horror.

I leaned into the conversation and said, "He didn't mean to help me. I tricked him. I hedged my butts."

"Unfair enough!" the publican returned.

I demanded: "Why is there a gap at the top of the list? That displays bad organisation, doesn't it?"

The publican beamed. "In Swansea, *bad* is a high standard to attain. But originally there wasn't any room. We booked a fellow from Africa by the name of Franco Luambo Makiadi, but he didn't arrive. I suspect this is because he died in 1989."

"Bill fits the bill instead," Goodbut said.

"I like the UPLANDS TAVERN already," I confessed, and it was true, I did. So the publican bought me a round of complimentary drinks and I sat at a table and drank them.

It was still early, so the wait was long and I had time to get drunk and sober up again afterward. Goodbut went out to buy writing materials, so he could do his review from where he sat or stood or danced, depending on how good any of the bands were. I considered what to play when my turn came. I was working again.

The evening wasn't here yet, but I'd already decided on my favourite song in the world, which was a very big little number, an infinite smallish blues, you might say, called 'And Dug The Pigdog A Tomb.' Maybe you know it? Famous it is, among the avant garde, and just right, I surmised, for the bohemian set who I'd been led to believe patronised this pub. An Irish man wrote the original, but my own variation was far better, at least for my present circumstances.

My banjo mightn't be equal to the task, but that didn't matter, because any song which stretches into infinity is never going to be completed, and so doesn't require a final chord, that last ringing sound which permits its listeners to appreciate or dismiss the song as a whole. Hard to judge *fine* or *poor* when something isn't there, and a song can't really be there until it's done, and this one was undone by definition from the start, and yet it still had a melody and words. That is how I was going to deceive the mob at my feet. I'm a cunning ugly.

Goodbut came back and joined me. We sank a few more pints of beer and finished our waiting together. The pub slowly filled up. Then the acts themselves started to arrive. Some had lots of equipment. A few just had guitars and mouths. First on was going to be Bridget Wells, an attractive and witty woman who (it emerged) had carried her instrument to Tenerife to give its neck and notes a tan. It certainly looked healthy. I guessed its sound would be exotic but just a little melancholy. I wasn't right, nor was I entirely wrong. I couldn't take any of my eyes off her and that's unusual when I have so many in reserve, and I felt unguarded and vulnerable for the first time in my mutant life.

I reckon it must have been about an hour after sunset when the indoor night properly began. The audience had been chatting away to themselves but now they mostly hushed, and chairs were angled to point at the stage. Bridget was already up there, slowly tuning her instrument, but she didn't have spotlights, just crimson candles all around her. There were two other musicians next to her, some guys named Marc and Tich, and the resultant sound was a web of chords which shouldn't be brushed aside, because it enhanced rather than tangled the shadows. One of her songs was called 'Rage Inside' and contained the line, "stay away from the dark one", and several people around my table took her advice and moved away from me. But anyway, Bridget was the lusty girl in pajamas whom I referred to earlier, but she didn't actually wear pajamas. She wore purple dungarees. Consider the pajamas a symbol for something else, whatever you like. I know what I like. It's her. She was talented and flirtatious, but I realised instantly she was not for me.

Then it was the turn of Satori. They played complex fusion jazz and its prog rock nephew with panache and ease. The bass player had funky thumbs and a fringe like rain to hide behind, a weather reporter turned sniper. That's not my metaphor, but Goodbut's, which I cribbed when I leaned over and took a peek at what he was scribbling, in the glare from the cigarette lighter of the girl who sat next to me. This band ambushed my expectations in other areas too, especially in the reeds. The utterly bald singer used his remarkably powerful voice to great effect in all the songs, particularly in the symphonic composition 'On The Steps At The Front Of My House With A Mobile Phone', and the epic finale, a song titled 'Red Haired Wife'. At one point he sang without amplification. He didn't need it. And it was cheaper.

Grampa Chaff was a more primitive act. He played his anatomy with mallets. They weren't soft mallets neither. His ribs were a xylophone with a surprising range of tone colours. His heavy skull was a gourd, like one of those pumpkin drums I'd heard they have in Slovenia. He was an old fellow, broken veins all over his face, but maybe they were due to impact injuries rather than age. Yes, in fact, if it wasn't for his giveaway name, I don't think I'd have been able to judge his age at all. There was too much blood for one thing. It poured out of his nose and ears and puddled on the floor but nobody in the audience raised an eyebrow. This was Swansea. I was the only one who clapped at the end. The pub was filled to bursting with applause. But it wasn't that the listeners didn't appreciate his music, just that they were very cool, and he seemed to realise this. Goodbut had written a single word in his notebook: "Knockout!" But this was plainly a lie. Grampa was still moving!

The Rag Foundation were a folk rock outfit, which makes them sound like the sort of citizens who wear cardigans under studded leather jackets, but I soon learned to keep that sort of archaic opinion to myself, or to lose it altogether and honestly change my mind, because a fool in the audience made a similar remark and the fiddle player, a petite but ferocious woman named Kate threw her violin at his head. It bounced off and back into her hand in the middle of a solo, and this tiny pause added to the phlegmatic power of the song, in the same way that a sigh contributes to a laugh over dinner at your best friend's house, when something has gone sour but it's a feeling instead of a rational certainty, and the song which was improved by this act of violence was about miners or cider or possibly love, or all three, a lovestruck miner drowning in a large vat of cider, and I knew this combo were the real thing, and that their shadows on the wall behind the stage would never usurp them.

I asked Goodbut: "Why are none of these acts better known outside the Swansea area? It's strange."

He shook his head. "Not really. This city exists apart from the rest of the universe. It is protected by obscurity and always will be. Even if (for example) Napoleon was still alive and tried to conquer Europe again, but without making any mistakes this time, he couldn't get as far as Swansea. All thanks to the miasma."

It explained everything, this miasma, which wasn't a physical smell but a psychic stench. You could blink at it only with the third eye, the mind's eye, and I had many of those, thrice three at least, so I understood and felt pity for myself. Mental blocks were the best defence against it, so I thanked my reluctance to ever enter therapy and have mine cured. But to be honest, I did once try to visit a therapist. He ejected me the moment I crossed his threshold. He didn't want to be infected with madness and I can't really say I blame him. He won't say the same for me, because I *was* to blame, apparently. So it goes.

"Besides," he added, "some of these acts *have* played in foreign parts. The miasma must form a variable shield which can be penetrated on rare occasions. Don't tell Napoleon!"

I noticed that there was a problem with the timing of the evening. The pub had to close at 11 PM, half past at the very latest, and it was already quarter to the hour. But The Rag Foundation were closing their set and I felt happier, for I assumed that because I was heading the bill, the other remaining act would make room for me by playing less songs. This was not to be. I clapped my myriad hands even more vigorously now, hoping to hurry the band off the stage with the noise. It almost worked. But they were going anyway, so perhaps not. I gave myself credit for it anyway. I like to do that. I'm very lonely.

Now Toni Trumpet got up alone and puffed some stuff. But no, I'm not going to describe what it was like. It was too paradoxical . . . the weird and impossible colour of azure red . . . the beat of a monkey's wings . . . the sheen of vacuum, density of hope, awe of epicycles . . . I can't say whether there was one song there, several or many, or none at all. The music was inside my head already, a distant and unobtainable memory, and it sprang awake for the first time. So there was novelty and nostalgia at exactly the same moment . . . Wheels inside my soul had been set in motion, springs I never knew I owned were winding down and powering unique feelings in my heart in the same way that windmills can be employed to drain knees, stir pots of stew or ventilate shipyards, anything unexpected but perfectly valid, just never attempted before.

The audience was spellbound and from the darkest corners watched things not human or alive. I realised they were the angles where walls met the ceiling. Even geometry had been seduced by the gutsy magic. That's quite a first, I think. I've never heard of that happening before. I suspect they cried afterward, those intersecting planes, slaves to theorems, tasting amusement on their sentient debuts.

It was done. One minute to the hour. Sixty seconds left to perform my infinite song! I didn't think it was possible. Yet I wasn't ready to give up faith. I needed some sort of reputation, I was desperate for recognition, and this was the only opportunity within sight. So I hefted my banjo like a frying pan and mounted the stage.

I was going to play an *extract* from my song. At the start of the gig, I'd planned to play as much of it as possible. I'd revised this intention when Bridget, Satori, Grampa and Rag had run over their alloted times. Toni had kept it trim, but only in the same way that life is short, which is always a saying but only generally a truth or feeling. It had became clear to me that I should just play a dozen verses of 'And Dug

The Pigdog A Tomb', and then just one verse, and then just one line, and then just one bar, and then just one chord, but now I knew it ought to be only one note, a single note, the best note in my favourite song, the best note in musical history, the one perfect note.

That's all I had time for, but it was enough. The note in question and also in answer was G sharp, not any old G sharp, but the G sharp in the sixth line of the 498th repeated verse of 'And Dug The Pigdog A Tomb', a G sharp which is superior to all other G sharps in all other compositions due to its context, what came before and after, but I was going to attempt the audacious and remove it from its context while retaining its quality of ultimate superiority. If I could pull that off, I could tug anything, so guard your hair and teeth, doubters!

Much later, when I sat in a different bar on my own, I worked out how it had gone wrong. Do you know the words to the song I chose? They loop round on themselves, which explains how that tune lasts forever. The first line is a standard opening. It goes, "A pigdog came on the lawn," and the second line continues, "and walked around alone", and it's like a promise of a lazy story, but the third line subverts this by saying, "Then gardener swung a hoe," and the fourth adds, "and broke its funny bone", to which the fifth line responds, "Then all the pigdogs came grunting", which may not have been deliberate of them, but in fact was, because, "and dug the pigdog a tomb", is the sixth line, and the seventh explains what they did with this tomb, which was "And they carved upon its door," and now the eighth explains why, "for the eyes of pigdogs to come", at which sombre point the song reverts to the first line again, which is the text they carved there: "A pigdog came on the lawn . . . "

And on and on to eternity. Dig it?

Actually it's a horrid song, because the pigdog wasn't dead when they dug it a tomb, just injured in the elbow joint, and they ended up burying it alive while it begged for mercy.

Like I said, this is a variation on the original, but popular music works that way. I'm not bothered by accusations of plagiarism or anything of the sort. Besides, what does it matter to me? Can I be sued in court? I hardly even own a crust of bread. More likely that a crust of bread somewhere in this wide world owns me! I'm pretty certain it does, the only pretty thing I can ever be, so I cling tight to it. That's a tendency I have. What's yours? Don't care to examine that, I bet.

Anyway, I ditched most of the song long before Toni Trumpet came down from the stage, but by the time I was climbing up on it, I'd resolved to pluck my note, the ultimate G sharp, as I've mentioned. The audience licked its lips, unsure of whether I was a solo player or a band. I like that ambiguity. It's my version of androgyny, a look very many musical stars cultivate. I can't do that, I have too many masculine chests to depilate, too many rugged cheeks to powder, so I just make the most of what I've got, which is lots of much. My support acts were watching me too, drinking and relaxing after their performances, and I briefly considered dedicating my perfect note to Bridget. Fear of rejection prevented me, rejection not just by the woman in question, but by the fabric of the cosmos for daring to presume too much. She was lovely.

I stood there and flexed my thumb.

To my astonishment, Goodbut called out a request: "That obscure Bavarian number, if you please."

"Which one do you mean?" I muttered.

He said, "'I Feel Like Hound Dressed Up As Swine Tonight'," and I realised he was trying to assist me, trying to make the pigdog soul of my banjo seem deliberate and right.

I loved him for that. Music reviewers don't earn enough money in my opinion. He was able to keep his car on the road, true, yet I still think he deserved a small wage increase.

But I retorted, "Don't know that one."

He shuddered just a little, and I added, "No, my set for tonight is sure to be remembered in myth long after the destruction of Bavaria, however and whenever that happens."

"Because," I continued, "it's the best . . . "

And then I roared, "Listen!"

31

And I plucked the G sharp. And it flew out of my banjo and filled the pub to its most hidden corner.

I knew something had gone amiss before the ripple of sound struck the nearest tables to the stage. I wanted to run forward, pull off my coats and gather it up, this ripple, whose circumference was already growing bigger than any item of clothing. Yes, gather it up and push it back into my instrument! But I stayed where I was and let the damage make itself known. It did. I leaned over and blew out the crimson candles which had been left flickering to themselves since Bridget arranged them there, for I craved darkness for the payback.

What had I done? What was my mistake?

Playing a sharp on a flattened instrument! The note just wasn't right. It was shifted a semitone backward, which wouldn't have mattered usually, it'd just be a major tone, but not in this case, because I had suggested the context with the note, as I indicated earlier. A bum note. It was *infinitely* bum. That stinks. So I flushed. My embarrassment was severe enough to calcify hedgehogs. That's warm.

The glow of my shame returned sunset to the interior. The UP-LANDS TAVERN boiled itself alive. The people ran out. Somebody was plucking at my sleeve. It was Goodbut.

He said, "You imbecile! You're finished."

We ran away somewhere. Turned out we were headed toward the only late night drinking venue in this part of Swansea, a bohemian place called MOZART'S. It was just down the road. I don't believe Goodbut wanted to go there with me, but the momentum of acquaintance carried me through the doors in his wake. It was cramped inside. Most of my audience were already there, together with my support acts. They tolerated me without a flicker of compassion. This was good enough for me. I didn't expect any sort of forgiveness. No quarter, not by half. I moved into the back room, which was slightly less full.

I recognised one person there, Brian, who I'd last met at Darren's party a few weeks before. He sat with his friends, Chris, Pete, Reshmi, Louise, and his hairstyle, Ginger. He guessed something was up, so he treated me like an unwanted bill, which is the overused pun I truly was.

He deferred me indefinitely, like the climax of my song. It still hasn't been performed in its entirety, so I've heard.

Somebody had left a newspaper at the bar, so I perched awkwardly on a stool and sat reading it. Anything to appear unobtrusive. The front page was bursting with news about trouble in distant lands. Lots of revolutions had broken out at the same time. The nations of Africa, the Americas and Asia had overthrown their governments. There were angry mobs in every street demanding globalisation and a single world state. As they marched to victory they sang anthems. I recognised these. I'd written them with the Cussmothers. The songs from our first (unsuccessful) album. It was clear what had happened. The secret societies had finally made their move. My former colleagues ruled much of the planet now. I felt like the fifth Beatle or the sixth sense, left out of things but still there, cheated, frustrated and helpless, an orphan of cuss.

I folded the newspaper and returned to my immediate surroundings. I needed to confront my own mess.

Some of my support acts began strumming guitars for their personal pleasure, while Goodbut kept repeating to himself and anyone else who would listen: "Infinitely bum! Infinitely bum!" And the beers and glasses of wine slipped down all other throats smoothly, but not down mine, and parts of me wept for the rest.

The very bald singer from Satori came up next to me. "That gig wasn't big enough for the all of you."

I nodded every one of my heads.

The atmosphere in the room became strained. The songs which came out of those guitars were painful. Every time a G sharp was sounded, the walls sparked red. There was shame and heat. The people winced. Even though these G sharps should have been different to the one I'd extracted from 'And Dug The Pigdog A Tomb', the horror was there. My fault for welding it to one specific context! The note was alloyed with that context forever now, tainted and ugly.

A mirror for my existence.

I felt a strong grip on my biggest shoulder. Bridget Wells was standing behind me. Then she growled:

"You've destroyed G sharp! You've ruined an entire note. Never again will anyone be able to play that semitone. There were only twelve in a full scale and now there are just eleven. All musicians must regard you as an enemy from this instant. You'll never get a gig anywhere. You should go home now. Leave us forever."

"I have no home," I replied miserably.

"Just get out of Swansea," Goodbut added. "I'm sure the miasma will part itself especially for you."

"I'll finish my drink first," I said, and I raised my pint to my lips, but I didn't taste it. I suddenly found myself surrounded by grinning people. So many happy faces! I felt light and immersed in compassion, warm and at peace. This is the way it should always be! I laughed my typical laugh but the sound was a fraction softer.

Then I realised that I was lying on my back parallel to the bar with my feet still resting on the stool. I was upside down and the grins were sneers and pouts. The warmth was gore. There was a gouting neck where one of my heads had been. I felt a fraction more stupid. But I rapidly worked out what had happened. Fed up with my delaying tactic, Bridget had punched me. Don't mess with that girl!

I crawled away, out of the room, out of the door, onto the street. It had started to rain. The sky washed me. Cars helped by splashing puddles. All the moonless gutters were damp and crooked. I didn't enter any of them. I crossed the road and found a patch of soggy greenery, Cwmdonkin Park, it was. There was no real shelter here, but I lay flat on my back again and thrust my legs up into the air.

All songs are now played without G sharp. Strings have been removed from pianos across the globe. Banning this note may even become law in the utopia of the new world order.

I sang a tune to myself while I was in the park, an obscure Atlantean number called, 'I Feel Like Urchin Dressed Up As Octopus Tonight'. It was appropriate. The membrane which connects all my thighs acted as an umbrella. There are no notes in Atlantean music, just bubbles. It is sure to surface in popularity again.

In the morning I'd begin the journey back to Cardiff. In the meantime I'd linger in a world where every twisted leer was a grin. A planet of grins discovered and colonised and exploited by me, but liberated by standing up for nothing in particular.

NOWHERE NEAR MILKWOOD

I needed a manager, that's what, because without one I was going nowhere. And nowhere is probably an unpleasant place. Already I'd been
to Swansea, so I had an inkling, though I'm disinclined to judge the
two places exactly alike, for the simple reason you can return from
Swansea. Plus there's a difference between going nowhere and *going to*
it. Yes, a manager was called for, and I called for one, wrote actually. I
placed an advertisement in a local magazine.

I should have chosen a publication devoted to the music business, I
appreciate that now, but they were too expensive. I picked one I could
more easily afford. I wrote out my advertisement, keeping it short and
enigmatic. Then I waited in my rented room for a reply. I was living in
Beresford Road at the time and the flow of traffic outside my window
resembled the excited murmuring of the audience I'd never known. In
the evenings, the glare of the headlamps pierced the curtains, illumi-
nating the peeling wallpaper that was all I had to look at.

To say I saw patterns there would be interesting, but I didn't. I tried.
The swirls of faded colour, possibly never bright, flickered with the in-
tensity of a dull headache, but they never congealed into the forms of
living things. I slept in the chair which was the only item of furniture
in the room. There was movement above me, other lodgers, feasibly
happier than I, going about their own penurious affairs. I never saw
them, though we dwelled in close proximity, nor had I any vast desires
in that direction. Anonymity seemed right for this place and time.

One morning there was a knock on my window. I stood and parted the curtains and peered out. A moonface was pressed to the glass on the other side. By this, I don't mean a round face, jolly and pock-marked, but a thin curved one in profile, fused to a crescent head. He was listening, whoever he was, for sounds of activity within. I obliged by rapping a selection of *my* knuckles back, and he sprang away from the pane in pain, but then he turned to regard me directly, winked his cold blue eyes and mouthed the words, "May I come in?" and grinned when I nodded.

I went into the grimy hallway and opened the heavy ugly door and invited him into my humble, very bare, abode. He stood uneasily in the dust, wringing his hands and forgetting to blink, and I shivered, but the temperature in my room was always a few degrees lower than it ought to be, whatever the season, so I dismissed this. I would have offered him tea, coffee, fruit juice, weak and salty beer, but I had none, so I reached into a pocket and drew out a small piece of bread, which I was saving for my dinner, but he declined this gift. I replaced it grate-fully and we stared at each other helplessly.

After a while, he said, "I'm here."

"I agree," I replied, "but who are you exactly?"

"The answer to your advert."

"Of course!" I exclaimed.

The tension, which had been unbearably abstruse, was broken. We shook hands, a ritual which lasts an hour with me and is best avoided. But I was overjoyed, for I believed the answer to my problems had materialised, a manager, my ticket to delayed success, the balm for my soul, worn out by years of hope deferred. He was my guide on the path to fame, a man with an astronomical head, and a mind for such figures too, for those would be my profits when I hit the big time, if there was any justice in the world, whether the world of elements or the insub-stantial one of business. I didn't care! A mentor, seemingly congealed from the early traffic fumes, here with me at last!

"When can we begin?" I asked.

"Right away," he said.

"Let's go!" I enthused.

"Fine," he replied. "I'll give you a lift to my factory."

I was so excited I neglected to question this suggestion until it was too late. I merely followed him out of my room, not even bothering to lock the door behind me because I knew I'd never return, and climbed into the sidecar of his motorcycle, whose chrome side was emblazoned with the image of a speeding glacier, ice crystals vaporising from its surface and flaring off behind like a rocket's exhaust trail. The engine didn't start. He turned the key in the ignition again and again and finally it clattered and groaned into some sort of life, undoubtedly alien and doomed. We roared off at walking pace and joined the more competent traffic. This should have told me something.

But it didn't.

We passed under a railway bridge, where the road was in a dip and flooded with dirty rainwater, and almost failed to make it out safely, but our destination wasn't far. We went down Tweedsmuir Road until we left the domestic streets behind. Now we were in the district of Tremorfa, where an industrial zone lurked like a temple complex dedicated to boiled eggs. It was depressing and therefore familiar, though I'd never been here before. We spluttered to a halt outside a grey building, a perfect cube, set on its own among black earth and patches of dead grass.

There were no windows in its walls and the main door was metal and chill to the touch. We entered. A freezing mist enveloped us. It was at this point that the first doubt assailed me. Frost cracked on my eyebrows as I knitted them, knitted them not warmly enough, not like cardigans, to display a mild confusion. No, it was severe, my frown, by necessity of temperature. Then I asked him plainly:

"What sort of manager are you?"

"I run a cold storage company. This is it."

"I wanted a music manager."

"Yes, but you advertised in the REFRIGERATION GAZETTE, so you have nobody to blame but yourself, unless you deem multiple heads too many to hold just one responsibility."

"I don't," I confessed sadly.

"Well, I'm your manager now. I answered your advert."

"I need gigs," I said.

He pondered this and blew on his hands. "I'll do my best to provide. Have you considered looking for them in the future?"

"The one place I haven't."

He gripped my shoulder. "Let's try there!"

He led me to a chamber at the core of the factory and shut me within. A dim light filtered through an observation slit in the hatch. The interior was bare, almost the same as my room in Beresford Road, but without wallpaper. The sides were ceramic and hard. I squatted and waited, glancing uneasily at the intake pipes in the ceiling. I heard my manager turning valves outside. Then I was sprayed with a very cold fluid, perhaps liquid nitrogen. It lapped around my ankles, my calves, my thighs. My mind began to shut down, suspend its duties, cancel its appointments with ideas. I was being sealed in ice! It didn't worry me too much, no more than anything else in my life, which was already infinitely bothered. It's better to be a cube than a square.

A cube which eventually melted. I was free again, but my manager had gone. So had the factory and its machinery, including the chamber which was my prison. So had the industrial zone of Tremorfa and its bordering streets. So had the rest of Cardiff. I crouched in a region of lagoons and a grim wind made sluggish ripples on the metallic waters, which reflected the light of an overcast sky. There was no vegetation, just a crude and sloppy mud tower at the limits of my vision. I reached for my pocket and my piece of bread but it had gone, crumbled to atoms. For that matter so had my pocket and clothes.

Nude, I started limping down the paths between the gelid pools. I had terrible cramp. I wondered how my garments could decay while I was trapped in ice. I guessed I must have been thawing for a long time and the bitter coldness of my present environment had delayed the return of my consciousness. That was it. By the time I reached the tower, circulation had returned to forty of my legs. A figure sat on a stool in the doorway and squinted at me. He was doing nothing, but I'd obviously interrupted him. I didn't feel sorry.

"Whet du yua went?" he sneered.

"Information, breakfast, celebrity," I replied.

"Qaeont eccint," he snorted. "Uat uf wurk ectur, eri yua? Git ewey, lievi mi eluni. O'm basy, cen't yua till? Baggir uff!"

"Just as soon as I get what I need. But you don't look busy to me. You're just sitting, twiddling, scowling."

"Nu, O'm pritindong nuni uf thos ixosts et ell."

He gestured at the entire landscape.

I sympathised. "Keep trying. Don't give up. But I need a gig."

"Will, yua wun't fond uni hiri!"

"I suppose not," I conceded.

He seemed to soften. "Yua mast gu tu thi Osli uf Chrumi. Ot's thi unly pleci whiri masocoens mey fond wurk."

I frowned. "The Isle of Chrome? What's that?"

"Thi cepotel uf thi lewfal plenit. Fulluw thos peth antol ot bicumis e prupir rued, thin kiip guong elung ot woth nu dovirsouns end yua woll onivotebly git thiri. Guud lack!"

He gave me a fruit for my hunger, but no celebrity for my reputation. The fruit was bruised and ugly. Before I left, I asked him: "Who are you?"

And he snapped, "Thi furmir Prisodint uf thi Wurld . . . "

I believed him, His bitterness was proof.

"Goodbye," I said, and he replied:

"Nuw O cen't ivin jaggli! Ivirythong guis et lung lest!"

And I peeled the fuit and bit into it, because I felt it was expected of me. It was sweeter than its appearance promised, and I hoped this was a metaphor for myself. It hadn't been so far. But I'm an optimist, always looking to the future. I was living there now, so it had to deliver or I'd be left with nothing. I walked. I left the lagoons behind and reached a very smooth plain, bland and unremarkable, the path dividing it in two, and I wondered if I had wandered into limbo, a future where erosion had flattened every protuberance, each crinkle and crease on the planet's surface. Not sexy, that. An infinite Belgium of the mind. And cryogenic freezing is a one-way ticket. I was stuck.

The clouds began to break and I glimpsed a pale pink sky beyond. The sun, wherever it was, had started to set. It was going to get even colder. I needed clothes or shelter, but neither were available. There was nothing left to do but run to generate heat. I hate running on empty stomachs, but my options were limited. So I accelerated over the plain and soon the friction warmed my cheeks. I kept under the one hundred miles per hour mark, because of the speed wobble. A sprained ankle at that rate and the ground becomes a big bruise just waiting to pass it onto you when you land. But the terrain was perfectly level, without holes.

As the ambient light dimmed into a muddy dusk, the silhouettes of low hills appeared on the horizon. I gasped in relief and slowed my velocity. The clouds had thinned out even more and stars were visible. I knew I was heading the correct way, though the path hadn't become the promised road. Behind the lower hills were higher ones, and beyond those true mountains. I was too weary to be inspired, but I saved the memory for later, when I'd have my feet up on a constellation of couches, if that astrological-comfy conjunction ever occurred. I couldn't feel confident at present it would. I was ravenous and my eye alighted on the first plants I'd encountered, but they weren't edible. Not yet. A few bluish mosses. Later I encountered ferns and tumbleweed too lazy to roll. No, not lazy. Square. The dice of desolation . . .

I ran up a slope into a forest of thin trees. They wore their branches bare and I wondered where the man in the tower had got his fruit from. Not from here. The trees were so thin I could almost pinch the thickest between finger and thumb, like the neck of a distant banjo which forgets to grow bigger when you approach it. There were mushrooms in the next forest, wide enough to curl up on, but not quite warm enough for a nude sleeper. Then I was racing between boulders, bandit friendly terrain, if old novels and romantic lithographs are to be believed. They probably aren't. So don't! Go on then, have it your way. Reckless. My elevation had increased considerably. I was passing between the hills and catching up with the mountains. They glistened with no colours in the unanimous night, no purples and silver. I slowed my pace again, for I was weak now. I cantered rather than galloped.

Dawn found me weaving through one of the high passes in the range of mountains. On the other side, I paused to look down. Astonishment sent my tiredness to bed. I was fully alert now and aghast at the scene below. Two armies clashed on a field. Bent shields and snapped pikes soon littered the ground. Each side carried lanceolate flags, by which I mean rounded at their ends, but these displayed no symbols of creed or nationality. They were different colours, but blank. As I watched, men died in sordid ways. Within the hour, there were only a few dozen left and I deemed it safe to begin my descent. By the time I reached the field, the battle was down to just two fellows, who took it in turns to hit each other with axes. Both were bearded and dressed in similar attire, though one wore a blue scarf around his neck and the other a red. They stopped when I appeared.

"Agly matent," said the first.

"Shell wi koll hom?" asked the second.

"O'll du ot!" the first insisted.

"Nu, ot wes my odie. Lit's foght fur thi roght!"

At this point I understood what had happened to language. Vowels had evolved. If monkeys, ragtime and milk can evolve—into humans, jazz and butter—then why not vowels? The problem was that they hadn't evolved into anything *else*. There was simply nothing for them to change into other than themselves. They were only letters, after all. But they had done their best with what they had. Each vowel had turned itself into the next one along in the alphabet. The last one had looped round to the beginning, like a sequence of support bands in a Swansea pub. The instant I worked this out, I had less difficulty grasping the meaning of such sentences as I heard in my subsequent adventures, which is why I now render them in an ordinary manner, for these *subsequent* adventures began almost immediately.

I said: "Don't slay me. For some reason, I love life."

Together they cried, "Which cause do you support? The rebels or the revolutionaries?"

"Neither," I returned. "I'm a musician."

They stroked their beards. "That's feasible. There was a musician once who was washed up on the Aracknid Islands. He had many arms. Word went round he was available for gigs and many theatre managers booked him. They assumed he would be able to play lots of instruments at the same time. But his arms were tentacles, and he just stood there on stage, unable to play anything!"

"I'm better than that," I confessed.

"They pitched him back into the sea," came the reply.

I said, "My destination is the Isle of Chrome."

The one with the blue scarf declared: "That's the only decent place in this land. Follow the path to its end. It forks once. Choose the right road. The left goes all the way to Paraparapara."

"Which is beyond a joke," said his opponent.

"Beyond *three* jokes," corrected the other, though he didn't specify what they were.

Then they returned to fighting.

I didn't loiter to watch who won. That's too immature a thing for me to do. I stole clothes from some dead warriors and continued along my way and the path became a road and I reached the fork I'd been warned about, and I bore to the right.

Now the landscape was softer and more civilised. The sky was filled with balloons and aeroplanes with mystic pictures painted on their wings. Groups of men marched up and down beside me. It made me nervous. I wore no scarf and thus was safe, for it quickly became apparent that the colours blue and red represented the similar but opposed philosophies of *rebellion* and *revolution*. With neither hue about my neck I declared my neutrality, trusted by none, but keeping my heads on my shoulders, apart from my long lost one, rather than on poles or plates or pickled in jars, all of which I saw when I passed the camps of one or other of these armies. I've never been a political animal, just a beast of mysterious origin and equally peculiar sorts. Safer that way.

I passed through small towns and then larger, and I slept in orchards and stole fruit. My health was adequate by the time I approached the outskirts of a vast city. It occupied a whole island and was reached across a bridge of tarnished gold. I walked along it and found myself standing at the entrance of a gateway which had been left open. A note fixed to one of the stone lintels announced: GONE TO LUNCH, PLEASE REPORT TO POLICE STATION ON YOUR OWN. And I passed through and searched for the building in question. Few citizens were out, for it was lunchtime, but I soon found the specified edifice. I assumed I had to register my presence there. The Station also featured a gate, but this one was guarded. A small boy levelled a primitive gun at me and I raised my hands in excessive surrender.

"Just following instructions," I said.

He shook his head and wiped his running nose with a dirty sleeve.

"Will you let me in?" I asked.

He prodded one of my stomachs with the barrel.

"Then I shall leave," I sighed.

He shook his head again and I grew annoyed.

"Listen here, young man," I began, "I can't stand here for the rest of the day, or for however long you think I ought to, because I've come a long way, through time as well as space, and I want to do the right thing and settle down here and find some work, for I'm a musician, so let me register my arrival, or whatever I'm supposed to do, and do it fast so I can be on my way looking for gigs, or I'll be forced to snatch that gun from you and break it over my knee, do you understand?"

He didn't, so I did. And he burst into tears.

A tall man came swaggering out of the building. He was imposingly absurd in his uniform, which was faded and unwashed. He wore a helmet of patently daft design and a long truncheon on his belt which interfered with his walking. He cried:

"What's going on here then?"

And I answered, "The youth of today have no respect, neither in the today of the past nor the today of now. It's the same lack."

"I might dispute that," he cried with a frown, "for everything changes over time, and in our era we make much use of chrome, whereas former civilisations favoured flint, iron and plastic. Thus I declare our modern lacks are more shiny than ancient ones."

His speech was nonsense, but he observed me with profound interest.

"The boy was unreasonable," I added sourly.

"Really? This surprises me. Percy is our most trusted sentry. The position of guard to the Police Station is hereditary and his father died before he was born. He is now seven years old and can actually aim his musket. He was much less use to my predecessor, who knew him only as a foetus and gurgling infant."

"Your predecessor?" I asked.

"Giotto Pucker, the Prefect of Police."

"And you are?"

He snapped to attention. "Tiepolo Bunter, the latest holder of that honourable title."

"I see," I said. "The big cheese."

He licked his lips. "Yes, now that the President is stuck in exile. But let's not waste time standing here. You look like a unique individual, a special visitor to our city, and you should permit me to give you a guided tour of our major attractions."

I accepted the offer. He barked an order to the guard and the gun was lowered. It was safe to pass. I followed Tiepolo through the gate. As I did so, I asked:

"Will Percy be your sentry for life?"

"Yes, and no more. If he survives to old age, he will doubtless serve one of my successors as faithfully and stupidly as he has me. It's unlikely I will last here much longer. Prefects of Police change quite rapidly. It's the enormous stress of the job."

In the grounds of the Station stood a series of statues on plinths. One was labelled with the word RADISH, but the sculpture which loomed up there was not a vegetable. It was a man. Peculiar. I noted that Tiepolo was excited by my appearance. He kept measuring me with his eyes. Against my expectations, he didn't lead me into the

Station itself, but up a ladder bolted to a wall. We gained the roof. It doubled as the landing pad for a curious flying machine. I blinked. It had more of the salad about it than any viable engineering principle. It soon became clear this device was going to convey us between the most notable features of the Isle of Chrome, if it didn't destroy itself first.

"What precisely is it?" I enquired.

Tiepolo beamed. "An invention of my most capable employee. The celerycopter!"

"Is it safe?"

"Of course not! Get in!"

His tone didn't encourage a belief that any objection was possible. I seated myself inside the contraption and he joined me. Vinegar dripped from the control panel onto my knees. The whole thing was more rickety than my very first gig, performed when I was in college over the public address system of a residential block for students. My reward for that show had been a week locked in a communal tumble drier in the deep basement, while the clothes of the students grew more and more thirsty for a wash, and armpits became so sweaty that young lovers ended their affairs, but they felt the cost was worth it to get back at me. Anyway, the machine lurched into the air at last and Tiepolo steered us over the red turrets of the domestic areas. And so my tour began. And it took all day. He was grooming me for something, I gradually learned what, and I was both thrilled and appalled. But first a few highlights of my trip, for they were genuinely impressive.

Imagine a temple as grand as a guitar must appear to an ant. This was the Temple of Bridget, a girl from long ago, worshipped as a goddess because she punched off the head of the man who destroyed G sharp. I chewed all my lips at this news. I nervously asked my pilot if this story was a myth or whether he believed it. He shrugged. Then I wanted to know more about the man she had attacked. Had his description been preserved? Tiepolo shook his head. Nothing much was known about him, but he must have been evil, ugly and an idiot. To destroy a note was a mean crime, but he had done it. If the glorious Bridget hadn't punched off his head soon after, he might have proceeded to spoil the other notes too. That is why the world was grateful to her. I smiled painfully. Her Temple was amazing, and to continue my earlier simile, if an ant encountered a guitar it would surely feel an overwhelming sense of utterly submissive frustration, for it would know it had exactly enough legs to play every string at once, and yet wouldn't be able to stretch far enough across to do so. It would probably crawl into the hollow body instead and reside there, sobbing formic tears.

We also visited the Bowl of Tunes, a stadium where all performable songs ever composed were played chronologically in relays by prisoners and slaves trained in the art of music. I say *performable* because anything which featured a G sharp had been censored, and the instruments had been modified over the ages to render the playing of that note impossible or at least very difficult and subject to monstrous penalties. We alighted in the centre of the Bowl and listened for quarter of an hour. These G sharpless melodies were a heavy emotional burden on the shoulders of my ears, and I was grateful when we departed, though the strains of the current piece, the 'Wurst Hassle' song, an irritating hotdogger, followed us into the low clouds. And these clouds were like curtains covering my shame, which was climactic. Then we flew onward and landed next to the National Museum.

I expected something mighty from such an institution, for Tiepolo had informed me there was now a one world state and that the words *national* and *global* were synonymous. The Cussmothers, it seemed, had realised their political dreams. Their meddling in my own time had led to all this. Over the centuries, the secret seeds they planted in the separate countries of the world had sprouted and grown and tangled themselves into one big permanent knot. That's a bad analogy. A better one might be that the plots and schemes of my former colleagues were the acids which dissolved borders until there was only one country left in the world, the world state itself, governed from this city which was also an island. Not bad for a musical band! I felt a brief pang of regret I hadn't remained with them during their time of success, but in fact our fates were still linked in a remarkable way. Not that I had an inkling of this yet, though Tiepolo kept looking at me in a significant manner.

We entered the museum and approached the first exhibit in the first room and he pointed at the glass and said: "Music was a martyr to him. This belonged to the dirtiest traitor to melody."

A shudder ran the length of my body, starting as a slight quiver and ending in a tidal wave of flesh which crashed against one set of ankles. My shudders have enough room in my frame to gain phenomenal power. I regarded the skull on its cushion and panted: "The lost head of the man who destroyed the note G sharp? The head which was punched off his shoulders?"

"The very one," winked Tiepolo.

I sobbed. "What a marvellous woman that Bridget was."

"You have become curiously sentimental."

I gripped the edges of the case to stop myself fainting. "Yes, but this is a totally unique exhibit."

Tiepolo laughed. "One of many. It's a fake."

My relief was tangible but I concealed it well. "Really?"

"A plaster replica. Like all religious, political and cultural *relics*, there are thousands of originals. Let me show you some others."

And he led me through a series of adjacent chambers, each of which contained a glass case with a skull resting on a cushion. Some replicas were superior to others. A few were too good, too flawless. Others were shapeless lumps of baked clay. Those of average quality were just right. The same probably holds true for the souls in my different bodies. There were no exhibits of any other description in the museum. This explained why we were the only visitors. Tiepolo declared:

"Before the countries of the world were united, many museums in various lands all claimed to possess the one true skull. Once the states were merged, so were the museums, and then it became apparent we had a surplus of authentic heads. Now we pretend to display them here, but really they are in storage."

"You can't throw them out in case one isn't a fake?"

He rubbed his chin. "Are you hungry? Let me buy you a meal."

I agreed to this proposal with alacrity.

We left the building and took again to the air. This time we landed at the edge of the city, beneath a smoking mountain. There was a cellar club in the side of this formidable cone of rock. It was called *UNDER THE VOLCANO* and was unlike any restaurant I'd ever visited. I wondered if this might be a possible venue for gigs, but it wasn't that kind of place. Food was grilled over natural vents in the floor, behind which magma seethed. There wasn't room for a performer. Tiepolo ordered two vast toasted cheeses and a jug of wine, and we alternately seared and cooled our lips until we were satisfied and tipsy. I knew he wanted to reveal something to me. He wiped his hands with a napkin and asked: "Where are you from exactly?"

"Not from this age," I admitted.

"I guessed as much," he replied, "so maybe I ought to fill you in on the history of the world state. That's what I'll do."

And he did. He told me a garbled account of my own time, when the Cussmothers had started the process of uniting sovereign governments. This centralisation of authority had taken millennia to complete. There had been relapses, some even recently, into patchworks of tiny kingdoms, but those were just glitches. The applied ideals of globalisation were too strong to reverse. There was a single supreme leader, the President, who ruled his global domain with a road of chrome, hard but shiny, though in reality his power was limited, or at least frustrated, by those who worked for him, in particular the Prefect of Police, of whom he, Tiepolo Bunter, was one of the finest examples ever. They were living in a fabulous era of prosperity and peculiarity. Or rather they *should* be living like that. But something had gone wrong, seriously wrong, recently. It had to do with a safety mechanism which had been built into the workings of modern dictatorship. Listen carefully.

To stop the people feeling oppressed by the many injustices integral to the running of an autocracy, it had been arranged that the acting President would be regularly overthrown by an insurrection. After his overthrow, he would go into exile. Then chaos would reign. The people would realise their mistake and call the President back from exile. They would actually welcome the re-establishment of strict laws and unfair order. Anything other than the utterly random misery of no rule at all. These systematic insurrections provided a much needed release of pressure for the general populace. They were arranged by the Prefect of Police and his underlings. Each period of total chaos lasted an average of two or three months. This time, however, it had been raging for more than a year, so long indeed that the original insurrectionists had clustered into two opposing groups, the rebels and the revolutionaries, each dedicated to overthrowing the other, whom they considered to be the culprits of the disorder. It was an ironic and hazardous situation.

"A year?" I cried. "Why so long?"

Tiepolo said, "Every insurrection demands a different place of exile, to stop the people realising the thing is rigged. Our current President has been almost everywhere, even to Cus and Yam-Yam. This time he went to a region of drab lagoons. A place of grey skies."

"I saw him there," I replied. "He was wearing a big wide hat."

"That looked like a crescent moon on his head? Yes, that sounds like him. Well this region of lagoons occupies the site of a lost city, a city with a romantic name which stood there ages ago. It was called Cardiff. Anyway, it seems there was once a road in that same city which kept all people stuck to it in a mystical manner. Once they stood on it, they couldn't leave, at least not easily. Although this road has long since gone, its influence somehow remains. Our President wandered onto it by mistake as he searched for a comfortable place to spend his exile. Now he's trapped there."

"Can't you pull him off?" I spluttered.

Tiepolo blushed. "We've tried that, but the mystic force is too strong. We used pulleys and levers, but nothing worked. The *adhesion* exists in the minds of the road's captives. The true solution is for the President to free himself by doubting the road. So he must doubt the entire landscape first. A desperate measure but the only one."

"I see," I said, "but I approached him rather closely. Why didn't I get stuck?"

Tiepolo frowned, and then he smiled. "He must have succeeded in doubting the power of the road for all others. He's making progress! One day he *will* be free."

"To relcaim his authority?"

"Exactly! To return organised corruption to the world!"

We lapsed into a silence that was by turns glum and hopeful. Finally I spoke to myself, but loudly enough for him to hear: "All my working life I looked for the right gig, for a place that actually wants to hear me play. As a last resort I came to the future . . . "

"A fine resort. We have crystal piers."

"You misunderstand me. Even the future isn't my venue. I've seen the instruments you have here and none are capable of sounding G sharp, not easily at any rate. I know that I'll never *want* to master instruments that can't play my favourite note."

A profound feeling of self-pity came over me, but it was at this point that Tiepolo sprang his suggestion.

He cried: "Since I first set eyes on you, I realised you might be the answer to my prayers, and I pray every night, to Drigg and Peekant, sometimes to Bridget, once to myself. Yes, I pray and have prayed many times for one such as you to come along. One did recently but some idiots threw him into the sea. Anyway, now you are here and I have been given a second chance. I didn't befriend you and give you a guided tour because I'm a nice man. On the contrary, I'm a horrible one. I did it because I guessed you could be useful to me. And useful to society. I want to offer you a job. It has nothing to do with music. Because you have so many arms, you always assumed that a career in music was your best option. Your failure in this area is a shattering not of your life, as you believe, but of an empty dream. Fate has reserved you and your mutation for something much bigger."

Then he made his offer.

And I accepted.

Woman was not made from a man's rib, but from that one area of his back where an itch is beyond a scratch. I always imagined a President would never feel short of female attention. I believed he would have his pick of girls and their physical charms. I soon learned this was not the case. If anything, success with the ladies becomes even more elusive than before. Bearing in mind my life has been once of enforced celibacy, this is a remarkable statement. I find myself in the position of having negative allure. Don't ask. I'm not able to explain. If I could, it might rub off on you, if it hasn't already. Best not to know.

I'm sitting at my desk. It's a grand desk. I have other desks in other offices and I'm currently occupying them all. At this one I am relaxing. I'm indulging a new hobby, the writing of fiction. I'm composing little stories as practice for writing what you are reading now. These stories won't be read by anybody, but that doesn't matter. I'm honing my skills. I doubt I'll even finish any of them. I've just started a new one. This is how it begins:

"Come into my parlour," said the domestic goddess to the handsome devil.

That's how I met my wife.

Her name was Reshmi and she had long black hair.

My name is Ug and I am from 20,307 BC.

I am bald. A sign of strength.

But she overpowered me when I first saw her. Muscles count for nothing when the heart which feeds them blood begins to melt.

I shake my head, scratch out the third line and rewrite it thus: "Her name was Lola and she had nuclear bosoms." Yes, that's more like it! More racy. I'm learning fast. This is more fun than the official report writing I have to do at my other desks. Now I hear a noise outside the door. The sound of a man clearing his throat. This signal is used instead of knocking for urgent situations. I call for him to enter. It's my Prefect of Police. He is holding something pale and grinning under one arm. I flinch but quickly recover my composure.

"Good morning, Mister Caretaker President," he says.

I throw down my pen. "What's up now, Tiepolo?"

"Another assassination attempt, I'm afraid."

I squint and mutter, "Successful?"

He shuffles his feet. "Yes."

I shudder once and then cry: "Well, let's fix it. Not a big deal really. How many have we got left, by the way?"

He holds up the plaster skull. "Several thousand. There are store-rooms under the museum. We're on schedule."

I accept this news with relief. "Good."

"Shall I fit this one now?"

I wave a consenting hand and he proceeds past my desk and through the open windows onto the balcony of my tower. Fragments of previous skulls crunch under his feet. The crowd surge below in the public square. My headless body, the one punched all those centuries ago, sways to the rhythm of collective feet, not my own. The mob are departing. Tiepolo fits the new false skull onto the pillar of my neck. He glues it there, and suddenly there is a President standing on his balcony again. The assassins have been cheated. This is the job that fate has decreed for me, perhaps the only one. But there are hobbies as well as careers. I'll get back to that point later. Meanwhile, let me add that there are speaking tubes which run from each of the offices and merge into one hollow pipe which curls around the leg of the President on the balcony and up his waist and torso and over his right shoulder. It ends in a flared amplifying horn and any of my mouths can talk through it from the safety of our desks. We take it in turn to make speeches.

Tiepolo returns through the windows, wiping his hands on a cloth to free them from the grease associated with my neck. I ask him, "What other news?"

He replies: "The real President has already started doubting his mud tower. Soon he'll be free to reclaim his position. You'll be his Caretaker no longer."

"I'm ready for that," I say, but this is untrue. I'm enjoying myself too much here. So I add, "Anything else?"

"Yes. I'm pleased to report our scheme is working perfectly. There's less fighting in the provinces. Some groups of rebels and revolutionaries have decided to disband and make peace. The warriors of Butter Wood have melted down their weapons."

"I know of no such warriors nor place."

"They are the descendants of the original inhabitants of Milk Wood. They were forced to change its name when the region was churned by an earthquake."

"Damn earthquakes! Think they can get away with anything . . . "

"Well, that might change soon enough!"

I smirk. We've already discussed the need to create new legislation. But I'm bored now. Or rather I have an urge to be alone. I wave him away. He goes. I have all the necessary qualifications to operate as the ultimate Caretaker President. My many bodies give me an advantage. I can mollify the mob with speeches and calm the chaos from my balcony, while doing the real work indoors at my desks *at the same time*, a thing no other man can do, which is why nobody has been chosen for this role until now. My speeches are spoken transcripts of the best songs of the Cussmothers, my own songs, which I heard on the news while I was in Swansea, chanted by the first rampaging mobs to set foot, or feet, on the long road to the single world state. They are old standards and I know them by heart. They work.

I can't be overthrown. Part of me is always somewhere else. There's just too much. And my public body on the balcony can be assassinated again and again by headshot after headshot. The skulls from the museum are a perfect fit. I pretend this is a coincidence. My assassins are usually followers of the old President who fear I have usurped his position. I probably haven't. Sometimes it is Percy who assassinates me. I am happy. But my scars still throb. The surgeon who operated on me is the same fellow who invented the celerycopter. He's efficient but weird. Complete separation was impossible. I would die. My individual bodies were not separated but *relaxed*. They are connected now by long taut fibres. At night, when I am completely alone, I can play these fibres like the strings of a zither. I can even play the forbidden note, my favourite note. And because my tower casts such a total shadow over the streets and squares below, blocking out the whole sky, I can send down one of my lesser bodies with a bucket to collect inspiration from the moonless gutters of the future.

TALLER STORIES

PROLOGUE

———➤◆◄———

Somewhere down near the Docks lies a road which doesn't exist in our space-time continuum. Like many roads, it has its fair share of shops and houses and even a pub. However, these buildings are no more real than the road itself. Some people declare they are phantom structures left over from another age. The argument runs something like this: if men and women can become ghosts, why not bricks and mortar? I have to agree with them. Not only have I explored this road myself, but I have often entered the pub for a drink.

It is an odd pub with a stranger set of patrons. The beer it sells is strong and not respectful of brains. It is brewed on the premises by the barman, who is generally only known by his first name and his final wink. He is called Hywel and was born far to the west in the village of Lladloh. Why he left his home to work in Cardiff is a minor mystery not worth solving. It seems he was once a baker, but lost his nerve in an incident with a high-wayman, and now prefers to serve anything not in a tricorne hat, whether man or monster.

He accepts payment mostly in tales. One evening he resolved to take more care with his accounts and asked me bluntly if I would invent some new stories for him, to balance his books and fill up this one. His pub was already crowded with professional authors, so I declined and pointed out that I was the only one of his customers who never composed fiction. Unfortunately, he considered lack of talent to be an ideal qualification for his fraud. He wanted the style to be clumsy but light, to cheat the Inspector of

Metaphors if he called.

So if you are ever near Mountstuart Square, and you happen to see a road that wasn't truly there before, take a chance and walk down it. The adventure will be absurd but safe, a brief flirtation with rare spooks. The pub in question is the friendliest tavern you may hope to visit, and a pint costs less than whatever you pay when you talk in your sleep. No, that is untrue. I am not permitted to depart unless I find a replacement for my unbearable task, and for that I am desperate enough to trick even you over this impossible threshold . . .

RAINBOW'S END

Although the *TALL STORY* on Raconteur Road is a pub that doesn't exist, takings are always high. Its richest patrons are potbellied council overseers who step through its doors during lunchtimes. They step, as it were, into another dimension where imagination becomes reality and truth takes a siesta on one of the benches in the beer-garden.

The landlord of this dubious establishment is none other than Hywel Price, a beery auroch of a man, whose hands are too large for the piccolo and yet too small for the fiddle. Consequently, he can neither shortchange customers nor assail their eardrums with unwanted music. This is doubtless the source of his popularity.

When I entered the tavern yesterday afternoon, business was brisk. So brisk indeed that Hywel had decided to close the bar. He was leaning with his elbows on the counter, talking to Flann O'Brien and declaiming on subjects he knew nothing about. This is a peculiar habit with Hywel. It is probably why his popularity won't last.

"Now take your modern rainbow," he was saying. "It has neither the consistency nor the vibrancy of your good old-fashioned rainbow. When I was a lad, rainbows were something special. But your modern rainbow looks tired and a bit worn around the edges. Personally I blame the Martians. That's where all these newfangled rainbows come from. They just don't make them like they used to . . . "

I coughed and signalled for a drink, but Hywel ignored me. His voice took on the drone of a wasp caught in a jar that had once held

Mrs Owen's jam: anger mingled with relief. I attempted to win Flann O'Brien over to my side by tapping him on the shoulder, but he was completely absorbed in his Guinness. The *TALL STORY* tends to be a pub where everybody talks but nobody listens.

"And that's another thing about your traditional rainbow that your modern ones don't have," Hywel continued. "A crock of gold, that's what! There used to be a crock at the end of every one when I was small. Well do I remember hauling back a big pot in the evenings after a summer downpour. There was never much gold in them though; just an apple, an orange, a few brazil nuts and a penny. But that isn't the point. We were happy in those days."

Flann O'Brien finished his pint and remarked that he knew a man who had chased a rainbow all over County Wicklow only to find an old wellington boot at the end of it. The situation was growing desperate. I realised that drastic action was called for if ever I was to be blessed with a drink. On a sudden impulse, I cried:

"I knew a man who chased a rainbow right here in the city. It happened two years ago, during that heatwave that set tongues a-lolling and eyes a-rolling. We were all waiting for a drop of rain to soothe our fevered brows and eventually a lonely blue cloud answered our prayers. There has never been a sweeter shower or a more magnificent rainbow."

"Oh yes?" Hywel looked up. I had finally attracted his attention. His fingers flirted with the pump handle of my usual. I licked my lips and sweat stood out on my brow. "Go on," he said.

"Well it also happened to be the week that the Reptile Circus was in town. Don't you remember? *Dr Slither's Performing Snakes and Salamanders!* Anyway, what occurred was that the reptiles were allowed to splash around in the Castle moat to cool down. There were big snapping caymans and crocodiles, enormous pythons and thick-tongued monitor lizards. There was even a Komodo Dragon from . . . er, Komodo."

Hywel gave me a cynical look and opened his mouth to resume his conversation with Flann O'Brien. I saw my chance slipping away. In blind panic, I added:

"Well I had this friend who decided to follow this rainbow I mentioned, to see if there really was a crock of gold at the end of it. I told him not to go, but off he went toward the Castle. He had to hurry because the rainbow was already beginning to fade."

Hywel turned back to face me. I had won a reprieve but still had to prove myself. I said:

"This friend of mine finally reached the Castle moat and there, lo and behold, was the end of the rainbow! So he took his shirt and shoes off, placed them neatly on the side, pinched his nose and jumped in. Down into the depths he sank, faster and faster. But he never came up again . . . "

"Why? Did he find his crock of gold?"

I sighed and shook my head sadly: "Alas no! It wasn't a Croc after all. It was a 'Gator."

Hywel burst into forced laughter and the bar was back in business. I took my pint of dark out into the beer-garden and sat on one of the benches next to sleeping truth. That is the trouble with the *TALL STORY* on Raconteur Road; every time you want a drink you have to tell one.

GHOST HOLIDAY

———◦—◦—◦———

I was sitting in the *TALL STORY*, listening to one of Hywel's sombre and unlikely tales, when a thin nervous-looking man added a comment of his own. Now there are two things about the *TALL STORY* that every prospective customer ought to know. The first is that it does not exist; the second is that Hywel must never, under any circumstances, be interrupted.

How he became landlord of a nonexistent pub is a secret that Hywel likes to keep to himself. Indeed, considering his size, strength and (even more importantly) the sheer nastiness of his pickle sandwiches, it seems probable it will remain a secret forevermore. And this is surely nothing to complain about. Some things are best left unsaid.

Anyway, Hywel was discussing the habits of the ghost of Hugh the Miller, who still haunts all wholemeal loaves and Danish pastries within a quarter of a mile of the spot where he died; he fell in a lagoon. Students and young couples picnicking on the shore have been known to find bloody fingers in their soft rolls and, once or twice, even a nose.

"Like all ghosts he has grown too fond of the place where he died. He despises intruders and does his best to frighten them away."

It was at this point that the thin stranger shook his head and made his comment. Hywel turned purple and shuddered. I stood meekly and waited for the storm to break. The little fellow said:

"Ghosts are not fond of the place where they died. You are mistaken there. Ghosts become bored very quickly with one area and long to move on. Many ghosts are actually itinerant spooks; travellers and strollers. The romance of the road is in their congealed blood—or lack of it. That is why they linger at crossroads. There is so much choice that they find it difficult to leave."

I studied the little man more closely. He was dressed all in black, with a dark cape, a top-hat and muddy boots. He had long greasy hair and bushy side-whiskers. He carried a spade and there was the stench of the grave on him.

"Of course," he continued, "some phantoms simply can't afford to live that way. They have to work for a crust. Instead, they spend a lot of time each year planning holidays and then they generally look down on their freer counterparts. Who can blame them? They pay their taxes like everyone else."

"And who might you be?" Hywel had managed to control himself. I had thought for one moment that I was about to witness a throttling, but now it seemed that Hywel would content himself with merely a stomping and a gouging. I swallowed my drink hastily and held my breath.

The little man lowered his gaze modestly. "I collect ghosts. I have quite a few now. I keep them in glass bottles in my cellars. I am thus able to offer my guests a selection of spirits." He chewed his lip and tears rolled down his dusty cheeks. "Unfortunately, I don't get many guests. None in fact. So I talk to the ghosts instead."

"Well that's all right then!" roared Hywel sarcastically. "I didn't realise I was in the company of an expert. So what is your name, friend?"

"Alas!" The little man shook his head. "I'd rather not say. It seems to put people off. Just pretend I'm an ordinary customer. Now let me tell you about one of my favourite specimens. He's quite a decent spectre."

I was about to reply that there was no such thing as a customer in the *TALL STORY* who could be considered ordinary. It is, after all, a pub that lies in another dimension, somewhere between dawn and sunrise and adjacent to both infinity and eternity. But before I could even begin to explain all this, the mysterious stranger had launched into his anecdote.

"His name is—or was—Jocky McJocky and he was born in a castle near the remote Kyle of Tongue. There is a mountain there called Ben Hope which he used to climb without hope; he was a dour fellow when alive. After his death, his spirits improved and he took to haunting his fellows with great glee. Can you guess what happened? Well, he became a tourist attraction. Americans would relish the chance to spend a night in a haunted castle and, in the early hours, would often hold conversations like this:

RONALD: What's that noise?

NANCY: What noise?

RONALD: It sounds to me like a dim rumbling from afar.

NANCY: Oh, that's probably just the head of Jocky McJocky, executed in the courtyard with a rusty axe for drowning Lord McBroth in a pot of soup. He rolls his head up and down the corridors.

RONALD: I see. But what's that other noise? That hideous screeching and wailing?

NANCY: Oh, that's just the old woman.

RONALD: What old woman?

NANCY: The old woman who made the soup.

As you can imagine, McJocky soon had his fill of tourists. Whenever he materialised in front of them, headless and bloodstained, they would insist on taking a photograph. They were never able to develop the prints, of course, but that didn't stop them from coming back next year and trying again."

The little man paused and licked his lips. He adjusted his hat and made a series of pained faces. It was obviously an uncomfortable fit, his hat, for he kept holding on to it with both hands as if it was about to spring into the air. Hywel leaned over the bar until his nose was within an inch of the stranger's own.

"So what happened next?" he demanded.

The stranger sighed and rolled his eyes. "He eventually decided that he needed a holiday. Now tell me, where would you expect a ghost who lives near the beautiful wooded Kyle of Tongue to go on holiday? Where would a soul used to rugged landscape and natural wonders go to find peace of mind?"

"Transylvania," I suggested.

"Shangri-La," countered Hywel.

The stranger shook his head. He twiddled his thumbs in some mordant satisfaction and uttered a little laugh. I was reminded of the rustle of bat's wings in a cave lit by a single candle—that is going out. His laugh became a whimper.

"No, he moved into a bedsit in Birmingham for two weeks, living (if that's the right word!) on chips and lard sandwiches. He started drinking cheap lager and sitting in front of the television all day. He wore a string vest and picked his ghostly nostrils with an insubstantial finger. He forgot to wash under his arms and never brushed his hair. He claimed afterward that it was the best time he has ever had."

Hywel turned to face me with a look of disbelief etched on his ruddy features. I gazed at the bottom of my glass and wished for a rain of stout. I even contemplated making my farewells. The little man nodded.

"When the holiday was over, he returned to the drab comforts of an entire castle, with its silks and gold and home-brewed mead. But every year he dreams of returning to the simple life of egg on toast and damp wallpaper. He's been saving up to buy a time-share there."

At last, Hywel could contain himself no longer. He seized hold of the stranger's collar and half-dragged him over the bar. "Before we accept your tale as true," he said, "we need to have some proof. How is it that you are in a position to collect ghosts when no-one else can?"

The little man was just about to reply when the doors burst open and a crowd of dead Irish writers stampeded toward the bar. It was lunchtime, of course. I recognised many faces among the poets and authors: Joyce, Beckett, O'Casey, Brian Merriman, Yeats, Flann O'Brien, Brendan Behan. But I soon lost sight of the little man. His hat was knocked off in the crush and then he had disappeared in a sea of thirsty bodies. Hywel had released his grip when the first literary foot had crossed the threshold.

I peered around frantically and finally spotted him creeping toward the door. Without his tall hat he appeared ludicrously small. I was still curious to hear more about his collection of ghosts, so I called after him: "Mr Burke, you've forgotten your hat!" He turned around to face me with a scowl and then vanished through the doors. I was desperate. "Mr Burke!" I cried again.

Hywel had been pouring a continuous stream of velvet pints, but my shout attracted his attention. Leaving the Irish writers bellowing in dismay, he relaxed his grip on the pump-handle and frowned at me. "How do you know his name?" he demanded. "He refused to give it."

When Hywel demands something, it is best to let him have it. And so now I held up the little man's hat—which I had picked up from the floor—and reached inside it. What I pulled out explained everything at once to all who were present. It hung there by its ears and twitched its nose.

A Mad March Hare.

THOSE WONDERFUL WORDS

As the *TALL STORY* is the second grandest pub in the universe, a fuller description of its layout and facilities may not be out of place here. (The grandest pub of all is the one that awaits the loyal Beamish drinker on the other side of the Pearly Gates, where auburn-haired *houris* pour pint after creamy pint and where traditional folk-sessions take place every night; Guinness and Murphy's drinkers go straight to Hell.)

The *TALL STORY* then, is a rather drab and chilly building on the outside; the windows are like glazed eyes and the walls sport a spider-web of hopeless cracks. Once inside, however, the traveller is astonished by the warmth and vitality that suffuses the aged bar and even older lounge. The cedarwood beams that hold up the sagging roof are scored and pitted with the marks of a million foreheads and the bottles and stools that nestle behind and before the bar are scored and pitted with the marks of a million . . . well, foreheads.

The floor of this remarkable establishment, however, is constructed of a truly unusual substance. In old Norse legends, it is told of a ship called *Naglfar* that will sail at the end of the world and is made entirely out of toenails. You may imagine anxious relatives of some recently mangled Viking taking due care to remove his toenails before he breathes his last—in an effort to delay the building of the ship and thus the end of the world. This is absolutely true.

The floor of the *TALL STORY* is not made out of toenails, but something far more offensive. It is made out of unnecessary words. All the words that are spoken for no good reason end up on this floor. That is why the floor keeps expanding toward the roof and why more and more drinkers keep striking their heads on those cedarwood beams—one day the floor will touch the ceiling.

This partly explains why Hywel winces whenever someone says something which contains more words than it should. If Harold the Barrel or Billy Belay ever cry over their jackstraws "Look here, see," or "I'll be there now in a minute," Hywel cringes and hides his face. Both the "see" and the "now" spin out of their ungainly mouths, like shooting-stars, and add their bulk to their brothers and sisters that lie trampled before them. It really is appalling.

To discourage customers such as Harold and Billy, tyrannical Hywel keeps a rather heavy reminder behind the counter. This reminder is made out of oak and is tipped with iron. It is about four feet long.

When Harold the Barrel and Billy Belay are not playing jackstraws in some dark corner, they are usually arguing with each other about which of them has had the more incredible life. They are both committed eccentrics. Harold is convinced that he can fly; sometimes he will stand on his chair and leap off, flapping his arms furiously. Billy is no less modest. He claims that he is a ghost and will often attempt to prove his point by walking into the pub without opening the door. Failure in both cases does not seem to deter them.

Other regulars are equally weird and wonderful. There is Madame Ligeia, the half-Gypsy mystic who lives in a tie-dyed caravan and who can only foretell the past—never the future. She is passionately jealous of rivals and once threw a fellow psychic bodily out of the tavern. She explains her brooding hatred of her magical colleagues simply by saying: "Too many sayers spoil the sooth."

Even more menacing is Dr Karl Mondaugen, the mad scientist of Munich. He is a cryptozoologist by profession but his hobbies include inventing bizarre and terrible devices the purpose of which eludes everybody, including himself. With his wild hair and little round glasses he certainly looks the part. He sometimes sits at the far end of the lounge, right in front of the low stage which is used every Tuesday night for lengthy jazz sessions.

"He has more than five-hundred inventions to his credit," Hywel tells me with a wink, "and most of them are utterly useless. They include such inspired works of genius as:

The Solar-Powered Torch.

The Wind-Powered Fan.

The Wave-Powered Whisk.

And that is just a sample of the most successful ones! I ask you, what can be done with someone like that?" Hywel blinks and offers me an exasperated grimace. I can only shake my head in reply.

While we mull over the sheer strangeness of life, the doors swing open and three weary climbers make their way painfully over to the bar. They are a ragged trio, rucksacks hanging like deflated sacks from their shoulders, ropes trailing in the dust behind them. They order double whiskys each and then retire to a long table near the blazing hearth. I note that two of them maintain a slight distance from their companion.

"Those are the Three Friends," Hywel informs me. "I could tell a tale or two about them for sure. But I'd rather tell you about the time that Karl Mondaugen built a fridge so powerful that it could freeze things instantly. Unfortunately, he put the components in the wrong way round and froze the whole world solid. Luckily it made no difference at all to anything and no-one noticed. It froze things so quickly that they all remained warm."

"I don't believe you," I say. I have even less faith in Hywel's stories than he has in mine. Occasionally we each like to humour the other; more frequently we attempt to uplift a hogshead of gentle scorn over his head.

"Well let me tell you about his latest project then," Hywel replies. "He's building a machine for me that will be able to recycle all those unnecessary words that clutter up the floor. The idea is that whole new sentences can be put together from all the leavings of the old ones."

I make a wry face and gaze beyond Hywel at the rows of jars and bottles that stand beneath the tall impossible mirror (why it is an impossible mirror is another story!) Among the pernod and rum crowd a few dubious-looking green-glass affairs within whose murky depths flicker strange shapes.

Inside the mirror, which often shows false scenes out of sequence, two figures seem to be arguing about fruit. These men are Byron and Julian, but I don't know that yet. Nor that the girl who has just entered, panting with exhaustion, is called Laura and has been chased through a forest. Further along, on the very edge of the reflection, a man by the name of Charlton Radish is proposing a new type of police force with powers over the laws of nature as well as society. It's a ridiculous idea, and so will probably come true.

"If I talk about any of those people . . . " Hywel begins, but he is cut short by a sudden crash. We turn around to find that Harold the Barrel and Billy Belay are wrestling with each other on the floor. Harold has attempted to fly again and has landed on the head of Billy who, confident that solid objects can pass right through him, has made no attempt to move out of the way.

"I'd rather know more about those two," I answer with a smile. "Why do they believe what they do? Why does Harold think that he can fly? And why is Billy convinced that he is a ghost?"

Hywel nods his head in agreement. "Now there's a ripe pair of tales for you! Pull your stool in a little closer and let me pour you another drink and I'll explain everything. It really is a startling sequence of events."

I take out my notebook and pen and wait for Hywel to commence. It is difficult writing and drinking at the same time, but I am willing to learn. Despite what people say, it is not all play in the *TALL STORY*; sometimes we work as well.

LEARNING TO FLY

When Harold saw the advert in the paper, he grew very excited. His breath came in short gasps and little muscles in his neck twitched. The advert said: LEARN THE SECRET OF FLIGHT. Harold sighed with pleasure. This was the chance he had been waiting for.

He had always wanted to be able to fly. Even as a boy he had dreamed of being an owl. Flapping his huge tawny wings, he would swoop down from the trees and soar over the river. At night, he was convinced that his spirit left his body and danced with the clouds.

And now, at last, it seemed that his dream would come true. At the bottom of the advert there was a name and address. Dr Lithiums, World Levitation Expert, 66 Park Road. Harold memorised the address, pulled on his coat and set off to find it.

As he made his way down the streets of the old town, he extended his arms and glided around the pedestrians who stared at him in amazement. Once, a woman in a large fruity hat attacked him with her handbag. But Harold did not care. He felt completely at ease.

Before long, he found the address and knocked on the door. It was answered by a pale woman with hard features and a thin smile. She gazed at him with a sneer. "I've come about the flying lessons," he said shyly. "Is Dr Lithiums here?"

The woman's expression brightened. She led him into a filthy room stuffed full with broken furniture. A small seedy man sat hunched over a flickering television, a bottle of whisky clutched in his fingerless gloves. Harold guessed that he had not washed for a long time.

"This is Dr Lithiums," the woman announced.

"How do you do?" Harold offered him his hand. The man ignored it and rolled a cigarette. He began to chuckle and mumble to himself. His chuckle turned to a cough and he wiped spittle from his lips with his sleeve.

Harold recoiled and stepped into a plate of curry that had been left on the floor. As he hopped on one foot, trying to clean his shoe with a handkerchief, the woman glowered defensively. "We could spend most of our time flying through the air," she said. "We don't need to keep our floors clean."

At this mention of his favourite subject, Harold forgot the squalor and closed his eyes. He imagined himself floating above the smoke-stacks of the city, bobbing along on currents of air like a helium bal-loon. He opened his eyes and began to laugh. "I also want to fly," he said. "That's why I'm here."

"It's expensive. Twenty-thousand pounds for the secret."

Harold's jaw dropped open. He reached into his pocket and pulled out his wallet. It was empty.

"You can pay in instalments," the woman suggested.

Harold groaned. The bubble of his dream had burst, leaving noth-ing but a little soapy water on the wallpaper of his life. He stumbled over old milk cartons and cereal boxes toward the door. His soul dragged in the grime behind him.

"Wait!" The woman raced in front of him and barred his exit. "There is another way. You can earn it."

With bowed head, Harold listened to her proposal. The next morn-ing, he returned with a dustpan and brush. He cleaned the floor and the grate, painted the doors and polished every surface. He mended the broken furniture and washed a pile of dishes so tall it touched the ceiling.

Throughout all this activity, Dr Lithiums remained silent, staring at the battered television. When he had drained his bottle of whisky, the woman would prise it out of his hands and replace it with a full one. This seemed to represent the only contact between them.

Harold attempted to talk to the man, but the man merely muttered obscenities in return. Harold wondered if this was all part of the necessary preparation. He returned to his task with renewed vigour and disturbed the thick dust on the man's bald head.

As the days passed, Harold grew weary, but his enthusiasm did not wane. However, when the days turned to weeks and the weeks became months, he finally began to suspect that he was the victim of a deception. One cold morning, he arrived at the house and the woman said: "You're five minutes late. Go into the kitchen and make my breakfast."

Harold threw his duster down in disgust. "I've had enough of this. I demand that you tell me the secret."

The woman frowned. "You haven't earned it yet. There is still much work to be done."

Harold raised himself up to his full height. "Either you tell me the secret now, or I'll break your television." He clenched his fists while the man in the chair whimpered.

The woman sighed. She whispered a few words into his ear and Harold managed a sarcastic laugh. "Utter nonsense! I should have known this was all a trick. It's obvious now. Why have I never seen either of you fly?"

"You don't understand." The woman watched him depart and shook her head sadly. She regarded her clean shiny home. She could not afford to lose such an excellent pupil. "Perhaps I should have explained," she said to herself. "Perhaps I should have told him the rest."

But as he walked down the street, and she noticed the gap between his feet and the ground, she knew how to get him back.

Moving to the writing-desk and selecting a piece of paper, she planned another advert. She wrote: LEARN TO GET DOWN AGAIN.

LEARNING TO FALL

Southerndown is a village maybe fifteen miles west of Cardiff; a wind-swept, dramatic place with towering sea-cliffs and a rocky shore that is like the surface of the moon. There are few coastal areas in the whole country that can compare with it for natural beauty. The tides are enormous and the breakers pound the sloping beach like monstrous tongues, refilling rock pools with wide-eyed crabs and starfish and breaking open new caves in the limestone walls.

Billy Belay had set off from Southerndown toward Nash Point with a bag that contained an anvil and a rope. He passed Dunraven—with its mouldering castle and picnickers—and carried on for another mile or so. The weather was warm and perspiration dripped the length of his nose. When he had found an isolated spot along the cliff-top path, he took the anvil out of his bag, secured it to his neck with the rope and hurled himself over the edge.

What he was really trying to achieve is anyone's guess, although the obvious should not be overlooked. At any rate, destiny had different plans for him; the tide was in, but somehow he was washed up onto a patch of dry sand, anvil and all, suffering no more injury than a bruised nethermost. At the same instant, he fell into a kind of swoon and it was some long minutes before he regained his senses.

When he did, he was bewildered. There seemed to be no explanation as to why he was still conscious. "But I'm dead!" he cried. As far as he was concerned, the fall had killed him outright. "I must be a ghost," he finally decided. As he thought about the prospect more carefully, it began to delight him. As a ghost he was released from all earthly ties and constraints. He would be able to do as he pleased. There were no rules anymore. He was free.

"I'm a ghost!" he repeated. He picked himself up and removed the anvil from his neck. It did not suit him anyway. He brushed the sand from his clothes and gazed around warily. No-one had witnessed his demise, and yet his body had disappeared. If he was a ghost surely he would be floating above his mangled frame at this very instant?

Dismissing the question from his mind, he made his way painfully along the beach back toward Dunraven. He supposed that he was not the first ghost to haunt this particular stretch of coastline. Indeed, he remembered a legend about a wrecker who used to lure ships to their doom with false beacons and whose spectre was still said to fret and howl on stormy nights.

Billy wondered if he would meet this wrecker, whose name he had forgotten. He did not know if ghosts were confined to the area in which they had died, but he assumed that they were. He pressed on regardless and before long had reached Dunraven. Here he paused and scratched his insubstantial chin.

Throughout his life, he had never played a single practical joke on anyone. This was not because he held such pranks in contempt but simply because of cowardice. He had been frightened of reprisals. Certain of his acquaintances, such as Alan Griffiths and Gareth Thomas, were forever tormenting each other with elaborate tricks and he had always viewed their antics with a measure of jealousy.

Now, however, he was safe from reprisals. As a ghost, he could cause as much mischief as he liked to anyone and everyone. Ghosts were allowed to do things like this and nobody criticised them for it. Indeed, it was acceptable behaviour on their part and sometimes even encouraged.

As he pondered on this, he happened to espy a lone fisherman sitting on a rock and gazing out to sea. He resolved to flex his ghostly muscles at once and crept up behind him. Placing his mouth to the man's ear, he yelled: "Boo!"

Instantly, the fisherman leapt up, dropped his rod and line and began running down the beach—his face as white as a summer cloud. Billy felt very pleased with himself. It works! he thought. I'm a real ghost! I'm a real phantom!

His second victim was a boy who was busy eating an ice-cream. Billy snatched the ice-cream away and thrust it into the boy's face. The boy burst into tears and the tears mixed with the ice-cream smeared on his cheeks. He too fled, arms waving.

I'm a ghost! Billy thought again. He was truly elated now. He opened his mouth and cried: "I'm a *GHOST*!" It was as if he wanted the seagulls to take up his cry and spread it far abroad, so as to leave no doubt in anyone's mind that here was a phantom not to be trifled with, unless of course the trifle was a strawberry one. (Billy wondered if ghosts needed to eat; he hoped they did.)

While he congratulated himself on his quick thinking in hurling himself over the edge of the cliff, becoming a ghost and adapting to his role with such alacrity, he came across a bizarre sight. On his hands and knees a strange figure was engaged with a peculiar contraption. As he moved closer, Billy saw that it was made of two glass bottles joined neck to neck. The figure was muttering to himself: "Common hour-glasses have sand on the inside and the world all around—my hour-glass will have the world on the inside and sand all around!"

Billy knew the man as Karl Mondaugen, the mad scientist of Munich, who now lived in Ogmore-by-Sea. Billy peered closer at the glass device and frowned as he seemed to see moving figures within it. Shrugging, he reached out his ghostly hands and gave the eccentric academic a spooky tickle with his icy phantasmagorical fingers. The scientist shrieked and fell onto the contraption, smashing both bottles beneath his body and wailing in terror and dismay.

Billy rubbed his hands together and walked on. By the time he had reached the village of Southerndown, he had committed another eleven acts of ghostliness, including disrupting a group of geology students by dancing around them with great whoops and hideous chuckles. As he headed inland toward the village, he had already acquired a considerable taste for mischief and saw no earthly reason why he should not gorge himself sick on yet more courses.

Ruining a funeral was next and snatching a postman's sack, casting letters all over the road, came after that. The main feast, however, was the incident with the poodle. Out of the Church Hall, haunt of the local Amateur Dramatics Society, came ungainly Mrs Featherstonehaugh, carrying her poodle under her arm. She had been rehearsing *Blithe Spirit* with her colleagues—a delicious irony, although Billy was unaware of this. He simply crept up behind her and . . .

At this point it may suffice to relate that she was found not more than ten minutes later by a policeman, with the end of a lead protruding from her gaping maw. She was quite blue and bloated. By this time, Billy had entered a shop selling cream cakes and was busy hurling them, one at a time, at the frightened owner of the establishment. The constable who had discovered Mrs Featherstonehaugh instantly repaired to the shop and confronted Billy. He was attacked with an unsheathed chocolate éclair. His eye was poked. Cream spurted.

To a casual observer newly arrived at the village, the sight of a wild-eyed figure being chased by a vengeful mob made up of ham actors, geologists, mourners, postmen, pastrycooks, a battered policeman and sundry others, may have been amusing. Billy also found it amusing—he grinned, chuckled and span as he ran. "You can't harm me, I'm a ghost!" he called back. "I'm impervious to mortal blows!" But his pursuers seemed disinclined to abandon the chase. Somehow they were able to see him. Perhaps Mrs Featherstonehaugh had also turned into a ghost and was directing their pursuit. He wondered.

Eventually, of course, he reached the cliff-top path that led from Southerndown to Nash Point. This was the course he had earlier followed. He raced down the path, but now he was puffing and panting. The crowd behind him was catching up. He tried to imagine what would happen if they caught him. Perhaps they would entrap him in a bottle and take him to an exorcist. Perhaps, when they had collected enough ghosts like him, they would force him to pay a hefty fine.

There was, after all, duty to be collected on imported spirits . . .

There was only one thing left to do. Reaching the point he had already jumped off once, he launched himself into space again. "I'm a ghost!" he cried once more. He fell in a graceful arc, tumbled head over heels and flapped his arms with gusto. No harm could come to him. He had already died once; he could not possibly die a second time. He was certain that his logic was watertight.

This time, however, the tide was out.

THE BANSHEE

Not all the writers who drink in the *TALL STORY* are dead and from Ireland. Many are local and very much alive. Among the published names, however, are a good few unpublished authors who languish in the beer-garden, trying to outwit each other with bitter observations on the injustice of life. One day it might occur to them that for their work to be printed, they first have to send it off. Until then, they seem content to grumble and moan about the same things.

I can see one of these hacks from here, crouched over a napkin with a pencil. I don't know if he's writing anything, but his dietary habits must be gross; his dribble contains the legs of ants. That's typical of the revolting standards of these so-called literary types. It's doubtless the reason why Hywel insists that they sit outside in the beer-garden, even in winter, and why he encourages the jazz musicians who play in his pub every week to make as much noise as they can.

"Did I ever tell you the strange tale of Walter's Head?" Hywel asked me one night. The worthy in question had just tottered out of the bar, his open neck glistening with the frothy bubbles of his stout.

"No," I replied, "and you have never told me the tale of the three mountain-climbers either." I indicated the group of battered adventurers who had unlaced their boots and were warming their woolly socks by the roaring log-fire, two of them eyeing the third suspiciously.

"Well that will keep, I dare say. Until then, let us drink each other's health, for as Omar Khayyám almost said:

> Come fill the cup, and in the Fire of Spring
> The Winter Garment of Repentance fling
> The pig of Time has but a little way
> To fly—and Lo! the pig is on the Wing."

"I don't know about that," I responded, "but I'm quite amenable if you're paying. Besides, Omar never had a taste of Mrs Owen's elderberry wine. It would have turned him teetotal overnight."

Just at that moment, I felt a hand clamp down on my shoulder. I was sure for a moment that it was Mrs Owen herself, and that she would punish me by making me take home a year's supply of nettle marmalade, her answer to the tongue-searing curries Hywel had started serving in the bar.

As I cowered in fear, a rasping voice tickled the nape of my neck and I heaved a sigh of relief. I recognised the voice as belonging to Madame Ligeia, the resident clairvoyant and mystic who had done much to throw her profession into disrepute. As I turned around, I found myself confronted by a veiled figure. No-one knows what Madame Ligeia looks like; she wraps herself so tightly in a cloak of mystery, complete with hood, that only her two eyes are ever visible—glowing like dim coals.

"What is the meaning of this?" she demanded. "I want that woman out of the pub now! Do you hear? Now!" She pointed a quivering finger at an empty chair around an empty table.

Hywel sighed and gave me a knowing look. "I'm pleased that you two have decided to become friends. Mutual trust is so important these days."

"Either you kick her out or I'll box your ears, you ill-mannered lout!"

"And to think that only yesterday you were insisting that I throw her out and threatening to box me around the ears!"

During this conversation, I was less bewildered than might be expected, for I knew something about Madame Ligeia which explained everything. Madame Ligeia is a mystic who can only see into the past. She never knows what is going on in either the future or the present. Consequently, she lives a whole day behind everyone else. That is why holding a conversation with her is so difficult: you have to provide answers to questions she will not ask until tomorrow.

The reason why she had her hand on my shoulder and was talking to me as if I were Hywel was because Hywel had sat on this particular stool the previous day—during one of his many breaks. To clarify matters further, it is best to linger awhile in this previous day and to note what happens:

Hywel is sitting on my stool and I am standing at his place behind the bar (just to help out, you understand) when a dishevelled figure enters the pub and walks up to us. I am astonished by this figure's appearance. It resembles a banshee, with long tangled hair and wild eyes.

Now the banshee, as everyone knows, is a spirit that follows old families about and wails before a member of that family is about to die. However, it is not quite as sinister as some people like to make out. Indeed, the day before, I had discussed the matter at some length with W.B. Yeats, who told me: "The banshee differs from the general run of solitary fairies by its generally good disposition."

So I am not too afeared when it comes up to Hywel and points a finger at an empty chair around an empty table.

"That woman keeps glowering at me and making rude comments," it says. "I want you to tell her to stop."

Hywel shrugs his shoulders and blows his nose in a handkerchief. "It is very heartening to see that you have resolved your differences. Life is too short for bickering."

"If you don't tell her to stop I shall twist your ears off!"

"And to think that tomorrow you were planning to twist my ears off and telling me to force her to stop sitting in that chair!"

After it has left, I turn to Hywel with a quizzical look. Hywel taps his forehead with a smile and winks.

"She is my guest. I invited her here personally."

I am dumbfounded. "What do you want a banshee for? Isn't Mrs Owen frightening enough for you?"

Hywel chuckles and explains that it is not a banshee but Madame Berenice, a mystic who can only see into the future. She never knows what is going on in either the past or the present. Consequently, she lives a whole day in front of everyone else. She is as difficult to talk to as Madame Ligeia is—for the opposite reason.

"But this is a disaster!" I cry. "You know how much Madame Ligeia hates rivals! There will be trouble over this, mark my words!"

Hywel shakes his head emphatically. "They both hate the idea of each other, true enough. But when they meet, the day after tomorrow, something will click into place. Madame Ligeia can only see into the past, whereas Madame Berenice can only see into the future. When they meet, they will both cancel each other out. At long last they will be able to see into the present!"

I scratch my head and pour myself a glass of cognac. "You mean like a seesaw of time? Madame Ligeia on one end and Madame Berenice on the other?" I am impressed when Hywel nods. "And you did this as a favour for them?"

"Wait until the day after tomorrow and then we'll see how things have turned out." Hywel snatches my cognac away and downs it himself, handing me back an empty glass. "Keep your fingers crossed until then."

The day after tomorrow comes soon enough and this time I am sitting on my stool while Hywel is behind the bar. It is a Tuesday night and musicians from far and near are setting up their equipment ready for the weekly jazz session. There is a lot of excitement in the air. A rumour has gone round that Tony Smith—one of the greatest jazz guitarists of all time—is due to make an appearance. Hywel nearly always manages to book fine acts. He has only had one failure, as far as I know, a fellow called Disability Bill who suffered from the delusion that he had lots of bodies and arms. The poor fool.

But above all the noise and hubbub of musicians tuning up and music lovers murmuring in anticipation, the raucous laughter of two women seated around a table drowns out all else.

"What did I tell you?" Hywel leans over the counter and gives me another one of his sly winks.

As I gaze at the two women, I can only shake my head in admiration at Hywel's ingenuity. The two women leave their seats and come over to join us. This time they address themselves directly to Hywel.

"We just want to thank you for introducing us to each other. We have so much in common. It really is incredible!"

Hywel puffs out his cheeks in pleasure. "It is very heartening to see that you have resolved your differences. Life is too short for bickering."

"For the first time in our lives we are able to live like normal people!"

"And to think that only two days ago you were insisting that I throw one of you out and threatening to box and twist my ears!"

Before I loose track of my senses completely, I decide to change the subject. I gesture toward a bottle of wine standing full among empty fellows. "I have heard this conversation before, or one very much like it. Now what was it that Omar never said?"

THE QUEEN OF JAZZ

Tony Smith entered the smoky pub and made his way to the stage. As he passed the bar, Old Bony thrust a whisky sour into his hand and winked. Tony took his guitar out of its battered case, plugged in and tuned up. He was vaguely aware of the admiration of the crowd, their love. "Right boys, what'll it be?"

"How about 'Clotted Cream'?"

"Nope. Let's make it 'Samarkand'." He nodded to the other musicians on the stage, the drummer, the hook-nosed bassist. They were all looking distinctly uncomfortable. It was probably the first time they had ever played with a living-legend.

As his fingers eased into the prelude, tickling the melody through all the complex time-changes, Tony allowed himself the luxury of a sigh. His superiority was beginning to tire him. He was beginning to wish, just for once, that he would meet his match. But that, of course, was impossible.

The musicians fell behind and he waited patiently for them to catch up, improvising on a former theme, his fingers a blur, his guitar the interface for a talent that was strong yet yielding. Though he could play faster than the eye could see, he never sacrificed delicacy of nuance for sheer technique.

"No doubt 'bout it! Tony Smith is the king of jazz!"

With the faintest of smiles, Tony nodded at Old Bony. This night was a free-for-all, a time when the cream of the local talent could show off their skills, stepping up on stage and dropping in or out of the performance whenever mood, or ability, suited them. Tony recognised many familiar faces in the audience. Most had brought instruments with them. None could hope to compete with him on equal terms.

Throwing up his arms, the alto-sax left the stage and sat down on a stool near the bar. He was shaking his head, his eyes alight with unfathomable awe. His place was taken by a more experienced musician, who also struggled with the rhythms Tony had initiated. One by one, the drums, bass and keyboards lost themselves in his web of shimmering sonorities and modal harmonies.

"Come on boys, let's try 'Purple Egg Head'." Tony attempted to inflect a note of enthusiasm into his voice, but it was a lost cause. Although he was the greatest jazz musician in the world, the most loved guitarist of all time, he had a problem. It was a problem that made the problems of other musicians seem insignificant. He had sold his soul to the devil.

It was the old, old story. Fifteen years previously, he had signed a diabolical pact in his own blood. The devil had promised to make him the best jazz musician in the world on condition that, after twenty years, he would give up his soul with the minimum of fuss. It had seemed a good idea at the time.

Almost immediately, Tony had found himself catapulted from semi-professional status to international renown. He had, in quick succession, conquered every possible style of jazz. He had taken trad, bebop, cool, fusion and even avant-garde to their logical extremes. Success, of course, had not brought happiness. But happiness was not a term of the contract.

At the end of the number, he instantly launched into another. "'Fleshpots'," he announced. The other musicians were sweating heavily. They were all duly replaced by a fresh batch. Once again, Tony calmly proceeded to blow them all off the stage. "'Pelican'," he cried, and then, "'Cryptozoology'."

Utterly exhausted, the musicians came and went. Tony alone remained the constant factor. He wrestled with trombones, cornets, marimbas, all manner of keyboards, flutes and even a rival guitar. His phenomenal ability swamped them all.

It was at the end of 'Nonchalant Pygmies', one of his most famous compositions, that a quiet auburn-haired girl stepped onto the stage with a large case. Tony frowned. He had not noticed her in the audience. He watched as she removed a long peculiar trumpet from her case, wiped it down with a cloth and moved toward a microphone. "How about 'Visitin' Angels'?" he said.

The girl shook her head. "Not quite. This one's called 'Judgement Day'. Just follow me if you don't know it." She raised the instrument to her lips. In the dim light of the pub it glowed with preternatural brightness.

"Never heard of it. And what kind of horn is that?" But the girl had already launched into the number, blowing a handful of notes of such unearthly beauty that he reeled backward. "Eh?" With a great deal of effort, he composed himself and followed her.

A hush fell over the packed pub. Even Old Bony stopped stamping and clapping. Tony suddenly realised that he was alone on stage with this newcomer. The others had tactfully withdrawn. As the tempo of her blowing increased, he struggled to keep pace. A surge of energy flooded his veins and his fingers took on a life of their own. He already knew he was playing better than ever before. But still the girl kept ahead of him, bouncing a melody of exquisite sadness back at him, bending his own desperate variations through impossible contortions.

He sobbed. She was leading him into musical dimensions he had never suspected could exist. He threw everything at her, changing key again and again, altering the time-signature with every note so that the whole took on its own supernal logic; but she swallowed it all up with the mouth of her horn and blew it out again, transmuted into something even more revelatory.

As if in a dream, he looked down at his fretboard. His fingers were bleeding. With a wrenching gasp, he struck a discord, another, and then it was all over. He gave up and watched with a curious mixture of horror and fascination as the girl finished the piece, sending a series of utterly perfect notes over the edge of the sound-spectrum, shattering every glass behind the bar in an inevitable, apocalyptic crash.

There was a deathly silence. Old Bony wiped his hands free of glass shards and foamy beer and whistled slowly through his teeth. "Tony Smith is no longer the king of jazz!"

Head bowed, Tony unplugged his guitar, placed it back in his case and hoisted the case onto his shoulder. When he looked up, the girl had disappeared. He stepped off the stage and made his way toward the exit. No-one tried to stop him.

Out on the waterfront, he paused and breathed the cold, pure air. He felt a strange mixture of emotions. He was pleased that he had finally met his superior. And yet, he was also worried. What would happen to his reputation now? Had he lost his soul for nothing?

As he walked deeper into the night, he saw that the mysterious girl was waiting for him. "Well!" he said, trying to sound as casual as possible. "I'd take my hat off to you if I had one. You're a fine player, to be sure. I thought you were an angel in disguise at one point!"

The girl brushed the auburn hair back from her face. "The opposite is closer to the truth. I'm more familiar with the other place. To put it bluntly, I've sold my soul to the devil in order to become the greatest jazz musician in the world."

"But that's what I sold mine for!" Tony blinked in surprise.

"I know. Let me explain. I've followed your career ever since it began. It always struck me that your talent was too vast to be natural. I guessed you might have made a pact with the devil. So I did the same. I said to the devil, 'I want to become a greater jazz musician than Tony Smith'. And he accepted my offer. I did it to save your soul. Now that I am better than you, the terms of your contract have been violated. You can demand a refund."

Before Tony could reply, the girl started to cry. Suddenly he understood the import of her words.

"My poor dear!" Taking her around the shoulders, he hugged her close. For the first time in fifteen years he felt free. So the devil had been cheated after all! A great weight had been lifted from his shoulders. He found it hard to repress his delight. He matched her tears of anguish with his own tears of joy. "Do you really mean it? Have you really sacrificed your own soul to save mine? Am I no longer destined to burn in Hell?"

The girl looked up. The tears stopped flowing. Tony drew back. She broke into a high-pitched laugh. "Actually, I lied. You were right the first time. I'm an angel in disguise. The Archangel Gabriel, to be precise. And yes, you are going to burn in Hell after all. I'm not a mortal so the contract still holds. Sorry! Just a little joke of mine. Can't help it, I'm afraid. What else am I supposed to do on my day off? Now don't lose your temper. Just a little joke. Nothing to get upset about, eh?"

Later, as Tony left the waterfront, he began whistling. A new number had already come into his head. 'Broken Angel Blues' would surely help him regain his rightful place as the greatest jazz musician in the world. But would he ever be known as the king of jazz again? Perhaps it was time for a change. Slowly, he held up a long burnished trumpet and an auburn wig. He wondered.

ANNA AND THE DRAGON

—◆—

The *TALL STORY* is one of the most cosmopolitan pubs in creation. Every night, men and women of a hundred different creeds and colours from all parts of the city mingle together as equals. The Docklands have always been a melting-pot of cultures and its reputation for lawlessness is certainly undeserved. Hywel has always encouraged the local Somalis, Yemenis, Chinese, Poles, Greeks, Swedes, Scots, Indians and even the English to enjoy each other's company and to exchange ideas.

He is even willing to serve students—one of the most mistrusted of all minorities. They often come in and treat themselves to a glass of cider—between ten. When they are feeling particularly flush, they will even splash out on a packet of crisps. Because they are disliked by so many, they make ideal scapegoats and the Government is able to grind them under the heel with few voices raised in protest. The poorest student who ever lived was called Michael, and the only thing he ever owned was a bad idea, but he doesn't drink in this story.

Some of these students are young couples—filled with an idealism and enthusiasm that have long since abandoned Hywel and myself. They often sit by tables near the windows, arguing politics and philosophy and the merits of tinned vegetables. Hywel regards their colourful clothes, their scarves and books of bad poetry as a father might regard the toys of a favourite child.

"See those four over there?" he said to me one day. "Well I could tell many a tale about them that would make your hair stand on end! Some of the oddest tales I have ever heard!"

Business was quiet that evening. In front of the fire, the three climbers still rested their weary limbs, one of them shunned slightly by the other two. And there were only three writers present: James Joyce, Dylan Thomas and Gabriel García Márquez. They were engrossed in their own affairs, laughing and joking. There was also Dr Karl Mondaugen, the mad scientist of Munich, who was busy building a new machine from spent matches which he picked out of the ashtray.

Apart from these, there was a quartet of students, chatting by the window. I knew their names but had never spoken to any of them. I am less tolerant than Hywel (I foolishly believe that students have easy lives.) There was Claire and Peter Elliot and Anna and Gareth Thomas. I had heard that Peter was not a nice man; Gareth, on the other hand, was a friend of Billy Belay and had a reputation as a practical joker.

The girls were both quite shy and I knew very little about either. Hywel had hinted that Claire had already been married once—to Alan Griffiths. But it was Anna he wanted to talk about.

He said: "You would never guess, would you, that she is an expert on dragons? I mean, real fire-breathing dragons! Let me tell you how and why. Ever since she was little, she has been fascinated by stories of knights and dragons. You know the sort of thing: fierce dragon takes up residence in a cave and terrorises local village; village leaves a help-less maiden each year as a sacrifice to placate dragon; brave knight slays dragon and rescues maiden. Usually the knight then marries the maiden and they live happily ever after."

"I know the type of story," I replied. "The old tales of chivalry and heroism. St George and all that."

"Exactly. But for Anna they were much more than mere stories. She believed implicitly in them. She amassed an enormous collection of books about the subject. Secretly, you see, she envied those maidens and wanted to be one. She wanted to be rescued by her very own hand-some knight."

I studied the group of students more closely. I was always amazed at how Hywel seemed to know so much about his patrons.

"But she ended up with Gareth instead?" I asked, innocently.

Hywel waved me aside. "Wait for it! Anyway, as I was saying, she longed to be a helpless maiden in peril, a damsel in distress if you like, and thought about little else. One day she was reading such a tale for the umpteenth time in an old story book—one of those collections of legends with illustrations on every page—when a voice spoke to her. Do you know what it said?"

I had to admit that I did not.

"Well it was a magic voice and it said something like this: 'Anna, there are few of us left now and we need your assistance. Will you help us?' And at the same time, the picture in the book came alive. It was the picture of a maiden chained to the entrance of a cave, watched over by anxious villagers. A dragon was emerging from the cave and, in the distance, a dashing knight was riding into view."

"That seems a bit unlikely," I muttered. "Are you sure this story is entirely accurate?"

Hywel ignored me. "As she watched breathlessly, the mystical voice continued. This time it said: 'Anna, few people are willing to take our place and we desperately need volunteers.' Although Anna couldn't be sure, she was convinced it was the maiden who was talking. So she replied: 'Yes, of course I will help you. Of course I will take your place.' And she clapped her hands for joy."

I mumbled and rapped my fingers doubtfully on the counter. But I knew better than to protest too vehemently at this stage. "So she was drawn into the picture and became a maiden?" I asked cynically. "And I suppose the knight rescued her and they were married?"

Hywel shook his head vigorously. "Not at all. She was drawn into the picture, sure enough, but when she looked down, it wasn't the body of a maiden that she saw. Oh no!"

"What then?"

Hywel stamped his foot and roared with laughter. "Scales of course! It was the dragon who had spoken to her!"

This was too much even for me. I refused to join in Hywel's mirth.

Very soberly, I straightened my tie and replied calmly: "That is the most absurd tale you have ever told me. I simply refuse to believe it. If it really happened, then how come Anna is sitting over there now? I demand you tell a sensible story for once."

Hywel was suitably chastened. "Would you like to hear about those other two and their disastrous trip to Ireland?"

I responded in the negative and gestured at the mountain-climbers. "Tell me about those. Why are two of them so wary of the third?"

"Ah, the Three Friends! By all means, if you insist, but you may wish that I hadn't afterward. Just a friendly warning."

"Why?" I asked.

Hywel squinted up his eyes. "Wait and see," he said menacingly. And those eyes twinkled.

THREE FRIENDS

The three friends were mountain-climbers who had trekked to the roof of the world. They had encountered many dangers on the way and each had taken a turn to plunge down a crevasse. Bound together by ropes as well as friendship, it seemed they had all escaped death by the narrowest of margins. One by one, they had praised their luck and had agreed that teamwork was wonderful.

After the end of one particularly difficult day, as the crimson sun impaled itself on the needle peaks of the horizon, the three friends set up their tent on a narrow ledge. The first friend, who had survived the first crevasse, boiled tea on his portable stove and lit his pipe. Stretching his legs out as far as the ledge would allow, he blew a smoke-ring and said:

"The wind whistles past this mountain like the voice of a ghost, shrill as dead leaves. The icy rock feels like the hand of a very aged corpse. Those lonely clouds far away have taken the form of winged demons. Everything reminds me of the region beyond the grave. I suggest that we all tell ghost stories, to pass the time. I shall go first, if you like."

Huddling closer to the stove, the first friend peered at the other two with eyes like black sequins. "This happened to me a long time ago. I was climbing in Austria and had rented a small hunting-lodge high in the mountains. Unfortunately, I managed to break my leg on my very first climb and had to rest in the lodge until a doctor could be summoned. Because of a freak snowstorm that same evening, it turned out that I was stuck for a whole week. The lodge had only one bed. My guide, a local climber, slept on the floor.

"Every night, as my fever grew worse, I would ask my guide to fetch me a drink of water from the well outside the lodge. He always seemed reluctant to do this, but would eventually return with a jug of red wine. I was far too delirious to wonder at this, and always drank the contents right down. At the end of the week, when my fever broke, I asked him why he gave me wine rather than water from the well. Shuddering, he replied that the 'wine' had come from the well. I afterward learned that the original owner of the lodge had cut his wife's throat and had disposed of her body in the obvious way . . . "

The first friend shrugged and admitted that his was a very inconclusive sort of ghost tale, but insisted that it was true nonetheless. He sucked on his pipe and poured three mugs of tea. Far below, the last avalanche of the day rumbled through the twilight. The second friend, who had survived the second crevasse, accepted a mug and nodded solemnly to himself. He seemed completely wrapped up in his own thoughts. Finally, he said:

"I too have a ghost story, and mine is true as well. It happened when I was a student in London. I lived in a house where another student had bled to death after cutting off his fingers in an heroic attempt to make his very first cucumber sandwich. I kept finding the fingers in the most unlikely places. They turned up in the fridge, in the bed, even in the pockets of my trousers. One evening, my girlfriend started giggling. We were sitting on the sofa listening to music and I asked her what was wrong. She replied that I ought to stop tickling her. Needless to say, my hands were on my lap.

"I consulted all sorts of people to help me with the problem. One kindly old priest came to exorcise the house. I set up mousetraps in the kitchen. But nothing seemed to work. The fingers kept appearing on the carpet, behind books on the bookshelf, in my soup. I grew more and more despondent and reluctantly considered moving. Suddenly, in a dream, the solution came to me. It was a neat solution, and it worked.

It was very simple, actually. I bought a cat . . . "

The second friend smiled and sipped his tea. Both he and the first friend gazed across at the third friend. The third friend seemed remote and abstracted. He stared out into the limitless dark. In the light from the stove, he appeared pale and unhealthy. He refused the mug that the first friend offered him.

The first two friends urged him to tell a tale, but he shook his head. "Come on," they said, "you must have at least one ghost story to tell. Everybody has at least one." With a deep, heavy sigh, the third friend finally confessed that he did. The first two friends rubbed their hands in delight. They insisted, however, that it had to be true.

"Oh it's true all right," replied the third friend. "And it's easily told. But you might regret hearing it. Especially when you consider that we are stuck on this ledge together for the rest of the night." When the first two friends laughed at this, he raised a hand for silence and began to speak. His words should have been as cold as a glacier and as ponderous. But instead they were casual and tinged with a trace of irony. He said simply:

"I didn't survive the third crevasse."

THE RAKE AND THE FOOL

"I didn't like that story," I said to Hywel, after he had finished the tale of the three mountain-climbers. "And I no more believe it than any of the others you have told."

While he had been talking, the *TALL STORY* had filled up slowly with faces new and familiar. I recognised various workers from the nearby County Hall. They rattled their chains and gnawed at their manacles as they waited to be served.

"Actually that tale is absolutely true," Hywel insisted, "but I admit that I made up the nonsense about the dragon. In fact, I could tell you another story about Anna and Gareth."

"Only if you make it brief," I mumbled.

"It concerns a goblin . . . "

To be honest, I was tired of Hywel's more outrageous flights of fancy. I said: "Put that one on hold and try something more culturally relevant than usual, will you?"

"Cross my heart," Hywel replied, but he did no such thing. "This one is so true you can have a year's supply of free drinks out of me if you disprove it, I swear!"

I grimaced at this prospect, for a *TALL STORY* year is made up of twelve bitter months, and eight is my usual limit. Unlike ordinary months, in which all the days are used up before moving onto the next one, Hywel's variety always leaves a few at the bottom and he collects the dregs into whole Winters of Discontent, Summers of Love, Broken

Springs and long Falls down the Stairs. It is awful.

"Go on then," I stammered.

Hywel stretched and gestured at his customers, seated at various tables throughout the tavern. People were chatting to each other, making plans or jokes, loathing or loving comrades, rivals and relatives, exchanging trivial or profound insights, just spouting gibberish when necessary. They included Byron and Julian, the former delving in his pockets as if searching for lost dice, a criminal frown on his brow.

Also Claire and Peter Elliot, crouched over a map of Ireland, marking out possible hiking routes with little flags on pins. Under the map, heads creased the paper at the right places to represent the hills. Two of these heads belonged to Flann O'Brien and James Stephens and this incidental acupuncture had cured them of sundry ills. Alas, most of that ill was their talent.

The main point which Hywel's gesture jabbed into me, though without medical justification, was that his patrons were *communicating*, however inelegantly. All except one, who sat alone. He was a pale individual with white eyebrows and colourless eyes, though he didn't seem old or unhealthy. It was almost as if he was a new type of human being. I thought he was drinking Guinness, but in fact he cradled an empty glass. Despair at his inability to make contact had filled it with a black swirling bile.

"A tragic situation," whispered Hywel.

I rolled my eyes. "He doesn't have any friends. I suppose you want me to go over and talk to him?"

"You misunderstand. He's not a lonely man. He's the *loneliest* man, and that's more serious than having no friends, in the same way that a knob of butter is worse off than a pint of milk. The latter can be returned to a cow's udder with a syringe, but the other is forever divorced from the mother beast. Why? Simply because butter is a fatal illness of milk. When milk is badly shaken on a voyage it becomes travel sick and vomits its own content outside its form. Thus butter will never get better!"

"Are you implying that society can reabsorb lonely men if they have luck and faith, but that the loneliest man is fated to stay isolated for eternity because he has curdled himself beyond the typical definition of humanity? I'll soon fix that!"

I was about to walk over to the peculiar fellow, but Hywel held me back. "It's a cultural thing. That's what you wanted, isn't it? A story about diverse ways of living. Anyway, it's impossible to befriend that wretched soul. Shall I tell you his name? It's pronounced something like this: Asdgfxfkh Kuhfoashfubv."

I frowned. "What language is that?"

Hywel flicked away a slave with his grimy cloth. "Now we're getting to the point. That man is a Faskdhfgasdhian, from a little known, indeed completely forgotten, ethnic minority. Where is Faskdhfgasdhia, you ask? It's not a foreign country but the original name of that island you see across the bay. No need to look."

The windows were too misty anyway, and the *TALL STORY* is always at least one narrow alley and three imaginary corners away from the Cardiff waterfront. But I knew which island he was referring to. In our language it is called 'Flat Holm' and is hardly a noteworthy feature of the local horizon. Slurping waves like a greedy saucer a few miles south of the city, its only claim to glory is as the site of the first reception of speech by radio transmission. On 11th May 1897, Guglielmo Marconi sent the three words 'Are you ready?' to his assistant George Kemp, who was standing on the island and presumably was.

"That's an arrogant twisting of history!" boomed Hywel, as if he'd read my thoughts, "for in very olden times Flat Holm, or as we ought to call it from now on, Faskdhfgasdhia, had a lustrous civilisation all its own, unique and bashful, brave and odd, spicy and tortuous. When it was suddenly destroyed, sometime between the Dark and Magnolia Ages, it was as if it had never existed! For the inhabitants kept no written records and their dwellings and artefacts were constructed from seaweed. Without physical evidence of their culture, they were wiped from the official annals of human endeavour!"

"And yet there were some survivors?"

"Quite a few at first, yes. They emigrated across the shallows to Cardiff. One of their most respected Prophets had said that the island would sink into the waves for a washing. That's what happens when your homeland resembles a saucer. A hundred families made the crossing in a huge canoe. They settled in an obscure part of the city, between Pearl Street and Beresford Road. Later the island rose again but they didn't go back. The same Prophet predicted it would eventually be haunted by a disembodied voice. Maybe he anticipated that radio message, or possibly I invented that bit. I can't remember."

"Did they flourish in their new enclave?"

"Not really. They were an introspective people and found it easier not to mix with outsiders. They didn't even bother to learn any other languages. So inbreeding and nostalgia became their guiding principles. They were ignored by Cardiff Council and this neglect was taken to such extremes that people actually found it difficult to see them. You know how it is when you stop noticing the wallpaper in your house, however exotic the pattern? That's because it doesn't try to interact with you. It just hangs around aimlessly."

I understood. "Ditto the Faskdhfgasdhians?"

"Slowly they started to die out. Eventually there was one couple left. Then less than that."

I nodded. "Right! So this chap is the very last member of his race? I can guess how he feels, standing on the edge of a genetic, linguistic and social abyss. But to extend your metaphor—if the wallpaper is stripped away, won't we suddenly notice a bare wall of crumbling bricks in our cosmopolitan environment?"

Hywel shrugged. "Who knows?"

We remained silent for a few minutes, and he took this lull in the profundity to serve his other customers, but by this time they had all been whipped back to work by potbellied overseers, who had selected drumming music on the ancient jukebox.

"This man—what's his name?—Asdgfxfkh Kuhfoashfubv!—has no way of relating to anybody else. No shared values, customs, concepts. He is utterly divorced from modern life."

"Correct again. No comedy in this tale, eh?"

An abrupt moral impulse seized me. I clicked my fingers at Hywel and cried: "The pickle jar."

Normally treating him with such rudeness would result in me having the jar forcefully set down on my head, which is actually what happened, but I was prepared for it, and it was the only way I could be certain of getting quick access to it, without yet another story nested inside this one, and I didn't care for a diversion. My hat cushioned the blow, and I left the vessel perched there as I stepped over to the poor soul. He had a look of extreme relief on his face when he saw that I acknowledged his existence, but I waved him back and offered him the jar with a deep bow. Maybe that gesture was an insult in his culture, for he blushed red. But for the sake of contact he repressed his feelings. He took the gift but didn't know what to do with it.

"There's joy in pickles," I said.

"You'll have to show him how," Hywel called to me. I unscrewed the lid and swallowed a gherkin whole.

Then I left him to it. I didn't want to look too soft, in case the act became a real part of my character and weakened my career hopes. By the time I had returned to the bar, Hywel had sharpened and polished a reprimand. "That was so irresponsible!"

"Not at all. It was an attempt at empathy."

"Would you give a terminally depressed man a loaded gun? Shame on you!"

I was confused, but not for long. Unable to bear his situation any longer, the last Faskdhfgasdhian had followed my example deliberately badly. He had stuffed not just one but several dozen gherkins into his small mouth at the same time.

"He's committing suicide!" I wailed.

"Worse than that," said Hywel. "When the average man kills himself, the world loses a single individual, a cell in the body of society. But what this chap has done is to wipe out an entire civilisation, with all its components. At a single choke he has eradicated a complete system of ethics, language, laws, aesthetics, fashion, science, religion. It's the ultimate crime. It's *auto-genocide!*"

"An indigenous religion, you say? I wonder what form that took? We will never know for sure now . . . "

"We can speculate," retorted Hywel. "I reckon the Faskdhfgasdhians were monotheists. Probably because I'm too lazy to envisage more than a single god for them. He was usually depicted as a clown holding a rake. A bumbling gardener, if you please."

"What do you base that reasoning on?"

Hywel leaned closer and winked. "Essentials of plot. Were you born yesterday? Now shut up and weep!"

I bared my teeth. "No! If I'm partly responsible for this disaster, it's up to me to put things straight! I intend to do my best to revive him. First aid and all that stuff."

"Too late! He's stopped breathing."

I rushed over to the casualty, who had collapsed onto the floor and was lying quite still. His throat bulged with gherkins. I roared: "Sound the alarm! Call for a doctor!"

"Ja!" barked Karl Mondaugen from a nook.

"Not you. We don't need a doctor of cryptozoology. We want a medical practitioner. Where's Dr Walnut?"

"Struck off decades ago! By a child with a catapult."

"Then I must pick him up." I hurried out of the pub but didn't get far. No time to explain why.

"What do you intend to do now?" sneered Hywel.

"I must unblock his throat!" I whimpered, as I returned to the side of my patient. "Any suggestions?"

"Perhaps you could try lubricant?"

"Not tonight, vaseline!" I muttered darkly.

"What was that?" demanded Hywel, but I shrugged and he didn't press for an explanation. He scratched his head and sought to recall the brief medical training he never had. In a nonexistent pub, that's feasible. He almost giggled as he called:

"Try the *kiss of life!*"

I groaned. I rarely care to kiss men, partly on account of their stubble, partly on account of mine, but mostly because I'm still in love with my past achievements. Mind you, I have a mistress too: my future hopes. Can't choose between them.

"Not sure I can manage . . . do my best . . . "

The smell of vinegar was abominable. My lips just wouldn't attach themselves to his. I tried pushing my head down with my arms, but they refused to work. The nearest I got was nose to nose, and that's still a handkerchief's breadth away.

"Ugh! How do women cope?"

Hywel cried: "Have you started yet?"

As I shook my head to reply in the negative, something incredible happened. The unmoving body beneath me sat up and spat out a stream of gherkins, most of which struck my face. The Faskdhfgasdhian known as Asdgfxfkh Kuhfoashfubv was better. He had got over his minor case of death with amazing abruptness.

I recoiled. "How did I accomplish that?"

Hywel rubbed his chin. "Of course! The people of Faskdhfgasdhia don't kiss as we do, with mouths. They rub noses! So you gave him the precise *kiss of life* he required!"

"Another forced *TALL STORY* coincidence!"

"I'm not sure if that's the right word," said Hywel with a frown. "I'd call it a rusty *deus ex machina*."

"You're such a snob! But look at this!"

I nodded at all the other customers in the pub. They were no longer engaged in their own business. They were turning on their chairs to gaze at Asdgfxfkh Kuhfoashfubv. It was as if they'd noticed him for the first time. There was excessive interest in their expressions. Even Byron and Julian were fatally distracted from their dice, or whatever game it was they were playing. Even Anna and Gareth stopped to stare. Claire and Peter too (and Flann O'Brien and James Stephens beneath the map). Also Mr Burke, Mrs Owen, Madame Ligeia, the Three Friends, Harold the Barrel, Billy Belay, Tony Smith. Everybody.

"Why the sudden fascination?" I wondered.

"A sad reflection on our society," sighed Hywel. "While the last Faskdhfgasdhian was still alive, nobody cared about him. After his death, it became open season on his culture. We all want to adopt it. He has become fashionable because he's the focus of a *revival*. We often seem to prefer reconstructions to the authentic product. Now he's set up for the rest of his second (bogus) life."

I noted that people had begun to try to dress like the new exotic celebrity. Someone had powdered the chalks provided for use at the dart board and was passing the dust around. This was being applied to cheeks and eyebrows. Clothes were being ripped and folded just so. Mouths were forcing guttural accents into the smoky air. And Asdgfxfkh Kuhfoashfubv was soon surrounded by dozens of admirers, fingers stroking his hair, tongues tracing his tattoos.

"Disgusting!" grumbled Hywel.

"Aren't you delighted he's finally receiving the attention he deserves?"

"No, because they won't get it right. When he choked himself on the gherkins, he really did expire for a short time. So the link between the authentic Faskdhfgasdhian culture and this new one was broken. It can't be the same."

"Won't he help to put matters straight?"

"How can he? Like I said, he did die. Thus he's also part of the revival. Probably some of his brain cells decayed while he lay prone on the floor—the cells containing the accurate memories of his customs and culture. So he'll have to go along with the recreation. It's just play-acting. Pure theatre."

"With plenty of opportunity to get things wrong? That's what happened with the Druids, isn't it?"

"Exactly. The crucial link was broken there too, and the modern 'Druids' have almost nothing in common with the ancient ones. I mean, the robes, the beliefs, the association with neolithic monuments: it's all incorrect. But what can we do?"

"Just watch and be superior, I guess."

Some of the drinkers were building a 'Faskdhfgasdhian' temple out of stacked beer-glasses. It was soon finished. Then they danced around it, calling out for the god which had once belonged to Asdgfxfkh Kuhfoashfubv alone, but now was theirs as well, to put in an appearance. I don't think they expected results. Which is why they were so shocked when a vague shape began to materialise in the entrance to the temple. They backed away as it stepped out and turned solid. It had hunched shoulders and was dressed like a rogue, with long dark coat, slouched hat and spotted necktie. It wore stubble on its chin and a filthy cigarette dangled from its lower lip. It had a squint and fingerless gloves. It hissed:

"Awright, me hearties? Wots up wid you lot then, eh? Leave it out, guv'nor. Get it sorted, mate."

In a grimy hand, it held a tub of strawberry yogurt.

Hywel smote his brow in despair. "They've even got the god wrong! The *rake* and the *fool* have been mixed up!"

I hadn't realised a rake was a kind of rogue . . .

There was a commotion at the main door. A policeman had entered the *TALL STORY.* It was Inspector Firbank. He was always late at the scene of a crime. It gave him a headache.

"Somebody has reported that an ultimate crime has been committed on these premises. Anyone care to own up?"

Hywel pointed at the god. "He's murdered good taste!"

Inspector Firbank nodded smartly and stepped over to the figure. He grabbed it by its torn collar and yanked it out of the pub back to the station. Blasphemy, hubris, justice!

I slumped at the bar. "Listen, I accept it was my fault for asking for a culturally relevant tale. I won't do that again. Grief! I could do with a dose of your most outrageous flights of fancy, however weak and corny. Now please take my order."

"What will it be?" asked Hywel.

"A triple of the worst you've got . . . "

GOBLIN SUNRISE

Anna shook her husband awake. Gareth blinked dreams from damp lashes. He struggled through the syrup of hypnagogic sleep. His yawn was as pink and large as the morning.

Anna kept shaking him. "Eh?" he gasped. His hands clenched the pillow and wrestled it over the edge of the bed. The reflexes of a tree, Anna thought derisively. His eyes snapped open.

"What is it? What's wrong?"

Anna lost no time. "There's a little man outside the window. He's wearing a floppy hat and curly slippers. He's laughing his head off. He's very ugly. He has a dirty beard and a warty face. Also, he's got horns."

"Ah yes, that must be the goblin I ordered."

"The what?" Anna cast a doubtful look through the frosty glass. She frowned. "Did you say *goblin*?"

"Didn't I tell you? I ordered one yesterday to do some work for us. Very hard workers apparently. Very efficient. Very neat. Good overall value." Gareth yawned again.

"Where did you order it from?"

"Little People Inc. A new company based in Cork, Eire. They provide goblins, gnomes, dwarves, elves and leprechauns for customers. Goblins are the cheapest of the lot. Not very bright, you see. But good workers all the same. Beautiful," he added.

Anna pouted. "I see." She lay back down on the bed. Gareth closed his eyes. Anna frowned once more. Gareth snored. After a couple of minutes, she turned on her side, propped herself up on one elbow and studied his face with its gaping, drooling mouth.

"What now?" He was somehow aware of her gaze.

"Let me get this straight. You ordered a goblin to do some work for us? What sort of work?"

"Oh, in the garden." He was dismissive.

There was another long pause. "I see," she said again. She scratched her nose. She introduced the toes of her left foot to the toes of her right. "Then why is he floating in the air? And why is he cutting at the clouds with a pair of clippers?"

"What?" Gareth woke with a start, jumped out of bed and squinted in the early light. The sun was big and red on the horizon. And there, far away, silhouetted by the dawn, a goblin was carefully trimming the rosy cumulus tufts.

Gareth opened the window, looked down at his overgrown garden, shook his fists at the sky and cried: "The lawn, you fool! The lawn!"

THE JUGGLER

On a morning as bleak and grey as his soul, Byron rose from his bed and avenged himself on his tormentor. And then, suddenly aware of what he had done, he fled out into the city.

He spent most of the day slinking down the backstreets and alleyways of the Docklands, convinced that the police were already after him. As night fell, and darkness wrapped itself like a cloak around his hunched frame, he grew bolder. Eventually, he decided that he needed a drink.

Entering a tavern, he stood against the bar and ordered a large whisky. As he was raising it to his lips, a hand clamped down on his shoulder. He almost spilled the drink and whirled in alarm, but it was only Julian, an old friend.

"What a surprise!" Julian was genuinely pleased to see him. He frowned. "What's wrong? You look pale."

"Do I?" Byron managed a thin smile. He shook his head, as if to clear it. "No, I'm fine. I'm just a little . . . tired. Nothing more."

"Come, let's find a table. We can talk about old times." Julian led him to a shady corner and offered him a cigarette. Byron declined and chewed a thumbnail instead. Little muscles in his neck twitched and quivered.

Julian talked for a whole hour, reminding him of more innocent days, student escapades and the dreams of youth. Byron forced himself to laugh at the right moments, but his eyes rolled in his head like those of a mad dog. Finally, he could stand no more and leaning forward, he hissed through clenched teeth: "I am evil."

"I beg your pardon?" Julian arched an eyebrow.

"It's true. This very morning, I took a kitchen-knife and cut that hideous throat from one ear to the other. He deserved it though. Five years of torture! Can you imagine it? Every night for five years! It's hardly surprising that I took matters into my own hands."

Julian opened his mouth and tried to speak. But no words would come out. He cleared his throat and gasped: "I think you should tell me all about it."

"Certainly." Byron nodded. He finished his long-neglected drink and wiped his lips with his sleeve. "Listen then. It all began when a new owner moved into the flat above mine. He was an Insurance Clerk, but his hobby was juggling. He also happened to suffer from insomnia. On sleepless nights, he would while away the hours by practising."

"I don't understand."

"He juggled with fruit. He bought some every day from the green-grocer across the road. I used to watch him through my window. He started with gooseberries and satsumas. These were not too bad. After a while, however, he progressed to heavier fruits. Apples, lemons, pears. Eventually, he was using melons."

Julian frowned and scratched his nose. He was beginning to suspect a joke. He wondered if he was supposed to chuckle. Lighting another cigarette, he studied the face of his friend, hoping to find a trace of humour in his stony expression.

Byron slammed his fist down on the table. His empty glass jumped. "Don't you see? He wasn't a good juggler! He was awful! That's why I had to do it. He kept dropping the fruit. A pounding on his floor all night. And his floor was my ceiling. I was nearly driven insane. I became a nervous wreck. I began to hate him more with each passing day."

Julian realised that it was not a joke. He had never seen anyone twisted with so much rage and pain. He shuddered.

"Of course," continued Byron, "after such treatment, the fruit would be bruised and useless. And so he would have to buy more. I tried to reason with him. I tried to point out that the juggling was damaging my health. But he ignored me. Every night the pounding would grow louder, and every day he would buy fresh supplies from the greengrocer. Well, what would you have done in such a situation?"

Before Julian had time to answer, Byron had slammed his fist down again. This time, the glass bounced off the table and rolled across the floor with a hollow drone.

"Yesterday, I was walking past the greengrocer's when I saw that he had arranged a dozen pumpkins on his stall. One of them he had hollowed out into a leering face. I remembered that it was Halloween next week, and last night I dreamed that my neighbour was juggling three of these pumpkin-heads. This dream was a warning. Do you know how heavy a pumpkin is?"

"So when you awoke you cut your neighbour's throat?" Julian sighed heavily. Sweat stood out on his brow. "In that case, you must give yourself up. The Judge might be sympathetic. You could plead diminished responsibility. After all, you endured five years of Hell."

Byron scowled. "That's just it! I didn't kill my neighbour. Why should I? All he ever did was juggle. The real culprit was the man who supplied him with the fruit."

"You killed the greengrocer?" Julian was incredulous.

Byron frowned. There was a strange glint in his eyes. "The greengrocer? No, I didn't kill the greengrocer."

"Then who?"

Byron smiled a superior smile. He rose to his feet and gazed down at Julian. "The pumpkin, of course. Who else? He deserved it though. You should have seen his face afterward . . . What a mess!"

And reaching into his pocket with a wink, Byron pulled out a handful of pumpkin-seeds and scattered them like dice on the table.

THE PEAT FIRE

Peter and Claire Elliot were lost on the moors. A fine drizzle had swept in from the west, chilling them even through their waterproof clothing and obscuring their view of the horizon. As Peter stepped forward, he sank a good ten inches into the soft clay that had been churned almost to liquid by the rains of the previous night. Cold mud surged over the top of his boots and forced itself under his toes.

"I hate this country!" he wailed.

Claire placed a comforting arm on his shoulder, but he pulled away with a scowl, losing his balance in the process and falling backward into the mire. He flapped aimlessly for a minute before Claire, struggling to repress a laugh, helped him to his feet. Once again, he shrugged her off and gritted his teeth. "Yes, I hate this country. And I hate you as well!"

"The holiday was your idea," Claire pointed out.

She turned her face into the oncoming sheets of drizzle. They washed over them with a regular pulse, as if dancing to the rhythm their feet had made earlier on the moors. It seemed as if someone was draping a succession of veils over the landscape, each veil a fraction of a millimetre thicker than its predecessor.

"I'm completely fed up!" Peter added, under his breath.

"Perhaps it will brighten up later?" Claire suggested. She knew it was useless now to remind him that he alone was responsible for leading them off the road into the wilderness. She attempted to smile and then began to whistle.

"Oh, shut up!" Peter growled. He raised a fist as if to strike her, thought better of it, and contented himself with spitting near to where she stood. "Let's just find our way out of here, shall we? Pass me the map."

"I gave it back to you," Claire replied.

She frowned as the blood rushed to his face. He was little better than a child, she decided. He stamped his foot, spraying mud and damp clay over an area considerably smaller than he would have liked. He tried again, and managed to spatter Claire's face.

"You liar!" he screamed. "Right, that does it! I'm off! You can find your own way back! Do you hear me? Find your own way back!"

Claire watched him stamp off, skidding on wet grass and lurching into low bushes. She sighed and shook her head. Doubtless, he expected her to race after him and apologise. But she had finally reached the end of her tether. He could drown in a bog now, as far as she was concerned. Enough was enough. Besides, there was always Michael at college, and he seemed a much nicer sort of man.

She waited until Peter was out of sight and then began moving in the same direction, slowly and carefully so as not to catch him up. She guessed that he would probably veer off at a tangent at some point and eventually end up walking in circles. His sense of direction was truly unique!

Before long, as the light began to fade and the rain increased in volume, she spied a lone figure making its way toward her. She assumed it was Peter and rolled her eyes in exasperation, but it was, in fact, an exceedingly thin stooped man with a strange, wild look about him. As he approached, he hailed Claire and began to chuckle. His hair was matted and he possessed but a single blackened tooth in his hideous wound of a mouth.

"Another visitor, to be sure!" he exclaimed. "And what would your name be?"

"Claire," said Claire, intrigued rather than alarmed by the fellow's appearance and strange high-pitched voice. It was a voice somewhere between the creaking of a coffin-lid and the scream of a bluebottle caught in a spider's web.

"Claire, eh?" The man screwed his face up and winked. "Not much I can do with a Claire," he said. "There's a County Clare though," he added thoughtfully.

"I'm lost," Claire replied, well aware that she should not really be divulging this fact, but feeling, for some reason, relatively safe in the company of this stranger.

"Come with me," the stranger insisted, taking her by the arm. "I have a hut. A bowl of soup and a peat-fire awaits you. Yes, potato soup and a real peat-fire!"

Claire let herself be led across the moors. As they walked, the stranger began to talk in a breathless monotone, nodding and tapping his warty nose as he did so.

"I'm a namesmith. I've been a namesmith for a long time now. I do things with people's names, you see. It's hard work too, I'm blasted worn out with it, but I enjoy it all the same. Peculiar things, names."

By the time he had finished, they had reached a hut, seemingly made out of turf, with a hole in the top to act as a chimney. Smoke issued forth and made a vain attempt to flee the rain. The man gestured at the open doorway. "Go inside. There's a bowl of soup and a real peat-fire. You're my second visitor today, you know."

Entering the darkened hut, Claire squinted at the oily fire that burned in the centre of the single room. It took her a full minute to appreciate what it was she was looking at. At first, she was appalled, but then she laughed. Divine retribution, perhaps?

Behind her, the little man chuckled again. His breath was chill on the nape of her neck. "Yes, I'm a namesmith. Well, what do you think?" He began to dance. "I'm still waiting for Old King Cole. Much easier to light!"

He danced in front of her and paused, attempting to gauge her reaction. "Well?" he repeated.

Claire smiled and shook her head.

"You can't spell, can you?" she replied.

KNIGHT ON A BEAR MOUNTAIN

At least the fireplace of the *TALL STORY* is never short of acceptable fuel. It burns the unpublished manuscripts of the writers who frequent its unforgiving domains. Nathanael West was in here the other day, searching for his cool million, which he'd misplaced a whole week, or dreamlife, before. He didn't reveal what the million was *of*. I don't think it was money. Nor locusts.

Perhaps he was hoping to find a sweetheart, a girl in a million, and in that case I wish him luck. Maybe I could set him up with another writer, say Mary Shelley or Christina Rossetti, but that's not really my job. I'm no Miss Lonelyhearts. Then again, it occurs to me that with a global population of ten billion, there must be 10,000 girls in a million running around at random. If they all decided to enter this pub at the same time, I would die of admiration and suffocation. Which reminds me: the ventilation is playing up.

There's a big grille set into one of the walls and a fan which sucks out the fetid air and cigar smoke and musical notes of the regulars. This grille resembles an ancient knight's helmet. Not that I've ever seen a visor. But it brings to my mind something Hywel told me a long time earlier.

I said: "What happened to that knight in the story about when Anna turned into a dragon? I mean, he barely came on the scene before you admitted the whole thing was a lie. I bet he was annoyed at being let down like that. I can't believe he just went away after getting all dressed up for action. Why not tell me what he did next?"

Hywel smirked to himself and something of his former profession returned to him as he rolled up his sleeves and kneaded my cheeks for a full minute. Then he fell back and answered: "Listen, Old Bony, we've become good friends and I feel I can speak frankly. You can't really leave this pub, though you've tried often enough. The street outside . . ."

I sighed. "No need to say more. But I wonder who built Raconteur Road? Laid the cobbles, I mean."

He was shocked. "Wash your mouth out with soapy beer!"

I did so, and swilled that taste clean with whisky. I grimaced at my reflection in the mirror over the bar. It didn't grimace back. It was fast asleep. I asked a safer question which had been bothering me for ages. "Why is that an impossible mirror?"

"You'll have to ask Titian Grundy."

"Who's he?"

"A man who lives in the future, so you'll have a long wait if you really want to speak with him . . . "

I decided to let the matter drop. "What about the knight?"

"That's the point I was coming to. Remember that it's *you* who's doing all the telling, as agreed in our original contract. I know you've arranged it to look as if I'm guilty for most of these stories, even though I haven't actually told a single one, but that's just a literary trick. I'm weary of it, to be honest, and I think you ought to accept your responsibility this time and let me have a rest."

I was disappointed by his reluctance to humour me, but I guessed it was only a temporary aberration on his part. However, I knew that two could play at this anti-game. "Well, I've decided to match your surliness. I don't have any words to spare."

"No problem." He indicated the figure of Karl Mondaugen huddled in its secret corner. The mad scientist was darning the sleeves of his strait-jacket with a toothpick and a guitar string. Faint notes of unholy jazz sounded as he worked. In the ashtray on his table, his latest invention waited to pass its first test.

I squinted at it uneasily. "So what useless thing has he created now?

A Wake-Up Call for an Alarm Clock?"

"Out of matchsticks? Don't be silly! I think it's: A Pair of Stilts for a Giant."

I tutted. "Fine, I'm sure. But how can that help me tell a story?"

"No, not that. Look at the other thing he's just invented."

I scratched my head. "I can't see anything . . . "

"Exactly! That means it's already up and running."

"But what *is* it?"

"Remember when I said that Dr Mondaugen was hoping to create a machine that could recycle all those unnecessary words which are scattered all over the floor, indeed which *are* the floor? Well, he's done it. And if you operate it, you'll be able to tell your new story without wasting any new words."

"Operate the machine! But where is it?"

"Outside this story, of course! You don't seriously expect to find the *implement* of composition within the prose it creates, do you? That would be totally absurd. No, it's located above the page."

"But I'm trapped down here, aren't I?"

"That's an illusion. If you are the author, you *must* be outside."

I was forced to concede the point. I took a deep breath and concentrated and the pub melted away. I grasped Mondaugen's machine, positioned it over the blank page and pressed the buttons to shuffle the reclaimed words. I dealt them like a true amateur:

"After the knight realised his services were no longer required in the rescue of a damsel, he galloped off in a huff. Fancy squeezing himself into this armour for nothing! It wouldn't do to take it off before he'd had his money's worth. He went looking for a substitute adventure. Across many lands he rode, through forests and over moors. Eventually he came to a very flat country on the edge of a stagnant sea.

"It was all marsh and swamp, with complicated routes winding between the lagoons and quicksands, and wills-o'-the-wisp at dusk to entice him off the path. In the day, wasps and will were lacking, but mosquitoes and dogged persistence urged him on. Catfish too, which leapt out of the pools to bite his lap. He was grateful to arrive at a settlement. It was a town in which every building was a windmill.

"Chief of this realm was Pungent Hugh, miller of millers, grinder of black bog-rush and pumper of bilge, who protected his people with dykes and towels. He welcomed the knight—Sir Jasper was his name—with a handshake and a meal. The bread was awful. Then when his guest had finished belching through his visor, he made a little speech. He said:

"'How grateful I am to meet such a noble hero.'

"'And why is that?' asked Sir Jasper, with much interest and not a little suspicion. 'Damsels?'

"'No, our women take care of themselves, I'm afraid. But we do need protection from a ferocious talking bear which roams these parts and raids our town at night. He smashes the sails of our windmills with his dirty great paws or spins them backwards until they break.'

"'A talking bear?' blinked Sir Jasper. 'In a swamp! Are you sure?'

"'Absolutely certain. I've heard it with my own ears. Oh, I know what you're thinking: bears normally live in the mountains, don't they? Well, maybe this one does too. But he comes down to visit us after sunset.'

"'I accept the quest! I shall sally forth to slay the creature!'

"And off he galloped again, glad to be fulfilling his chivalrous role at last. It dimly occurred to him that he might as well wait until the bear entered the town that evening, but there was something unheroic about not taking an active part in seeking danger. What true knight ever sits still and allows dastardly things to charge at him? The traditions must be followed scrupulously. Besides, he didn't like the town. So he kept going, looking for a mountain and a liar—I mean lair!

"Although the sun was getting low in the west it was still hot and he sweated profusely inside his armour. He was grateful for all the holes in his visor which let the air in. The sky was cloudless, but swarms of biting insects cast a little shade. He knew where he was headed thanks to an eccentric line of reasoning he had decided to pursue. North! For when the evening came and the stars appeared, the constellation of Ursa Major would be directly ahead, frosty and bright.

"What other sign would a talking bear choose to dwell under? Ursa Major is the Great Bear, and a real one which can articulate meaningful sentences must surely be the greatest of its kind. Sir Jasper peered anxiously into the distance, but there were no mountains. The land remained flat. The sun set over a large lagoon and the foam on his horse's mouth turned pink. Still there were no peaks visible. Twilight was followed by dusk, and the smell of decaying vegetation gave way to that of smoke. A volcano perhaps?

"No, it was a small camp-fire, and the bear sat warming its paws in front of it. A pot of porridge bubbled on the coals. Sir Jasper found it impossible to urge his horse forward, so he dismounted and creaked stealthily toward his foe. Ursa Major did indeed twinkle, above him and also on his armour, but the mountain was absent. No matter! He grimaced inside his helmet as the bear slowly turned its head at his approach, but realising that his expressions of fear were hidden, he drew his sword from its scabbard with a confident flourish and ran forward.

"The bear stood up. It fixed the charging knight with its wild eyes and demanded: 'Who the bloody hell are you?'

"Sir Jasper had known that this was going to be a talking bear, but actually hearing the words emanating from that mighty jaw was an experience he wasn't really prepared for. He went numb. The sword slipped from his fist. This was precisely the reaction the bear was hoping for. The tactic rarely failed. It opened its huge arms to receive its visitor, which it intended to crush inside the iron shell, rather than wasting time trying to get him out first. The plan almost worked, but Sir Jasper had a secret.

"Before he had become a knight, he had wanted to be an actor. He wasn't very good at it—critics said he was too wooden—but he'd gained some knowledge of the mechanical tricks used by theatre companies to increase the astonishment factor of a production. The most obvious and simple of these devices was the pantomime horse. Worked by levers and springs on the inside, a single man could operate it with amazing efficiency.

"Something in the bear's tone made Sir Jasper wonder if a similar trick was being played here. Instead of trying to brake his headlong rush, he accelerated and jumped. The bear closed its paws around nothing. The knight came down on the bear, straddling its shoulders. Sure enough there was a row of buttons running all the way down the creature's back. What's more, they looked ready to pop. Sir Jasper reached over and undid the top one. It was just enough. The costume burst.

"Unfortunately for him, there wasn't a man inside. Sir Jasper had assumed that bigger things hold smaller things, not the other way round. The object that stood among the tattered remains of artificial bear was—a hippopotamus! It rolled its huge eyes and lisped: 'Thank goodness for that! It was such a tight fit in there!' But Sir Jasper wasn't deceived. He undid the top button of this costume too, and the hippo burst to reveal an elephant, which trumpeted: 'A blessed relief to be out of that, what?' Yet Sir Jasper still didn't relax.

"Another undoing of a button, another fabric detonation and now the knight was confronted by a blue whale. Before it could utter a word, he fumbled for the next button. Now he was in the branches of a gigantic redwood tree. He felt dizzy. He screamed as he undid this final button, for what burst out of the tree was something he had suspected was the real villain all along, though he hadn't acknowledged the fact to himself—it was an impossibly high mountain. Its lower slopes were covered in snow and lost climbers, one of them wedged in a *third* crevasse. Sir Jasper clung tightly to the summit, but as the peak rose into the sky and beyond the atmosphere, he came to regret the holes in his visor which let the air out . . . "

The machine to recycle words was empty, so I switched it off and stepped back into the page. Hywel blinked.

"That's weird! You just seemed to vanish."

"I moved into a dimension where I had godlike control over scenes and situations. Anyway, what did you think?"

"Of the tale about the knight? Very poor. I'm not blaming you for that, of course. You only had a limited selection of previously used words to work with. But I pity our readers."

I nodded. "So do I. But if that's truly what happened to Sir Jasper (and I've decided that it was) then I can't be accused of dishonesty. I'm not culpable for the clumsy bits."

Hywel shrugged. "Very wise."

There was nothing more to say. We gazed around the pub in quiet despair. Nothing much had changed. There was no longer a floor to stand on, because the scattered words which had doubled as flagstones had gone, but the ineffable void which now occupied their place was no less solid, so it didn't matter. I gestured at Mondaugen.

"I wish he would stop fiddling with his strait-jacket. It's giving me unpleasant memories."

"Don't look at him in that case. Seek a distraction."

One came in the form of a figure who entered the *TALL STORY* wearing a knapsack on his shoulders. His boots left crimson prints on the surface of the polished void. Hywel said:

"That's Steven; and he must have trodden in Michael."

I recoiled in distaste when the figure approached the bar. As I did so, my foot struck something round and hollow which rolled under a nearby table. Hywel was delighted. "Ah, you've found Walter's head!"

I pointed in turn at the newcomer, the loose skull and the boot-prints. "Clear these up for me, will you?" I joked.

But Hywel did, worse luck.

121

SOMETHING ABOUT A DEMON

Steven Karlsen had one peculiarity, and that was his inability to understand sarcasm. Because the punch at Dr Mondaugen's annual party had been jokingly recommended, he had helped himself liberally to the foul brew. As a consequence, he had spent five whole days wandering the streets of Cardiff in a high state of delirium.

Where he had been in that time, what he had done, he could not say. All he knew was that his pockets, once full, were now empty and that his knapsack, once empty, was now full . . .

As the trance finally began to wear off, he was delighted to find himself in the environs of the Docklands. Feeling more than a little thirsty, he made his way to the *TALL STORY*, hoping to prevail upon some kind stranger to buy him a drink. Entering the establishment, he had the good fortune to recognise Alan Griffiths, an old friend, sitting at a table near the door.

Adjusting his knapsack and pushing through the crowded drinkers, Steven reached his friend and promptly sat down next to him. But the friend was not pleased. He tried to hide behind his drink, holding it so close to his face that Steven thought he must be trying to climb into it head first.

"Well!" Steven slapped his friend on the back. "What a surprise!"

Alan said nothing. He continued to pour the creamy liquid down his throat. Steven found himself forced to address his friend's oversized gullet, a particularly repulsive part of his anatomy. "Fancy meeting you here, of all places!"

"It was inevitable." Alan slammed his glass down and wiped his lips with his sleeve. "Cardiff Docks is the hub of the Universe and as such, all mortal souls are eventually drawn to it by its irresistible gravity."

"Really?" Steven blinked in surprise. "I never knew that before. In that case, it is not so odd after all."

"Sarcasm," Alan explained with a grimace. He lit a cigarette and blew smoke at Steven. In the half-light of the dissolute tavern, the smoke writhed like a pale and weary ghost.

"You are alone?" Steven glanced around into the heaving mass of humanity. "I am not interrupting anything?"

"I am waiting for someone," Alan replied. He spat contemptuously: "The most gentle and considerate woman in the world."

"Oh yes?" Steven raised an eyebrow. "Then I would very much like to meet her."

Alan was exasperated. "Sarcasm," he growled.

"Ah!" Steven nodded sagely, but he was completely bewildered. "I do not understand sarcasm." He lowered his gaze and twiddled his thumbs.

There was an awkward pause then. Alan cleared his throat and pretended to be absorbed in reading the back of his matchbox. Eventually, Steven summoned up the courage to ask him for a drink. "If it is not too much trouble," he added.

"Of course not! Nothing would give me greater pleasure!" Alan scowled with a viciousness that surprised even himself. "A bottle of the best champagne, perhaps?"

"Oh dear, no." Steven shook his head. "A lager shandy will suffice."

Alan sighed. He realised that even the bluntest sarcasm could have no effect on Steven. He decided to take advantage of the situation. "Have you lost all your money then?"

"Used it up," Steven answered. "My pockets were full five days ago, stuffed with notes. But somehow I have managed to spend them all. I dimly recall entering a succession of shops and purchasing various items. I remember nothing more." He indicated the knapsack, slung over one shoulder. "They are all in here, I presume."

"Tell you what," Alan suggested. "If you have anything of interest, I will exchange it for this." He held up his half-empty glass and swirled the soapy contents around.

Steven licked his dry lips. "Certainly. You are a good friend, Alan."

"Come then. Let us see what you bought." Alan snatched Steven's knapsack and emptied it onto the table. A torrent of mouldering junk clattered out before them. "Well, it seems that you have been visiting every antique-shop in the City. Antique spelt J-U-N-K."

"Is it all worthless?" Steven was disappointed.

"Heavens, no! Rarely have I seen such a magnificent collection of fine and tasteful pieces." Alan sifted through battered brass ornaments, cracked and chipped statuettes, iron globes with cords trailing from them and rusty candlesticks to pull out a broken clock, rotten frame sprouting springs. "Marvellous. Superlative. Exquisite."

"It is yours." Steven beamed gratefully. "And take anything else you fancy."

Alan laughed. It was a gruff howl of a laugh. The clock slipped from his fingers back onto the crest of the pyramid of junk. "Sarcasm, you fool! Are you completely stupid? I would not give a toenail for this mechanical analogue of horse-manure!"

"Sarcasm?" Steven scratched his head. "I am sorry. I thought . . . "

"I mean, look at this!" Alan held up a dusty blue bottle and waved it under Steven's nose. "What on earth possessed you to buy this?"

Steven peered closer at the bottle. He blinked. He thought he glimpsed a dim and fitful shape moving in the depths of the opaque glass. He grappled with thin wisps of memory. A dark and evil-smelling antique shop down a particularly obscure alley in a part of Cardiff he had never visited before. An old man with young eyes and a white beard. An aura of menace and an arcane secret concerning the bottle. Something about a demon and a single wish?

Alan pulled the stiff cork out of the neck of the bottle and sniffed gingerly. He wrinkled up his face and retched. He closed one eye and tried to peer into the bottle. "There is something in here. I cannot quite see what it is."

"If it is nothing of interest," Steven ventured, "perhaps you will buy me a drink for old time's sake?"

"Old time's sake?" Alan was aghast. His lower jaw began to chatter. Abruptly, it ceased and he bent forward, still clutching the bottle. "What exactly do you mean?"

"We are friends." Steven kept his eyes on the floor. "We were very good friends once. You told me that I was your best friend. You said that you admired and respected me for my intelligence, humour and compassion."

Alan curled his lips back in a snarl. "Sarcasm, you fool! I was joking. I always hated you. I thought you were the most mindless cretin I ever had the misfortune to meet. And you are not going to touch a single drop of my drink!"

"I do not understand sarcasm." Steven fought back tears.

At that moment, a tall, auburn-haired woman entered the tavern and, spotting Alan, made her way over to his table. Steven was impressed with her elegance as she wove through the masses, a skill that had always eluded him. She stood before them with a winsome smile and Steven instantly rose to offer his seat to her.

"What time do you call this?" Alan placed his foot on the vacated chair, barring her descent. "Eh?"

"I was held up." The woman was apologetic. "A meeting with my producer."

"Really?" Alan shook the bottle at her face. "Are you sure about that? Are you quite convinced that you were not, in fact, spending a squeaky session with him in the recording studio?"

"Quite sure."

Alan turned to Steven. "This is Toni," he said. "A girl so dedicated to jazz that she sees fit to blow any trumpet on offer, even when it belongs to a decrepit and rather dirty old man."

"I have told you before." Toni's lips quivered. "I am not having an affair."

Clutching his glass in his free hand, Alan kicked the table over. Steven's collection of junk crashed to the floor. The other drinkers began to stare. For once, silence reigned in the tavern. "Get out! You are no better than a common tart!"

After she had left, and the other drinkers had turned back to their own concerns, Steven set the table up and scooped as much of his possessions as he could reach back into his knapsack. "Do you really think that was wise?" he asked, ingenuously. "Creating such a disturbance? Are you not embarrassed?"

"Embarrassed?" Alan's face twisted again. "Of course I am embarrassed! I will never be able to show my face in Cardiff Docks again!" His voice was thick with scorn. He held aloft the bottle in one hand and his drink in the other, as if to weigh his shame on the scales of conscience. "I am so embarrassed that I wish the ground would open up and swallow me . . . "

Leaning across, Steven managed to catch Alan's drink. But he was unable to rescue the bottle. With a self-satisfied grin, he drained the glass and glanced around. Luckily, no-one had noticed. Shouldering his knapsack, he left the table and followed Toni out into the wide and mysterious world.

"I do not understand sarcasm," he said to himself.

Neither, so it seems, do demons.

THE FURIOUS WALNUTS

For more than a week, Walter had been feeling a trifle Scottish. It didn't help that his house was the colour of salmon. Nor that his wife was named Heather. He'd wanted a magnolia house and a wife named Patsy, but you can't have everything. A primeval force was moving within him, an urge to plunge through moor, lake and glen.

Over breakfast, a meal of sheep's stomach stuffed with lungs, he mentioned his condition. He wondered if turning into a Highlander would affect his career. He was, after all, paid to sell a chemical which removed ice-cream stains from trousers.

His wife glowered at him. Being a gentle soul, her glower was not hugely effective. If looks could kill, he'd be complaining of slight abdominal cramps and asking his pharmacist for aspirin. Fortunately, he felt sick enough already.

"You'll have to adjust," she told him. "My brother, Desmond, had a dose of Burma. Took to wearing rubies in his nose and making fishbone curry. But he kept his job in the Civil Service. And cousin Joseph was a train-spotter who became an Eskimo. Never needed to change his anorak, just noted down kayaks instead."

Rather than feeling reassured, Walter finished his food in anxious silence, wiped his knife on his beard and stuffed it into his sock. He wanted to hold forth on bridges and pneumatic tyres. But his wife hated lofty or inflated topics. So he dressed for work, shook the last drops from the bottle of woad and mounted his bicycle.

Around him, men and women were changing, shells of identity falling off and rattling on the pavement. Walter blinked. It seemed to him that whenever an identity clattered to the ground, a horde of imps rushed out of shop doorways and storm-drains and lifted it up. Then they fitted it onto the shoulders of some other pedestrian. They moved so fast, it was difficult to register their presence at all.

Walter felt he ought to investigate this phenomenon more closely, but at that moment he passed the bus-station. Lately, the bus-station had exerted a strange fascination for him. He spent the next hour or so hanging around the ticket-office, threatening commuters and demanding the fare back to Glasgow.

When he reached work, his boss was waiting for him. Mr Jhabvala was a yogi and astrologer who had invented *Caste-Away*, the ultimate frozen dessert stain eradicator, in Bombay. His prototype was so successful that jealous rivals had pursued him all over the subcontinent. Years in the Kashmiri mountains had taken their toll. His skin was pitted with cobra bites and his eyes glittered like opals.

He invited Walter to sit down, leant back in his swivel-chair and stroked his chin. A run-in with brigands had left him with only three fingers on his left hand. The missing digits on his right hand, however, were testimony to frostbite in the Hindu Kush.

"Listen, old boy," he began, toying with his cravat, "I've paid a lot of thought to this and I've decided to let you go. Awfully sorry, but you know how it is. Be a good chap and don't cry. Stiff upper lip and all that. Thing is, old bean, we can't allow a Scotsman to peddle our goods. Customers would take fright. Kindly accept this Cheddar as a parting gift and run along. Toodle-pip."

Sighing languidly, Mr Jhabvala pasted his kiss-curl back onto his brow and inserted a cigarette into a long holder. Walter ignored the gift and stomped out, cursing into his beard. On the street, he caught his new reflection in a tailor's window. His Scottishness was growing worse by the minute. The claymore in his belt interfered with the back wheel of his bicycle, the tam-o'-shanter keep slipping over his eyes. He'd have to visit his doctor.

Dr Walnut was a family practitioner. He greeted Walter cordially, offering him a hookah and rolling out a carpet for his benefit. Walter felt uncomfortable in the surgery, possibly because he'd never seen Dr Walnut in a fez before. Foregoing the hashish, he outlined his problem. Dr Walnut nodded, poured himself a glass of raki and clapped his hands. The receptionist, Miss White, came in and undulated her bare midriff on the desk between them.

"A little thin, no?" he chuckled, exhaling noxious fumes through flared nostrils. Noticing Walter's scowl, he held up his hands in a mollifying gesture. "You can't get the staff these days. Now what can I do for you? You are turning Scottish? Well there's a bug about. Rampant Internationalism. It's the rains we've been having."

Walter nodded. Dr Walnut stood up and moved to a filing-cabinet in the corner of his surgery. He opened the drawers and a scruffy child popped out of each. In their features, they were miniature replicas of Dr Walnut. They leapt to the floor and began riding hobbyhorses in tight circles on the gaudy central rug. Walter caught the flash of silk, the creak of leather, the acrid odour of mare's milk.

"My sons succumbed last week. Mongolianism, a severe outbreak. All my silver scalpels have been looted. Keep erecting tents in the kitchen. What can one do?" He inhaled deeply on his hookah and his eyes sparkled. "The little heathens! They're absolutely furious, no?" One at a time, he lifted them and deposited them back into the filing-cabinet, forcing the drawers shut with the toe of his curly slipper.

Walter wasn't interested in other people's children. He paced the room in dismay, his sporran swinging, "That's all very well. But what can ye do for me?" He scratched at the lice in his plaid. Dr Walnut gave a mysterious smirk and reached into the folds of his robes. He removed a murky phial and held it up.

"It is most fortunate you came to see me at this time. I have just finished distilling this liquid from my sons. It is poison to the imps who cause the ailment. I call it *Tartar-Source*." He winked slyly. "It is expensive, but for you there is special price."

"Och, give it here!" Walter snatched the bottle and swallowed the contents. For a moment he reeled and clutched at his head. Then he made his way gingerly out of the surgery. Dr Walnut followed, calling him the offspring of a dog and various unnatural partners. He brushed past Miss White, who had returned to Reception and was sugaring her body, and fell down the steps onto the street.

Over the next fortnight, a second transformation took place. Walter was at a complete loss to explain this one. He found his head was still eager to cycle everywhere but his abdomen wanted a bus. His arms had an urge to paddle a coracle. Most disconcertingly, his toes began to smell of fish and his neck of sausage. When he woke one morning to find that Heather had drawn isobars over his body with a felt-tip pen, he guessed he'd also have to swallow his pride.

Dr Walnut was very forgiving. He studied Walter carefully, tapped parts of his attire with a tiny hammer and grunted. "The cure was only partially successful. Your head seems to have remained Scottish while the rest of you has altered. You have become a walking analogue of the British Isles. Your body is England, your arms are Wales and your legs reach all the way down to Cornwall."

"That explains it!" cried Walter. "Yesterday, I was passing a cake shop and my feet were attracted by the cream. They went one way, my body went another and I slipped and landed on my Kent. But if I'm the mainland, where does Ireland fit in?" He saw the answer in Dr Walnut's pout. "My wife! What do you mean! Oppressed?"

Dr Walnut shook his head. "No, no. Green and gently rolling." He took Walter's pulse. "Any pain in your Lancashire?" Walter had to admit there wasn't. His Cleveland itched and his Herefordshire rumbled, but these were minor concerns. Something of much more fundamental importance had just occurred to him.

"What will happen if the Union dissolves? I've heard that Scotland stands a good chance of winning independence. If that happens will my head fall off?" he demanded.

"I think I know what your problem is," Dr Walnut replied. "You're a character in a short-story. Some amateur hack is writing this down even as we speak. At the end, to entertain the reader, he'll make the

Union dissolve and your head will indeed fall off."

"Isn't there anything I can do?" Walter was in tears.

"If the reader doesn't reach the end, you'll be okay. You'd better try to be boring from now on, in the hope they won't go any further. If you try really hard, they might throw the short-story away in disgust and do something else."

It was suddenly very clear to Walter. His fate lay in the hands of some non-accountable reader. But what was the best way of being boring? He thought about it. Whatever happened, the reader mustn't be allowed to reach the end of the story. He thought about it some more. He appealed to the reader to stop at this point.

His head fell off.

THE ILLUSTRATED STUDENT

The illustrated student also came apart, but in a different way. He woke to a morning dark as treacle with rainclouds. He climbed painfully out of bed, lurched to the bathroom and remembered that his name was Michael and that he was poor.

In the cracked mirror over the sink, his pale reflection accused him with a mournful eye. He opened his mouth and checked his teeth. They were all as loose as spare change. Yellow saliva dribbled free. Blood flecked his sallow tongue.

Back in his room, he listened for the hacking cough of his neighbour. There were seven other students in the house, all as despised and absurd as himself. They were dying of neglect. But he would refuse to die. He had decided to fight back.

On his bookshelf stood a heavy dusty volume, a psychology textbook he had stolen from the local library. Clearing his desk of long-empty beer-cans, mouldering plates of curry and overflowing ashtrays, he threw the volume down and flicked through the pages until he found the section he desired.

The chapter in question discussed the use of the Rorschach ink-blot test. The test had been designed as a method of showing the different ways in which people perceive the same image. A random splodge of ink would be shown to a subject, who would then have to say what the splodge looked like.

Michael remembered reading a story about a psychology lecturer who had painted a Rorschach ink-blot on his shirt and who had travelled the land, diagnosing people he met by their reactions to the design. Although this story was a fiction, it had given Michael an idea.

Staring at the example on the yellowing page before him, Michael scratched his head. Instead of an ink-blot, he saw a starfish. Or was it a sunrise over a mountain? He blinked. Perhaps it was a flight of swans? It was only after ten minutes of careful study that he understood what it really was. It was, of course, a hedgehog . . .

Selecting a plain white shirt from his wardrobe and laying it out next to the book, Michael began mixing his paints. He took a fine horse-hair brush, dipped it in the black viscous liquid and faithfully copied the design in the book onto both the front and back of the shirt.

Afterward, when the paint had dried, he pulled the shirt on and buttoned his coat up over it. Then he slung his bag over his shoulder, retrieved his piece of sculpture from under the bed and pocketed it. This piece of sculpture was essential to his plan. It had taken two days to carve from a piece of wood and stain to the correct colour.

Leaving his room, he tramped down the stairs to the musty hall. Old newspapers littered the floor; the plaster was flaking off the walls. He opened the front door and stepped out into the street. Above him, the clouds tumbled against each other. Pulling his collar up around his face, he headed toward the shopping-centre.

As he walked, a lorry pulled up by his side and the driver hailed him. Grumbling, Michael walked up to the cab-window. The driver wanted directions to the college. "I've been driving around in circles all morning," he confessed, "but I can't find it. I'm supposed to deliver an espresso-machine to the Dean's office."

"I'm a student," replied Michael. "I have no money. I have not drunk a cup of coffee for weeks. The Dean, like the government, doesn't care about students. Look at my teeth." Determined not to help the driver, he gave the fellow false directions and moved on. He felt guilty, but he also felt powerful.

Before long, Michael reached his destination. It was his local Post-

Office. He took off his coat and placed it in his bag. Then he took out his piece of sculpture and strolled into the lobby. When the people inside saw what he held in his hand, they fell silent and shuffled their feet.

"Nobody move," cried Michael, as he waved the imitation gun in the air. A large, muscular black man in the process of licking a stamp glowered at him, the stamp still attached to the end of his tongue. Michael frowned. He had not considered the possibility that anyone might disobey his instructions. "Or else . . . " he added vaguely.

"Do you want cash?" To his surprise, the cashier was already reaching for a bundle of used notes. He nodded and continued to brandish his piece of sculpture. In one way, he felt truly free for the first time in years. In another, he felt that events had somehow moved beyond his control.

"Just like in the films." An old woman shook her pension-book at him and chuckled. By her side, her senile, harmless husband swayed in his universe of drool. "Wait till Mrs Owen hears about this!" Her chuckle turned into a ghastly rattle.

"Listen." Michael began to suspect a plot. "I'm the victim here, not you lot. My gums are shrinking a little more every night. My new girl-friend, Claire, left me because I was so poor." He was almost tempted to aim his sculpture at the ceiling and pull the trigger. He mumbled and snorted angrily.

"How do you want the cash?" The cashier raised an eyebrow. When he failed to reply, she grew petulant. "Tens? Fives?" She counted out the money with professional efficiency. "Will two-thousand do? We're not a bank you know." Behind her, Michael could see a stunned assistant squinting at him.

Michael knew that his time was limited. He took the cash and stuffed it into his pockets. Then he jabbed the gun into his belt. Rushing out of the door, he bounded down a sidestreet. He was so excited he forgot to put his coat back on. He scarcely even looked where he was going . . .

The Police arrived at the scene five minutes later. Inspector Firbank had not had a good day. A migraine was forcing rainbows through a mincer at the corners of his vision. His unhealthy grey eyes bulged and he mopped his forehead with a damp handkerchief. He was convinced that he had somehow slipped through a wormhole into a dimension ruled by lunatics.

"You mean that you all had a good look at him, but none of you can describe him?" He was incredulous. He rubbed his chin and wrestled with all the metaphysical problems that arose from such a question.

"Oh yes, we all saw him." The old woman shook her finger in imitation of Michael's gun. "He didn't wear a mask. Not even a stocking."

"What did he look like then?" Firbank demanded.

There was a long pause. The customers and the cashier eyed each other. They scratched their heads. Suddenly, their faces lit up. All at once they opened their mouths and spoke:

"A starfish."

"The sun rising over a mountain."

"A flight of swans."

Inspector Firbank sighed. A quote from Nietzsche came into his unwilling head: The irrationality of a thing is no argument against its existence, rather a condition of it. He shook the quote free from his aching mind and tried to smile. His mouth, however, refused to obey.

"I see," he said, slowly. As they all waited, not knowing what to do next, a man came into the Post-Office. He was panting heavily. He made straight for the cashier and then spotted Firbank. He caught his breath and nodded. "Just the fellow. I came in to ask directions. I'm a lorry-driver looking for the college. I've been driving around in circles all morning . . ."

Inspector Firbank gasped. "You're covered in blood . . ."

The lorry-driver blinked. "Well, yes, I did hit something just now. It ran out in front of me. I tried to brake but it was too late. I got out to take a look, but it was nothing important." He seemed to notice the stains for the first time. He grew desperate. "Nothing unusual," he added in a small voice.

"But what was it?" Firbank cried. His day was growing worse by the minute. There were pains in his chest and his left hand had turned numb.

"Nothing unusual," the driver repeated, gazing around with terrified eyes. "It was an accident, I swear." His voice became a pleading mumble. There was genuine remorse in that voice, as well as the traces of a growing doubt. "Just a hedgehog . . . "

THE STORY WITH A CLEVER TITLE

Bang! This story starts with an explosion, to grab the attention of its readers. Once the dust settles around them, it can turn into a complex, profound, mature piece of writing, and they will probably stick with it longer than if there wasn't any action in the first sentence. That's my theory, and it clearly works, otherwise you wouldn't still be here. But I can't be bothered with the literary stuff, the bookish expression, so the opportunity has been lost.

I'm tired and fed up. I'm not claiming I enjoyed the trauma of the blast. Far from it! It knocked off my hat and medals. But all the same, it had power, and that's something I sorely miss. Plus I'm desperate to escape from here. The damage was minor. No big holes in the walls. Just a few broken bottles behind the bar. The juke-box in the corner had got stuck, playing 'Broken Angel Blues' again and again. What else? Oh yes, all our customers were dead.

We don't get many bombs going off in the *TALL STORY*. But I doubted Hywel would ever discover my responsibility for this one. There are so many terrorist groups devoted to so many whimsical causes that I could easily blame some imaginary faction or other. The Pacifist Brigade, for instance, or the LOMOJ, whoever they might be. Think up one yourself if those won't do. It was a crude device, but I hadn't made it. I just lit the fuse. I found it among the pile of junk left by Steven Karlsen on a table. Maybe it was an antique.

In the mirror over the bar, I saw that the pub was untouched. The drinkers were still alive. The potbellied overseers cracked their whips and the students shared a glass of cider and the Faskdhfgasdhian temple tottered over its acolytes. There was even a commotion in front of the fireplace, for the Three Friends had decided to climb up the wall to the rafters and the ends of their ropes trailed in the coals and strangled the sparks. Near the door, a convention of doctors blocked the exit. Dr Lithiums, Walnut and Slither debated the merits of Aerial Turkish Komodo Dragon's blood. There weren't any. Everything in this parallel world was normal and routine and facile.

"Fine for them lot," Hywel groaned. "But what a loss of business on our side of the reflection!"

He surveyed the mangled bodies with a frown.

"Shall I go through their pockets?" I suggested. "And maybe slip the rings off their fingers?"

"You know I only take payment in stories. I doubt you'll find many of those on them now. On second thoughts, search the writers for scraps of paper, notebooks, that sort of thing."

I did so. The usual suspects were a disappointment. Flann O'Brien had a collapsible bicycle in his pocket; Gabriel García Márquez had a phial of cholera, a clock and a heart; Anna Kavan had a puddle; Omar Khayyám had a winged piglet; Bruno Schulz had a hole. Felipe Alfau wore a coat made entirely of pockets sewn together, and all of them were full, but they only contained other coats also made of pockets, and so on forever, or at least until the pockets became so small they might only hold a single atom, and you can't generally write stories on those, unless you happen to own a quark-point pen, which you don't. And neither did he. No, the professionals were destitute. I guess they left their work at home.

As for the amateurs, Billy Belay and Harold the Barrel had diaries, but they were just full of graphs recording the number of times they had flown or walked through walls that week. The figures had been massaged. The numerical figures, I mean. The human figures, with their shoulders, spines and necks, all stiff, had probably never felt the touch of a Thai girl in the whole of their now absent lives.

At last I came across a corpse with a story. It had been scribbled on an old napkin, the ends of which were stuffed up his nostrils. I drew it out and wiped it clean on my own nose.

"What does it say?" asked Hywel.

I read it. "It says:

The Story With A Clever Title

Bang! This story starts with an explosion, to grab the attention of its readers. Once the dust settles around them, it can turn into a complex, profound, mature piece of writing, and they will probably stick with it longer than if there wasn't any action in the first sentence. That's my theory, and it clearly works, otherwise you wouldn't still be here. But I can't be bothered with the literary stuff, the bookish expression, so the opportunity has been lost.

I'm tired and fed up. I'm not claiming I enjoyed the trauma of the blast. Far from it! It knocked off my hat and medals. But all the same, it had power, and that's something I sorely miss. Plus I'm desperate to escape from here. The damage was minor . . .

"Hold it right there!" cried Hywel.

"What's wrong?" I said.

"Don't you see? It's *this* story, the very piece we are standing in. If you get to the point where I ask you to read it, we'll be stuck in a loop forever. A terrible fate!"

I kicked the body with my boot. Clots of blood jumped onto my sock. "I wonder who this person is?"

Hywel sneered. "Oh, I know him. He's a hack by the name of Hughes. Not sure of his first name."

"Has he published anything? Will he publish this?"

"That depends on who you are now. If you're him, reading this after having just written it, to check for mistakes, then maybe not. If you're somebody else, then maybe he has, unless he gave it to you in manuscript form. Perhaps you're an editor on the verge of writing him a rejection note? It's hard to tell."

"I'm reading it in manuscript form, I think."

"No, you're *standing* in it. Put it down. It's too dangerous. Have you any idea how uniquely horrid it would be to get stuck in a fiction loop?"

"No I don't. No I don't."

"Put it down. It's far too dangerous. Have you any idea . . . Wait! This isn't a loop. I just broke out of it."

"Well, I put it down. It must be plain déjà vu."

"Thank heavens for that! Now put it down. It's too dangerous."

"More dangerous than my bomb?"

"I didn't hear that. Obviously my ignorance of your part in the explosion has been written into the text."

"A bit implausible that, isn't it?"

"Not really. There are so many terrorist groups running around, it could be anybody. I reckon it was the LOMOJ."

"The Liberators of Mrs Owen's Jam?"

"That's probably what they are. Or maybe the Come Again Faction. They use déjà vu bombs, packed with that odd feeling."

"I have to confess that I did read the manuscript to the point where you asked me to read it. Maybe the déjà vu bomb knocked us back out of the loop? It took us back to a moment *before* I did read it. But wait! That's impossible. It wasn't a déjà vu bomb. It was gunpowder. I lit the fuse myself."

"I didn't hear that. I didn't hear that."

"This is getting boring. Shall we look for a different story? One without any paradoxes?"

"No point. You've searched all the bodies now. If you really want another story, you'll have to invent it yourself."

"I'm too disillusioned for that."

"Then you'll have to go without. I'm not telling one, because even when I do, it's really you doing the talking. Hang about! You can step outside the story again and use Mondaugen's word-recycling machine to write it for you!"

"No I can't. It's empty now."

"In that case, we'll just have to wait until enough unnecessary words accumulate on the floor to be recycled. Say something unnecessary. Tell me about your childhood."

"That will take too long. That will take too long."

Hywel sighed. "Well, that's a start. But you're right. We might be here for millions of years. At least you would get to meet Titian Grundy at the end of the wait. And then you could ask him about the impossible mirror."

"I can't waste time waiting around for the future. Isn't there a faster way of getting there?"

"We could use a time-machine."

"Great idea! Let's hop on immediately!"

"Sorry, they haven't been invented yet. But when we *do* reach the future the slow way, we can send one back to us here."

We looked around expectantly, but it didn't appear.

"Obviously we never got to the future, or else we forgot to send one back."

"Maybe we're too busy there. I wonder what the future's like, and what I'm doing? Hearing that story about Byron and Julian has made me want to learn to juggle."

"That's too mild an ambition for you. I bet you're President of the World and living in a mobile tower!"

"Will we *ever* get to hear another story?"

Hywel clicked his fingers. "I've got it! You know how your best stories are always polished with great care? The more care that goes into them, the better they are."

"True. But so what?"

"Well then, the less care you put into them, the worse they are. What if you put *no* care into them at all? What if you don't even write them? That really is minimal care!"

"They wouldn't exist."

"Ah, but how do you know that? Maybe they would just be very, very bad stories. But stories nonetheless."

"You mean that a tale might already have spontaneously generated out of total lack of care?"

"Yes, and it might be here at this very moment. It'll probably be a horror story, because bad horror stories tend to be the worst of all. If we search the pub, we'll be sure to find it. I'll take this side of the bar, and you take the rest of the room."

I found the story pasted to the noticeboard near the main door. I peeled it off and studied it.

"That's weird!" I said. "It has a number in front of it."

"What's the number?"

"18b," I replied.

"Well don't read that bit out."

"It's almost as if it's a story which is pretending to be a chapter in a much longer work!"

"Arrgh! No déjà vu! That hasn't happened before!"

"Yes it has! New things happen all the time!"

"Guess that's called déjà vu?"

"Shall I just read it out?"

"Just read it out, will you?"

And I did . . .

A Tale of Terror

Laura was running. She ran.

She ran through the forest. Through the forest she ran. Laura ran.

She was running through the forest. The forest was dark. It was scary. Her name was Laura. She ran.

A monster was chasing her!

("Awful title," remarked Hywel.

"Now you've interrupted the flow of the story!" I protested. "I'll have to start again from the beginning."

"Don't forget to include the title. For the sake of integrity."

I didn't ...)

A Tale of Terror

Laura was running. She ran.

She ran through the forest. Through the forest she ran. Laura ran.

She was running through the forest. The forest was dark. It was scary. Her name was Laura. She ran.

A monster was chasing her!

She ran from the monster. Laura ran away from the monster. Through the forest.

The forest was large. It was dark.

The monster ran after her!

After Laura ran the monster, through the dark forest. It was running. Laura was running. They both ran.

Through the forest.

She tripped as she ran. She picked herself up and resumed running. She tripped again. She tripped because she was running! Through the dark, creepy forest.

She picked herself up and ran.

The monster was behind her. It ran after her. It wanted to meet Laura some time. Maybe she would like that?

No, she wouldn't!

But the monster would! The running monster!

Like many running monsters, it ran. After Laura. And she was running too! Through the forest.

The large, dark, creepy forest!

There were trees in the forest. Like most forests, it had trees! Unlike most forests, it had a monster. A monster running through it. After Laura!

Who ran. She was running. Laura was running. She ran.

She tripped. She picked herself up. She ran.

Laura was running. She ran.

She ran through the forest. Through the forest she ran. Laura ran.

She was running through the forest. The forest was dark. It was scary. Her name was Laura. She ran.

A monster was chasing her!

She tripped and fell. There was a note on the ground. She picked it up. She read it. It said:

Dear Laura,
I'M BEHIND YOU! DON'T LOOK BACK!
signed
The Monster

p.s. Maybe we could meet some time? I'd like that.

Laura read the note. She was scared.

She read the note as she ran. In the forest she read the note. The short note in the large forest.

Not just large. Creepy too! And dark.

Like the note. The note which Laura read. Before she finished it.

She ran. Laura ran. She didn't look back. She took the monster's advice! It was good advice.

Good advice from a bad monster!

What are the chances of that happening?

Laura tripped. She picked herself up. She ran.

She was running. Laura ran.

She ran through the forest. Through the forest she ran. The forest was dark. It was scary. Her name was Laura. She ran.

The monster was chasing her!

Or was it? If it had left a note for her, it wasn't behind her!

It was in front of her!

It was in front of her in the forest!

The large, dark, creepy forest! The forest with trees!

She stopped running. Laura didn't run. She didn't run through the forest. She didn't trip, because she wasn't running! She didn't need to pick herself up and resume running.

If she ran, she would run into the monster!

Which was in front of her!

She decided to look for somewhere to hide. Somewhere to hide from the monster. Somewhere in the forest.

She saw a house!

She ran to the house. Laura ran to the house.

The door was shaped like a mouth!

She ran inside.

The door closed and ate her!

The door was a mouth! The house ate her!

The house was the monster!

But if the house was the monster, how did it chase her through the forest? How did it chase Laura?

It wasn't a house!

It was a caravan!

THE END

"Grief!" exclaimed Hywel. "What a load of rubbish!"

I nodded. "The worst story I've ever heard. Almost worthy of this hack. What did you say his name was?"

"Hughes. But which one?"

I spat on the body. "What do you mean?"

"Which Hughes? There are many. He isn't alone."

"I guess we'll never care."

Hywel sighed and mopped his brow with a sleeve. "Anyway, thank the Bugger Lords the story has finished. Bend over—I mean down—before them! You may keep your trousers on."

"I suppose we can't complain too much. After all, it was written by itself. And there were certain odd coincidences in it. The caravan, for instance. Was it tie-dyed? Did it belong to Madame Ligeia? And was the monster a vampire? So many questions!"

"Pity Mondaugen is dead. He could answer them."

"Yes, he was an expert on monsters. A professional cryptozoologist. But it's too late to ask him."

"He died with the others in the explosion."

"His body ruptured in his favourite nook . . . "

My estimate of our losses had been too high. There was movement in the shadows. Karl Mondaugen crawled to his feet. I was about to stroll up to him and finish the job with a broken bottle, but then I remembered that this would give me away. As for the mad professor, he had saved himself with his latest invention. He had invented:

Karl Mondaugen.

"But he can't do that!" I protested.

Hywel squinted. "Why not?"

"Because he has already been invented! It's plagiarism!"

"No, it's not. He was never patented."

"Ah well, maybe we'll get a proper story out of him instead? I'd like to know about his weirdest cryptozoological case."

"I'm sure he'll be only too delighted to tell us. But who will tell us about *him*? That's what I want to know. And what's that spherical object smouldering on that table?"

"What do you mean?"

"Which part of my reply does that refer to?"

"What do you mean?"

"Both bits, I take it. I might as well admit that I often suspect that Dr Mondaugen is his own worst enemy."

"And the spherical object?"

"It's a bomb! An antique! Probably not worth much when it goes off! Some idiot must have lit the fuse!"

"So the first bomb wasn't mine?"

"No, it belonged to the Come Again Faction, as I mentioned earlier. You assumed the explosion was your responsibility, but in fact the fuse on yours is longer and slower."

Dr Mondaugen picked his way to the bar. "So it is a tale you want? I will give you a tale!"

"What's it about?"

"My weirdest cryptozoological case!"

Hywel nudged me. "I think you should take cover with me behind the bar. If we crouch down, it'll protect us from the blast. But there's not enough room for the professor, so don't tell him!"

I took Hywel's advice. "Thanks!"

"You know how people's secrets often come out after their deaths? I reckon it will be the same with Dr Mondaugen. When this other bomb goes off, we should get to learn the truth about *him*. Let's hope he manages to finish his own tale first."

The mad scientist consulted his memory for the oddest case he had dealt with. It did indeed concern the monster in the forest which had chased Laura. And yes, it was a vampire. It was dark behind the bar, and creepy, but not large. Dr Mondaugen's voice stank like garlic as he leaned over, elbows on the surface, and related the events of:

THE SILVER NECKS

There was a vampire called Unthank who suffered from a raging thirst. His doctor suspected diabetes but the patient refused to take a test. Unthank drank from all the necks in the village, valley and forest, but he was still unsatisfied. It seemed he might deplete the land of victims, so his doctor took him aside and told him:

"This can't go on. You're giving the undead a bad name. The elders are talking about locking you up in a pyramid made from garlic. Luckily there's a solution. You must travel to Heaven, where you can sup as much as you please from the inhabitants without making them anaemic. They are immortal and have bottomless veins."

Unthank thought this a splendid idea and asked for directions. The doctor clucked his tongue and cried:

"If I knew how to get there I wouldn't be working here! You should look for a crossroads guarded by a burnished knight. For a modest fee he will allow you to choose one of the paths. But beware: three lead to a hideous doom. Only the fourth, which looks the same as the others, will take you to Heaven. The knight won't tell you which is which, though he sometimes drops hints like anvils."

Unthank, despite his name, was grateful and he wrapped himself in a sunblock shroud. He wondered what hideous dooms lurked at the ends of the three roads. But thirst overcame his anxieties and he flew off into the woods. He flapped for a long time until he came to a river. A canoe was moored to the bank and a knight in rusty armour sat at one end. Unthank controlled his appetite and asked:

"Excuse me, do you know the way to Heaven?"

"No, but I'll take you to someone who does. A burnished knight who guards a crossroads. It'll cost you, though."

Unthank paid him and sat in the canoe. The fellow paddled them with a sword wider than a jump. After a day they reached an estuary and in the middle of the estuary a large island. They disembarked on a wooden jetty and walked inland. Eventually they reached the intersection of four roads and the guide said: "Here we are."

Unthank squinted. "I can't see a burnished knight."

"One moment." The fellow took a wire brush from a compartment in his knee and scrubbed himself all over. Finally he gleamed like a full moon. He gave the vampire an apologetic look. "Chivalry doesn't pay much, so I earn a bit on the side."

"Can you tell me which path leads to Heaven?"

"I'm not permitted. If I try, I'll be turned inside-out: it's an old curse. However, I'm certain you'll pick the best road. When pilgrims come here the odds are against them, but in your case I feel confident. Follow your instincts and you'll do fine."

Unthank peered at the four paths: they were identical. He stroked a fang. "Allow me to go away and consider it. First thing tomorrow morning I'll be back to make my choice."

And so saying, he strolled off and hid among some bushes. When the sun went down, he cast off his shroud and flew into the sky. From above he was able to see where the roads went. Three led to hidden trapdoors, visible as vague outlines: the fourth led to a walled garden with a roof of crystal. Unthank glimpsed beings who wore halos and carried harps. He listened but there was no music.

The next day he approached the knight and said: "I've made my choice and now I'm off to sample paradise."

"You must pay me first. If you refuse, my magic sword will slice you into nearly four-thousand pieces."

Unthank grumbled, but he handed over the coins and walked toward the western path. The knight cried out in alarm:

"What a terribly stony road!"

Unthank winked. "The way to divinity always is . . . "

"Wouldn't you rather choose a more comfortable path? The others have all been resurfaced. Look at the gorgeous camber on the northern road! So tasteful and elegant. Consider also the gutters of the beautiful southern road! In absolutely perfect condition."

"They look just the same to me."

"A remarkable coincidence, I agree. We must discuss this matter over a pint of ale. There is a tavern halfway along the eastern road. Allow me to escort you there, arm in wing."

Unthank shook his head. It was obvious the knight was trying to make him change his mind. Did he earn a commission on the number of travellers who fell down the trapdoors? It seemed likely. These crude antics enraged the vampire and he briefly considered leaping on the cheat. But without a tin-opener he was at a disadvantage.

"If it's all the same to you, I'll persist with my choice. I'll send you a postcard written on a cloud . . . "

The knight shrugged and a sigh escaped the holes bored in his helmet like steam from a golem's kettle. Unthank ignored him and hurried as fast as his bowed legs could manage. The road ran straight to a locked door in the side of the walled garden. He rang the bell and waited. At long last, a voice answered. Unthank was astounded to recognise the icy tones of his doctor. "How did you get here?"

"I took a short cut. Some enraged villagers caught me after you left and drove a stake through my heart. It's your fault. The vampires and the humans got on well until you started drinking them dry. If I was you, I'd turn right around and go home."

"Don't be silly. It was you who advised me to come here in the first place. Open up and show me in!"

The doctor mumbled to himself and turned a key. Unthank stepped over the threshold into brightness. Everything sparkled painfully: he shielded his slitted eyes and struggled to focus his surroundings. Nothing matched what he had seen from above. The garden was made of metal: platinum, gold and copper. Osmium flowers exuded tetroxides and birds in aluminium trees clicked relays and preened magnetic feathers. Zinc fish darted in mercury pools with propellers instead of fins.

Even the halos of the blessed souls were electric. Unthank lifted a hand to touch the sparks looping from the doctor's antennae and was knocked to the ground. When he rose, he tried to open the door. The doctor shook his head. "It won't allow you to depart. It only works one way, like a diode. We're stuck here. Ever since God took a course in electronic engineering, rectification has supplanted redemption."

"I don't understand! Last night I saw harps."

"Bare wires," the doctor rasped. "Most of us undress before going to bed. We're immortal now, but the only way to live forever is to be re-born as a machine. You won't find sustenance here: our blood is molten silver. If only you'd taken a diabetes test!"

Unthank shed a gothic tear. It was plain as a grave that Heaven to a vampire was sheer Hell. "The knight tried to warn me off this path. But I thought he was aiming to mislead me."

"He's the one who made us. As I said, he drops hints like anvils. On these anvils he hammers out our bodies. When the Age of Chivalry finished he grew very lonely. He sees robots as kindred casings, advanced versions of the traditional knight. But he's a likeable enough fellow. I prescribe iron tablets for his metal fatigue. Now I might as well confess I'm not really that sort of doctor; I'm a cryptozoologist. But all the others are at a conference, so I had to step in."

"Where do the other three roads lead to?"

"Hades, Tartarus and Limbo. They would have been perfect for you. As a matter of fact, I believe the Devil is advertising for vampires to help his demons hassle the damned. You've got no-one to blame but yourself. If I was you, I'd attempt to bite my way through the roof. It shouldn't take more than a couple of million years."

"Fangs for the advice . . ."

And so we leave Unthank. This tale about him has finished just in time. The bomb is about to go off. When he escapes, the first thing he intends to do is take revenge on the knight. This is just as impractical as it is unfair: the knight is blameless. He is also quite empty. When Sir Jasper died on top of the tallest mountain in the world, his suit of armour left him behind and came down to work for this tale. But now it plans to resign from here too. Well, would you do the job for his pay? When travellers pick the road to Heaven, he gains nothing. And when they choose one that leads to the Hells, he earns a pittance.

BANG!

NEVER HUG AN AARDVARK

"Well that really takes the biscuit," said Dr Mondaugen. He was unsure which biscuit he was referring to. His fingers idled over the custard creams and finally settled on a ginger snap.

"But do you believe me?" The visitor leaned forward and gripped the arm of his chair. "After all, I don't know who else to turn to. I mean, would you confess to such a dark secret? Would you?"

"Hmm." Dr Mondaugen spat crumbs as hard as gravel and dipped his tongue into a cup of lukewarm tea. "I doubt it. Now if you had said wolf or bear, or even squirrel, I would be inclined to investigate your case. But an aardvark? I don't think so."

The visitor sighed and held his tragic head in his massive hands. Then he looked up and indicated the window. Dr Mondaugen peered through the glass, across a dark lawn broken up by a number of haphazard paths, and toward the tall trees of the horizon. Stark branches netted a swollen moon.

"The sun has gone down and the full moon has already risen. Within a short time, the change will come upon me. I will start to tremble and there will be a terrible pain in the centre of my head. My face will elongate into a sharp snout, my ears will stretch upward. My arms will become short legs and I will grow a tail. I will develop an insatiable craving for ants. This is not a laughing matter. You must help me!"

Dr Mondaugen shook his head sadly and wiped his lips with a napkin. "What makes you think that I can help you? Possibly you need to visit a different kind of doctor. A severe blow on the skull perhaps? Eh?"

The visitor pounded his fists on his knees. "You are the only person who is even willing to listen to me! You are Karl Mondaugen, the great cryptozoologist. The man who won a Nobel Prize for documenting a genuine case of lycanthropy and developing an appropriate cure and whistle. The man who spent two years in China tracking down the were-monkey in a banana-canoe! The man who tricked a vampire into entering Heaven and then secured a day-pass to check on its condition! If you can't help me then who can?"

Dr Mondaugen nodded solemnly, reached into his pocket for his pipe and began filling it with tobacco. He gathered up a few biscuit crumbs from the plate before him and packed these into the bowl as well. "I have my own reputation to think of. A were-wolf is one thing. A were-aardvark is quite another. I know that the moon is full tonight. But even if you change right before my eyes, why should I do anything but ignore you? An aardvark is a silly animal . . . "

The visitor snarled. "That's where you're wrong! The aardvark, which constitutes the *orycteropodidae* family, is over sixty-million years old. Its forelegs are so powerful that it can not only rip open whole termite nests but even fend off lions and leopards. What does this say to you?"

"Never hug an aardvark?" Dr Mondaugen raised a cynical eyebrow.

The visitor was exasperated. He rose up to depart. Ruefully, he offered the doctor his hand, more out of habit than any respect.

"I think I'll pass on that," the doctor observed, "if what you have just said is true. Tell me, when you say that you develop an insatiable craving for ants, do you mean small black insects or the sisters of uncles? Ho, ho! An important point, I assure you. I thought for one ghastly moment that the crux of your tale was going to be one of those awful puns. But don't take it too personally, Mr Hughes."

The visitor left with a sneer, slamming the door behind him and locking it with bolts and chains. Dr Mondaugen glanced around the room with a critical eye. It was hardly a fitting environment for a world-famous cryptozoologist. There were few books, for one thing, and the walls seemed to be made of some padded material . . .

Rising from his chair, he crossed over to his desk by the window, took up his pen and started writing a new page of his *Dictionary of Shapeshifters*. His hand moved at a phenomenal speed. At this rate, he knew, it would probably see publication within a year. He smiled to himself. The cranks always came to him at this time. Indeed, his own change had been completed an hour before. He was that rarest of all shapeshifters: the were-professor.

Glancing up through the bars of the window, he perceived the visitor on his hands and knees on the lawn. Doubtless looking for ants. Around him pranced and slithered the other patients in a variety of guises; tiger, snake, eagle, hyena and shark. This is what happens when you let the lunatics run the asylum, Dr Mondaugen decided as he went back to work.

EPILOGUE

There are many real pubs in the universe which forget to chase out their patrons after closing time, locking them in for illicit drinking orgies, and almost as many nonexistent ones which follow that tradition. But few indeed are the taverns which can't be left because of the drunkenness of the streets outside. Whenever I tried to escape from the TALL STORY, the cobbled surface of the adjacent alley rose up like a wave and crashed me back inside. The only way it might sober up was if Hywel stopped mopping the spilled beer out of the door. And the only way that would happen was if people kept a tighter grip on their glasses. Which relied on them not buying so many drinks in the first place. But there was little chance of that occurring while Hywel remained in business. And that would continue so long as I told tales about him.

However, I have now secured a replacement for my ordeal. It is you, dear reader, though you don't fully realise it yet. It should be obvious that imaginary pubs, however hard the roads which lead to them, can only properly exist as ideas in heads. I have erected this one brick by brick in yours, over the space of twenty feeble fables, and you have decorated and stocked it yourself. That's business, I'm afraid. By all means, take over; you have no choice. Beyond this epilogue, you'll have to deal with the biggest lies of the world on your own. I won't be there to help, nor even to lurk and gloat. I have more critical campaigns to return to. I'm ready to conquer Europe again. I've learned a lesson. One front good, two fronts bad; and winter won't be hearing from me this time. The next boat out of

Cardiff to Elba isn't mine.

After I sneaked away from my final exile, I wandered aimlessly over centuries and cultures, hoping to forget my failures. I went mad. Locked in the same asylum as Karl Mondaugen, I even started to believe I was an ordinary person, without megalomania or a funny hat. A were-man. It was ghastly. The birds spoke to me through the bars of my cell. They counselled patience and revenge. They broke open the walls with their beaks and told me to flee to Wales, a land where I might blend in without attracting attention. The capital city of that country is rife with short fat grumblers who do odd things with arms under clothes. I felt at home. I started to get better. I only popped into Hywel's pub for a quick drink to toast my forthcoming victories. Now I'm hoarse with tales. But having already taken you for a long one, this is where I ride off alone.

THE LONG CHIN OF THE LAW

(A PUNITIVE FANTASIA)

THE CATASTROPHE TRIALS

In the old days, of course, murderers were often locked away in dungeons while hurricanes and earthquakes went free. And let there be no doubt that they took full advantage of their freedom. They rushed and shook, shattered and toppled whenever it suited them. They had no conscience.

The first Natural Disaster we arrested was the volcano that erupted on the outskirts of our City when the President was making his inaugural speech. Without stopping to retrieve his hat and coat, he raced to the scene with many attendants and ministers. He did not hesitate to show his concern on camera. The ash had engulfed one of the richer suburbs, the President's majority.

There was a hung Parliament then, an economic crisis followed as share prices fell sharply. The President took to drink and gambling. Women were a mystery to him. His nose was too large. Before he had completely destroyed his liver, we decided to take action.

The trial was swift. Our Judges proclaimed the volcano guilty with due solemnity and sentenced it to life imprisonment. They stood on the volcanic glass and hammered off pieces as souvenirs. We solved the problem or removing the remainder to a place of security by constructing the prison around it. We used iron bricks. We threw away the key.

To be perfectly honest, the idea was not entirely my own. I knew a poet once who suggested it. She had long hair and a winsome smile. I loved her, but I could never give her any credit, not even of the financial sort, and thus it was I, Titian Grundy, Prefect of Police, who became the renowned and much-loved one.

There followed a period of prosperity then, hope, luxury even. There was a Golden Age of sorts. We expected a Platinum one to be just around the next corner.

The blue Tsunami rolled in from the east, towering so (I gesture here with upraised eyes) that we could not see the noontime sun. It bore an island with it, one of the outlying Aracknids wrenched free from the Continental Shelf, palm-trees and huts and village life all still intact upon the rich soil, although the latter considerably disrupted, and it crashed down on our wharves with the force of the Cosmic Serpent's own heartbeat. Our crystal piers became shards, glistening on the green waters of the harbour, a hazard to shipping for many years to come. Very pretty they looked too, those shards, more pretty even than the original structures, though that is missing the point.

We had greater difficulties with this one. After all, the guilty party had melted away into the greater ocean again. We had nothing to point the finger at any more. But we were not foiled so easily. We employed mathematicians to calculate the probable volume of water involved and we pumped this amount directly out of the sea. We were not above punishing innocent liquid if necessary, yet we felt sure that at least some of the molecules we had acquired had been responsible.

We took longer over this trial. We stored the water in a large outdoor tank and adjourned often, fishing or boating on the accused, thus forcing some Community Service out of it while we waited for the verdict. Naturally, the Defence Lawyer was outraged. He was also frustrated. We cut his wages, handpicked the Jury ourselves and let them make the correct decision. We tortured our captive with red-hot pokers.

During these revolutionary changes in the legal system, I never failed to miss my poet. I tried to behave like an ordinary man: I visited the President and played croquet on his lawns. I married a beekeeper and asked my poet to become my mistress. She turned me down, however, having had enough of such romantic entanglements. She adopted a cat and took in lodgers instead.

You know the way I feel about my work. I have had doubts, but they have been few. I do not believe that I must justify my actions. I have posed nude, grown a fiery beard and learnt to juggle. I envy the arty set, I suppose. I can no longer walk into a student pub without being jeered at. I love my poet more than ever. I have not yet forgotten her name.

I write this report as a story for good reasons. Last summer, a particularly vindictive tornado escaped from its reinforced bottle and wrecked my office. All my papers were shredded. My filing-cabinets were peeled back and my secretaries stamped through the floorboards. I was left without a single record of my achievements. That is why I must circulate this one more carefully. Perhaps it might even find its way into the pages of a fiction magazine.

These tornadoes, incidentally, were my first real mistake. We collected them in barrels at first, but these were easily burst. We tried jars before bottles. Our bottles were made out of stainless steel. We had to wait until the tornado began to die and shrink to the correct size before pouncing. This did not seem to deter others: they saw how much damage they could do before they were apprehended. They began to come in pairs.

The mistake I made was as follows: I issued instructions to bottle tornadoes before they had formed. We collected them before they had committed any crimes, and forged the documentation. The scheme seemed to work quite well. The number of arrests increased dramatically. I was awarded a bonus.

And then one day, I received a telegram from the pressure group Amnesty Interstellar. They had been making the rounds of the prisons. One of the developing tornadoes I had arrested had turned out not to be a tornado at all, but a dust-devil. I was disgraced. I had to resign and move into politics.

The President and I became firm friends. We both complained about the World, about life, about women mostly. I drank espresso and smoked fat cigars. The President wrote pamphlets and picked his nose, which were both tasks that could take all day. My captive tornadoes were released. An independent body was set up to monitor Police procedures. My statue in the plaza was defaced.

I am no longer handsome, but my poet is still beautiful. She now works as a Careers Officer. There is a man who wants to marry her. He takes her to restaurants in a solar-powered glider. I know: I have seen them. I will follow them one day in my hot-air balloon. I have kidnapped her cat.

The President keeps a typhoon in his cellar. A man I know at the prison smuggled it out to us. In the evenings, the President, the cat and myself, creep down the winding stairs and peep cautiously at it. We are careful not to open the door too wide, in case it escapes. We feed it model towns which it devours with great avidity.

The World is going soft. We will soon return to the old days, when (as I said before) murderers were often locked away in dungeons while hurricanes and earthquakes went free. Sentences are being reduced everywhere.

I hear that even the volcano on the outskirts of the City is due up for parole next year.

THE CRIME CONTINUUM

Yes, your King is in a bad position. My knights have devastated your ranks. Your Queen has fallen to a pawn (the shame!) and my rooks have yet to enter the fray. While you consider your next move, I will tell you a story. You are my only friend now; the prison guards refuse to listen to me. Whenever I try to talk to them, they simply open their hideous mouths and gibber. I can almost believe it when you tell me they are not men at all, but intelligent apes who have recently paid a visit to the barber.

My name, of course, is Titian Grundy. Once, I was the Prefect of Police. I had money, power, the love of auburn-haired women. I knew the President personally. My influence over him was profound. I taught him how to balance on a trapeze and how to juggle ugli-fruit. In return, he paid close attention to my suggestions concerning subsidies to elk farmers. Our relationship was one of mutual help and respect. We were a symbiosis. Possibly even a gestalt.

He lived far away from the City, in a field of blue grass by the banks of a tawny river; in a golden tower full of music machines. When an itinerant band of jesters, mummers and acrobats set up their yellow tents in his field, he asked permission to join their troupe. They refused, however, because of who he was. Yet the following morning, when the Carnival opened, there he was, juggling and tumbling with the best of them. I alone had arranged it for him. Nothing was too much to ask.

And similarly, when I wished to extend my elk farm high into the Carbuncle Hills, he lent me a pair of silver scissors to cut through the red-tape. In other words, I was granted a licence without so much as a murmur from the Ministry of Environment. Twice its former size, my farm earned me twice as much in subsidies. I even purchased a single elk and let it roam free on my grounds.

But I am already digressing. You are plainly not interested in pastoral reminiscence. Very well, I shall return to my story. The story in question concerns the day when I solved the very last crime in the history of the world. I recall every detail as clearly as a dandrum recalls a bugaboo. On that day, I threw down my pen, sat back in my chair and lit a cigar. It was obviously a time for celebration, yet a nagging doubt pulled at the corners of my mind. With astonishing ease, I ignored it and left my padded office. I have a genius for not taking things to their logical conclusion.

Out in the street, I mounted my powered unicycle and threaded my way through the Talking Plaques. Talking Plaques were men and women who had been recruited from the ranks of the unemployed. Their task was to recite a list of all the crimes ever committed on that spot since the world began. Thus, whenever I approached them they would call out things like, "Dorian Bilious dropped litter here on 13th November 2503," or "Thomas Major assaulted a minor here on 24th May 1762," or "Ug stole a piece of meat from Og here on 6th August 20,307 BC."

It was incredibly irritating, of course, to be assailed from all sides by these lists. But as the scheme had been my own idea, I felt that I had no right to complain. The Talking Plaques were sometimes clustered in large, dense groups, so dense indeed that wide detours often had to be made around them. When a particularly compact group was approached, the resultant cacophony was deafening and the actual words incomprehensible.

Few areas of the City were free of these groups. Indeed, few areas of the entire land. A great many crimes had been committed since the world began. I even had two such groups ensconced in my own home.

Eventually, I managed to steer my unicycle onto a road relatively free of the ghosts of past crimes and gunned the engine to maximum speed. This road took me out of the City and towards the President's tower. He was spending less and less time at work, as his obsession with juggling overtook his love of politics.

The President had built his tower on one of those very rare places where not a single crime had ever been committed. I was grateful for this. In the distance, I could just make out a row of Talking Plaques. But they were out of earshot and thus I was spared their hideous monotone babblings.

The President received me as cordially as always and poured me a cup of blue-green tea. Then he wound up his music machines and we enjoyed an hour or two of Cereal Music. After the machines had wound down, he offered me mulled wine jelly, but I could see that his fingers were itching to resume juggling. On the table next to his Presidential telephone stood a bowl of bruised and battered ugli-fruit.

Reluctantly, I declined his offer and got down to business. I kept an eye out for his wife but she was not there. In fact, she was hardly ever there. She had her own apartment in a geodesic dome located far beyond the Pallid Colonnades, where I often brought her gifts of artificial flowers and edible ribbons for her auburn hair (yes, I admit it. I was having an affair with her. We had spent many happy hours trying to occupy the same point in space-time.)

The President shook me by the hand and congratulated me. I had solved the very last crime in the history of the world, he said, and thus had made the globe a better place. Just out of curiosity, he asked me what this very last crime had been. Glancing at the notebook I kept in my top pocket, I told him. The notebook said this: "On 21st December 1999, Brian Willis did forget to brush his teeth."

So my job was finished, he added. After all, solving crime was what I was paid to do. The Police Department could now be closed down and I would be set free to retire to my elk farm.

At this I shuddered. This, of course, was the nagging doubt that I had successfully ignored earlier. I have, you see, a horror of elks. The last thing I wanted to do was to retire there among them, even though my herd consisted of only a single specimen.

I explained all this to the President. He listened attentively enough, his hands making little juggling motions under the table. My only other option, he said, was for me to declare myself unemployed and become a Talking Plaque. This was almost as unacceptable as the first option. Together we sat and thought deeply about the problem.

Eventually, prompted into inspiration by juggling-withdrawal, the President came up with a solution. He would change the law to make more work for me. For example, he would make illegal the possession of a nose over, or under, a certain length. This was an admirable solution indeed. Immediately this law was passed, I set about arresting those criminals whose noses were illegal, and researching the past to discover all those who had formerly possessed illegal noses and had thought they had escaped the long (but not too long) arm of justice. A clause exempted the President—whose own nose was formidable—from prosecution.

It was not long before I managed to solve these extra crimes. Many of the Talking Plaques were arrested and replaced by those whose noses were within the parameters of acceptability. However, the total numbers of Talking Plaques increased, as the jails began to fill up with owners of immoral proboscises.

Not that I was worried by the fact that all these extra crimes had been solved as well: I knew that I could rely on the President to change the law again. And, true to form, that is exactly what he did. This time, it was ginger beards that we made illegal. And, after that, dirty fingernails. In quick succession, we changed the law thirty-six times. Among others, things that had once been acceptable but were now heinous crimes included: owning pets, picking of the left ear, appendicitis, talking too quickly, talking too slowly and liking owls.

And then one day, when I arrived at the President's tower with a proposal to outlaw birthmarks, I found him lying face down on the floor, gnashing his teeth with rage. His tower was in disarray; broken music machines lay everywhere, bubbles of music floating free and bursting with resounding discords against each other. I thought, at first, that he had failed to perfect some particularly difficult juggling trick and had destroyed his tower in a frenzy of ugli-fruit collisions, but then I saw that the fruit in his dish were not bruised and I guessed that it was something more serious.

It soon transpired that my guess was correct. For the first time in three years, he had journeyed beyond the Pallid Colonnades and had visited his wife. There he had found a garment of underwear embossed with my own initials. I tried to deny the fact of the affair, but I blushed so pink that I gave myself away.

Tearing up my new proposal, The President suggested an alternative. He would make the solving of crime illegal. This alternative brought a chill to my bones. I was arrested shortly afterwards and brought to this very cell. My guards then were nice fellows. They even introduced me to the Talking Plaque who was going to recount my crimes. The Talking Plaque in question was a young girl with auburn hair. But she did not even look at me. I am not ashamed to say that I cried.

Naturally I appealed. And this was the crux of the whole matter. My appeal was a work of genius. I maintained that since the solving of crime was illegal, then the people who had arrested me had also committed an offence and should be jailed. And so on, until there was not a single person walking free in the whole world. I thought that this paradox would make the Appeal Judges see the absurdity of the charges levelled against me and throw my case out of court.

Unfortunately, after long and careful consideration, they agreed with me and promptly ordered the arrest of those who had arrested me. I was returned to my dank cell and I have remained here ever since. Slowly as I rotted away the months, the cells around me were filled: the chain reaction, once it had started, could not be stopped.

I suppose that one day soon the last human left on Earth will walk in here and lock the door behind them. I expect that the last human will be the President. And then, of course, apes or monkeys will have to guard the cells. I wonder when all this will happen?

Ah! You have made your move at last! It is a good move too. You know something? You look a little bit like the President yourself. Indeed, I would be willing to testify that you were him if it wasn't for the fact that you have no ugli-fruit with you. It is not so easy trying to juggle with bananas.

JUDGMENT DAY

Now I'm sitting quietly on my cloud, I can confess everything. It's not very often that I get a chance to sit back and relax. So I'd better make the most of it. Put the kettle on, if you have to, or finish writing that letter to the friend you haven't seen for absolutely ages, but do it quickly. I haven't much time left.

My name, as you are doubtless aware, is Titian Grundy. Until recently, I was Prefect of Police. I held the position for so long that I can't even remember what I was before. Probably a student of some kind. I vaguely recall skipping through autumn leaves with an auburn-haired girl and a multicoloured scarf, but this means nothing. I might have been a cheese-maker who'd simply lost his razor.

Anyway, to return to my tale, I was sitting at my desk one day, spinning paper helicopters through my open window when I received a telegram by carrier-pheasant. The telegram was from the President, an old friend of mine, and it announced that a meeting of Parliament had decided to make gods illegal. The motion had been carried by six hundred and sixty-six votes to one.

Jumping up, I held my chin in my hands and considered the import of this radical legislation. I knew the reason for the decision, of course; it was staring me in the face from the cover of yesterday's newspaper. Yet another leading citizen had been killed by an icy meteorite. It was generally held that the gods were responsible: throwing divine snowballs that concealed both a malicious glee and a fair-sized boulder.

The responsibility, however, once entirely theirs, now lay with me. Now that the gods were mere criminals, as opposed to omnipotent beings, it was up to my Department to arrest them. If I failed in this assignment, I would doubtless be replaced. My career would be over and I would have to seek alternative employment (for some reason, the position of cheese-maker occurred to me.)

Naturally, I was eager to embark on a raid of the Heavenly Realm as soon as possible. I was prepared to sign an arrest warrant at a moment's notice. The problem, as always, was transportation. I knew that the Force had several solar-powered gliders at its disposal, and had recently saved up to purchase an atomic trampoline, but even these shining examples of aerial-transport technology would be incapable of taking me up to such a great height. I was nonplussed.

Sighing, I left the office and went for a walk around the large artificial lake that ringed the Department like a noose. Huge mechanical locusts flitted around my head, an invention of my second-in-command, Satsuma Ffroyde. They had been designed to keep intruders at bay. I stared into the dark umber waters for many minutes, struggling to find a solution to my dilemma by means of a thought-experiment. I set up the test-tubes and retorts of my mind and mixed the isotopes and catalysts of my imagination. But all was in vain.

I could see reflected, quite clearly in the lake, the whole of the Heavenly Realm. It seemed to me then that I could jump down quite easily to my destination through this mirror of the ineffable. But before I was lulled into the attempt by the rhythm of the reflected clouds, a sharp crack assailed my ears and looking up, I perceived an enormous meteorite hurtling towards me. Luckily I was able to step aside as it plunged into the lake, shattering my own reflection into a thousand glassy shards.

My lakeside meditation had saved my life, of this I was certain. Probably the gods, learning of Parliament's decision, had sought to destroy the potential agent of their nemesis. Staring into the mirror of the lake had not only warned me of the approach of the meteorite but had also diverted its trajectory. Obviously the gods had mistaken my reflection for the real thing and had aimed at the wrong target.

This blatantly unimaginative assassination attempt stiffened my resolve to complete all my duties to the best of my ability. I was determined now not to beg the President to reconsider his new law, as I had been tempted to do. Instead, I returned to my office and called a meeting of all my high-ranking colleagues. Together, I felt sure, we would come up with a method of reaching the hide-out of these ontological criminals.

The meeting, however, proved to be a major disappointment at first. Few of the officers present knew anything at all about the heights of theology. They talked listlessly about helium balloons and giant catapults. Satsuma Ffroyde even confessed to being an atheist. He claimed that modern research in pendulum-physics had proved that the universe ran on clockwork. When I rounded on him in disbelief, he turned purple and added that this was merely a metaphor.

"This is ridiculous!" I cried, throwing my arms up in despair. "Is there no-one here who knows anything at all about the gods and how to reach them? I mean, who is their ruler? Do they have one? Is it Grunnt or Drigg? Perhaps it is Wheeze? Who is the god of meteorites? Gaap? Or is he the god of holes?"

"I thought it was Chyme," mumbled one of the officers.

"No, no! Chyme is the goddess of Aeolian-Harps!" countered another.

Exasperated by their ignorance, I turned to Dr Celery, the Police Surgeon Specific. He alone in the Police Department could be relied upon to say something worthwhile. But he was by nature a very reticent man and had to be goaded to speak. After a lengthy goad with a bundle of Napierian Nettles, he cleared his throat and said:

"Of course the gods exist and I know a method of reaching them. I have made a small study of the subject. I think that you may safely forget about helium balloons and the like. Physically, of course, it is impossible to enter the Heavenly Realm. However, it used to be said that a person's soul left their body at death and floated on up there without any other assistance. It is conceivable that I could temporarily kill you by freezing you in a cryogenic tank and then re-thaw you after you have completed your mission . . . "

This was the sort of information that had proved extremely difficult to obtain since all the priests and clergy had fled the land during the great ecclesiastical-exile order issued by the President the previous year (one of them, apparently had tried to seduce him during a confessional.) I was delighted with Dr Celery and dissolved the meeting at once.

The time-period of my demise was to be set at one month. This, it was presumed, would give me plenty of time to seek out and arrest the gods even if they fled to the furthest clouds of their pearly paradise. Accordingly, I submitted to Dr Celery's cryogenic machines, letting the sub-zero vanilla freeze the very blood in my veins and the very thoughts in my brain.

As I lost consciousness, I found myself floating down a blue tunnel towards a light that was bright yet gentle. In one hand, I clasped the arrest-warrant I had prepared the day before and, in the other, a magnum of Chablis I had taken as my sole provision for the journey. As I sipped from the bottle, the light at the end of the tunnel seemed to glow still brighter. I heard strains of unearthly music and caught my first glimpse of the afterlife.

The tunnel disgorged me with a convulsive spluttering noise and deposited me before the ivory gates of the Heavenly Realm. The gates were open and were unguarded. I guessed that Tourmaline, the three-bodied, single-headed Dog that was said to patrol the divine entrance-way had sneaked off for a moment to relieve himself. It was one of the problems to be expected with possessing three bodies.

I was grateful enough, of course, for Tourmaline is said to be quite bad-tempered and to bite even the most moral and holy of citizens as they file past. I was disappointed, however, that no-one appeared to greet me. Obviously, apart from the President, I had no friends on either side of the great divide between life and death. I sauntered through the gates onto the pearly meadows of the Heavenly realm. I became increasingly agitated and bitter when I discovered that even here there were no hordes of auburn-haired maidens willing to soothe my brow.

Anyway, as time is indeed growing very short, I shall briefly wind up my tale. I searched the Heavenly Realm for the gods but found only a large clockwork mechanism that seemed to be governing the Cosmos according to some pre-determined program. To this day, I cannot say whether the gods, aware of my approach, had built this device to rule in their place while they fled, or whether it had always been there. At any rate, I switched the thing off and allowed free-will to enter into the Universe for a change.

As for the blessed souls who cavorted around the Heavenly Realm, I couldn't prise any answers out of them either. They leapt around plucking harps and blowing trumpets in an incessant and extremely irritating manner. I rounded them up, arrested them one by one and imprisoned them in the vast palace that housed the clockwork machine. The President, of course, had earlier banned the use of musical instruments and therefore these ghosts and spirits were guilty of an offence under section G sharp of the Public Chord Act.

Alone in Heaven, I played at being a god myself. Monotheism had finally prevailed over the less-organised Polytheistic system. Playing god turned out to be harder work than I had anticipated. But I grew to enjoy the unlimited power; I let it caress me with its corrupting fingers. As I said before, at this very moment I am sitting on my favourite cloud, toying with the destiny of whole continents.

The only problem is that my month is almost up. It will soon be time for Dr Celery to re-thaw me and draw me back into my earthly body. I will have to give up this life of infinite privilege and become a mere Prefect of Police again, a servant of the State, mortal, fleshy and unliked. At least up here, I am reasonably content. Power, I have discovered, can be an adequate substitute for love.

Naturally I have tried to kill Dr Celery many times, to prevent him bringing me back to life, but I can't seem to get the hang of these meteorites. I gnash my teeth in fury, but all to no avail. At least, when I do return, I shall be able to avenge myself by telling him that the gods do not exist and that Satsuma was at least partly right. The destruction of his faith will be some consolation. However, my own faith is also starting to crack, although I am in a more secure position than either of my colleagues. If I were Dr Celery then the absence of the gods would be a savage blow indeed. On the other hand, if I were Satsuma then I would have to ask myself: who built the clockwork machine in the first place? It is more than merely a metaphor. Luckily, I have none of these problems.

Thank god I'm an agnostic!

THE THIRTY-NINE MILLION STEPS

Dare I say it? Dare I say that I—a mere cog in the workings of this great timepiece called the World (albeit an important one)—have prised myself loose from my bearings, rewound the coiled spring that keeps us all animated, redrawn the numbered face, replaced the hands with my own fists and even set the pendulum to swing on a rhythm of my own choosing? Dare I say that I—Titian Grundy, Prefect of Police—have changed society in a way more profound than any would previously have deemed possible? Dare I say such a thing?

Of course! False modesty was never a great talent of mine, though I practised mightily hard and long, especially in front of the President when diplomacy and a possible promotion were in the air. But that is another story. The President himself was no slouch at taking credit for things he had achieved—and many that he had not—and I see no reason why I should be any different. Besides, my public expect a full and frank confession and in this particular case humility and the truth are mutually incompatible.

So I will proceed directly to the very roots of my tale. There is no need for introductions. My previous exploits are already well-known enough to make any such preludes and preambles completely redundant. The Cabbage Affair was one of my remarkable successes: that time so painful in recent racial memory when a mutant Savoy threatened the very foundations of society. Cabbage soup was forthcoming to most citizens for months after the resolution of that corrugated case.

So too the affair of the Elk-Assassins, a curious sect that sprang up with the sole purpose of eliminating public servants and inaugurating an Elk republic. Despite my very real terror of the creatures (their antlers still haunt my dreams) I succeeded in breaching the walls of their clifftop fortress—and ending their machinations—with a dozen cannon specially converted to fire kayaks, snow-shoes and all those other northern adjuncts so inimical to the wellbeing of elks.

The case that I wish to discuss now, however, has served to make my name far more notorious than any of these. It began when I received a message from the President requesting me to reduce the crime rate to zero within a week. I was much vexed by this communiqué and spent long hours rolling around on the floor with my new assistant, Lola Halogen, in a state of indescribable agitation. Eventually I picked myself up and paid a visit to Dr Celery, the Police Surgeon Specific, in the basement of his private house. Being the most rational man I knew, I felt sure that he would be able to offer me some useful advice.

And so he did: after much tugging of his stringy beard, he helped to define the nature of the problem. Crime occurred in the first place, he pointed out, because criminals thought they could run away from the scene of their misdemeanours. What was needed was a method of preventing them running away; a sort of moral net to catch them in their tracks. For example, a state of altered gravity in—or near—the vicinity of their intended crimes would ensure their undoing.

I agreed with his conclusions but was bitterly disappointed when he went on to confess that he would not be able to help me further. He knew much about corpses and tweed but little about gravity. However, he then suggested that if I contacted the University, I may find some expert or other willing and capable of taking his ideas to their logical outcome. Accordingly I sent an express message by carrier-tortoise to the very hub of glorious Academia and within three days, found two intense and exceedingly proud individuals waiting for me in my office.

They introduced themselves as Professor Warp and Professor Woof, the two greatest experts on the subject of gravity. They were serious rivals and bore more than a little malice towards each other. This antipathy ran so deep that they even affected different tastes in clothing, women and food. The former favoured cravats, brunettes and peas. The latter preferred spats, raspberry blondes and beans. My own tastes, of course, are both renowned and irrelevant to this tale, but I will state them anyway: unbuttoned cuffs, redheads and cheese.

I outlined my needs and away they went, both determined to outdo and belittle the other. Professor Warp had decided that he was capable of constructing a machine which would reduce gravity by a factor of ten. This would ensure that criminals would not only be unable to flee the scene of their crimes but would not be able to reach them in the first place. Their ambitions would be left up in the air, so to speak. Professor Woof's chosen method, on the other hand, was to try to increase gravity by a factor of ten. Quite literally this would be a crushing blow to the naughty fraternity. In the first case, the Police would maintain the advantage by wearing weighted boots; in the second, by pounding their beats on spring-loaded shoes.

I left them to it and paced my office nervously, keeping one eye on the hourglass that dangled from the ceiling on a cord of braided hair and the other eye on Lola Halogen's impressive cleavage. If I did not complete my task within the time allotted to me by the President, I would be demoted and placed in stocks in the market square of the miniature village he had built out of spent matchsticks in one corner of his overgrown roof-garden. This was a prospect I did not relish. The President is a fair shot with the ugli-fruit crossbow.

To ease my mounting agitation, I determined to pay the matter no further heed and resolutely avoided contacting either of the Professors to check on the progress of their respective schemes. Thus the first I knew of the success of both was that morning before the President's deadline when I awoke to find myself lying in the centre of one of the walls of my bedroom with various knick-knacks and tasteful objets d'art lying in great profusion all around me. In short the wall had become the floor and the floor had become the wall.

I will skip over the ensuing chaos that reigned a full month after this peculiar discovery—the details are both too painful and too wearisome to recount. Suffice it to say that the natural order of things all over the world had altered. It seems that Professor Warp and his rival, Professor Woof, had both completed their gravity machines and had switched them on simultaneously. A strange thing had happened. Instead of cancelling each other out, as might have been expected, the combined manipulations of natural gravity had produced a force that exerted itself sideways. Anything that had been caught out in the open at the time had instantly plummeted laterally, parallel to the ground.

It was a laborious process adjusting society to this new state of affairs. For some reason—which was never adequately explained—the Professors insisted that it was impossible to turn their machines off. So we were stuck with a world in which a trip to the corner shop required scaling a vertical face by way of finger-holds and toeholds that had once existed as mere cracks in the pavement. The solution, of course, was to carve steps into this endless precipice we now all existed on. But everyday life was still an exhausting process, all ups and downs. A bit like life before the change, I suppose.

Visiting the President was the most hazardous venture of all. He had chosen to build his latest tower on the very tip of an exceedingly straight and narrow peninsula that jutted far out into the Coughing Sea. To scale this peninsula required the cutting of exactly thirty-nine million steps, and the erection of a bannister longer than any that had existed since the Supreme Roger accidentally fell into a machine which forced rusty trams through a pinhole to make wire for tightrope walkers. I would guess that this bannister was even longer than that.

It required amazing stamina to ascend these thirty-nine million steps—though it was great fun sliding down the bannister on the way back. What made the journey even more dangerous was the fact that all manner of objects were flying around through the air; pedestrians, ships, apples. All the things that had not been indoors or tied down when the great change had taken place. Such objects fell endlessly around the world, circling the planet on average twice a day.

Surprisingly, it was not Dr Celery who formulated the clever plan to save us from the menace of lateral gravity. It was myself—and Lola Halogen, of course—after a lengthy erotic session with a bottle of henna and a mouldy Cheddar. The two gravity machines were located in the catacombs of the University. Perhaps their proximity to each other was producing the bizarre effect. Possibly the removal of one of them from its inverted twin would nullify the anomaly. It suddenly occurred to me that, using the President's new tower as a pulley, we could hoist one of the mechanisms up to his end of the peninsula, leaving the other behind. There were arguments between the Professors after I announced my scheme to them. Neither of them wanted their machine to be the one that was moved. I settled the dispute by tossing a coin.

It was a one-sided coin—though never let it be said that I am unfair—and when professor Woof chose Heads, Professor Warp had no choice but to choose Sides, which was an unlikely prospect from the outset. And so it was Professor Warp's device, the one that lessened gravity by a factor of ten that was attached to the rope and yanked away from Academia and towards political turpitude. The fact that this machine was also considerably lighter than Professor Woof's may also have been a contributing factor in our very real delight that Professor Warp had chosen Sides.

Imagine, if you will, the scene of the great haul; the strange many-faceted gravity machine of one of our greatest scientists being pulled up the monstrous staircase by the members of the Police Department (how Satsuma Ffroyde grumbled!) with steady jerks and a sea-shanty. It bounced on each step and threatened to shatter into a billion fragments. Luckily, it did not. I had earlier scaled the thirty-nine million steps up to the edge of the peninsula with the length of rope between my teeth and had looped it over the President's tower. As the machine rose steadily higher, a peculiar thing began to happen. The force of the sideways gravity slowly began to decrease.

We now know that the simultaneous switching-on of two such radically different devices in such close proximity to each other had set up a Magnetic Latitude Effect, whereby gravity had started to tug in a direction diametrically opposite that of the planet's spin.

181

As we forced the machines apart from each other, the vortex set up by them broke down and they began to operate as originally envisaged. Thus, at the University, lecturers and research students were flattened into the second-dimension. As Professor Woof's machine neared the end of the peninsula, the effect grew steadily more dramatic. Eventually, when the device had actually reached the President's tower, something truly unexpected and bizarre happened.

I have mentioned that the President's tower stood at the end of the absurdly straight and narrow finger of land. I have perhaps neglected to add that the University lay at the other end. Thus the two gravity machines, both struggling to bend the laws of physics in different directions, were soon operating at maximum potential. The thirty-nine million steps carved into the peninsula comprised the longest continuous staircase that had been constructed during the crisis (which is why it had been chosen for the separation experiment.) Unfortunately, the peninsula was geologically very weak and it snapped off—the University end staying firmly attached to Earth, while the President's end flew up and crashed against the moon (now much closer than it had been in ages past.) Thus we were left with a ladder to Luna.

It is pleasant up here. We do not worry about having enough air to breathe—an ample supply followed us up. We can commute back and forth whenever we choose. I prefer to stay here for two reasons: it is generally quieter and there is an almost ceaseless supply of cheese. The President has built a new tower on the dark side. One day I may be invited there to tea and cribbage. The most lasting effect—as I have already hinted at—is that our natural body rhythms have altered. They now rely on the phases of the Earth. When she is full, I throw back my head and howl. When she is new, I sleep with a silver coin under my pillow and dream of merciless elks with eyes wide as craters.

THE IMPOSSIBLE MIRROR

I am a reflective man. I never used to be, it's a condition that came over me recently—like a dizzy spell. Sitting on a piece of driftwood in the centre of a bubble snorted from a nostril of Neptune, I have little to do but gaze at the concave walls of my prison and recollect the circumstances which led me here. It's a deep ocean and I have a long way to go before I break its surface and burst into freedom.

To pass the minutes of the ascent—not mine, which are barbed and can only be passed with difficulty, but yours (which happily are at least greased)—I sometimes chant aloud my story. Few fish have heard of my name or exploits. I have done a small number of remarkable things. I am Titian Grundy, Prefect of Police, catcher of miscreants blue-handed. (In other dimensions, the colour of crime may well be crimson. I do not intend commenting on these alternative cultures. In our society, the hue is indigo and the cry is salty).

It all began two years ago. I had just arrested the full moon for the crime of pouring honey on troubled seas (outlawed since my beekeeper wife ran off to join the Elk Liberation Army) when I was summoned by my old friend, the President. He had cut himself shaving that morning; his reflection had skipped out of the frame of the mirror. He wanted me to do something about it. "Jump into the mirror and apprehend the delinquent image," he cried. I told him that mirror-worlds were beyond my jurisdiction. He wrapped his fingers in my hair and tried to force my head into the silvered circle. My brow cracked the glass.

Finally, he conceded the futility of the operation. Because he has my prejudices, my toasted brutality, I did not complain. Indeed, I promised to launch an immediate investigation and offer a reward for the return of his image. He pulled his long nose and nodded, while I mounted my chariot and made my way back to the Police Station. The tortoises strained in their harnesses; before the sun had set in the Glib Ocean, I was sitting at my desk, lecturing my colleagues about the strange occurrence.

Amazingly, all had suffered similar experiences. In some cases, reflections had thumbed noses at their owners and made other rude gestures. "Why did no-one mention this to me?" I demanded. My colleagues shuffled their feet and admitted they had been scared of looking foolish. After all, if a man cannot control his own reflection, how can he stake a claim to his fate? There was no answer to this. So I wondered why I had been spared such an affront during shaving. Then I remembered: I have a beard.

I called for a mirror and angled it under my jaw. To my utter consternation, it showed a blank. "What is the meaning of this?" I roared, in my liquorice voice, black and very sweet. But, of course, there was no meaning; for logic had fled along with the reflection, doubtless mounted on its shoulders. I called for a cup of blue-green tea and, having received a particularly fine blend, dipped my nose towards its seductive wavelets. Yet even in these turquoise shallows, my handsome visage was not available. I was aghast.

I ordered a thorough search of the entire building. "Seal all the doors and windows! Make sure the reflections can't escape." I raised the cup to my lips and the entire beverage cascaded down my chin. Surprising how much we rely on an illusory kiss, the meeting of mirrored lips and real, to guide rim to palate! Nonetheless, dripping tea and authority, I stirred my orders and sugared them. My colleagues bounded into action: it did not occur to us that the capturing of images so ephemeral requires handcuffs made of uncle-of-pearl.

While they searched, I sketched portraits of myself in the excessive margins of official reports and fixed them over the redundant mirrors.

They were a poor substitute, but the alternative was hollowness, a dented identity. As I wielded pen and scissors (assisted by Lola Halogen, my glowing secretary) my most competent colleague—Dr Celery, the Police Surgeon Specific—returned with a heavy book cradled in his arms. I drummed the desk with my fingers. "The reflections are in there?" I inquired. "Well that makes sense. Traitors always turn to literature to justify their perniciousness." I was about to launch into a tirade further condemning the aberrant reflections, and drawing comparisons between various criminal activities and an appreciation of the arts, but Dr Celery stalled me with a shake of his tubular head.

He told me he had searched the archives in vain—the reflections were elsewhere. But while flicking through the musty collection of prohibited volumes in the darkest reaches of the basement, he'd chanced upon an interesting explanation for our dire circumstances. I urged him to share this insight and he dropped the tome before me, splitting it open like a giant clam and thrusting a wrinkled finger into its yellowing depths. I peered through the cloud of dust at the indicated passage and read aloud:

"In those days the world of mirrors and the world of men were not, as they are now, cut off from each other. They were, besides, quite different; neither beings nor colours nor shapes were the same. Both republics, the specular and the human, lived in harmony . . . One night the mirror people invaded the earth. Their power was great, but at the end of bloody warfare the magic arts of the Yellow President prevailed. He repulsed the invaders, imprisoned them in their mirrors, and forced on them the task of repeating, as though in a kind of dream, all the actions of men. He stripped them of their power and of their forms and reduced them to mere slavish reflections. Nonetheless, a day will come when the magic spell will be shaken off . . . "

I fell back in my chair and gnawed my knuckles. It was obvious that this ancient chronicle (for such it was) spoke truth. The Yellow President had existed over ten millennia ago, the sunniest ruler of the Spectrum Dynasty. The ordained time, when mirrors would once more become disobedient, was upon us. This was a calamity of ludicrous dimensions. I appealed for advice. Should I rampage through the cities of the world, smashing each and every mirror with a toffee-hammer? Should I order the immediate cloaking of all reflecting telescopes? Should I proclaim against ice?

Before I could receive an answer from either Dr Celery or Lola Halogen, the telephone rang and I found myself listening to our own President. He was no longer my friend, he claimed, and wanted me to return his chrome watering-can. I asked the reason for this enmity. He bawled that my reflection had appeared in his mirror in lieu of his own, but dressed in his clothes. I was thus an outlaw of the lowest order: a linen thief. Before I could stammer an apology, he rang off.

Dr Celery nodded sagely and dried my tears with one of his flapping cuffs. "It seems," said he, "that the reflections are already tired of rebellion and wish to return to their owners. But they've lost their way and can't remember which mirrors they belong to." And to emphasise his words, he picked up the looking-glass I'd called for and gestured at it. I found myself meeting the gaze of someone unknown to me, dressed in the uniform of a Prefect of Police. At once I was in a froth, roaring at him: "Impostor! Usurper! You'll get solitary confinement for this deception!" Heedless of Dr Celery's protestations, I instructed Lola Halogen to lock the mirror into a filing-cabinet and swallow the key. (Her mouth was too dainty for such a morsel, so I completed the task).

"But where is the President's reflection?" I demanded. "How can he comb his hair or pick his nose by gazing at me? I'm competent at neither operation. He'll grow annoyed and I'll be demoted again." I was frantic with worry. Dr Celery told me not to fret—we were, he insisted, all in the same bathysphere. There was probably no logical order to the jumbling of mirror-images. The President's reflection might be an unimaginable distance away, in any kind of mirror—suspended on a wardrobe door perhaps, in the boudoir of a widow, beyond the Pallid Colonnades; or gleaming in the burnished copper disc of an Amberzarian Potentate; or else, on one of the countless Aracknid islands, burning blackly in the smoky obsidian altar of some Sideways Priest, polished to virtue by his singular sleeve.

With Dr Celery's encouragement, I began to consider these, and other, types of reflecting surface as possible hosts for an endless procession of unknown faces. But what of warped mirrors? Would they distort the psychology of their unwitting guests? After all, an image that expects to appear in a harmless medium, such as the base of a saucepan, might be mentally injured by swelling instead in the convexity of a wok. The Police Surgeon Specific advised me not to dwell on arcane details. It was more important to think of some way to reverse the situation (pun charged, clubbed over the head and refused bail).

The lost reflections, it seemed, would never be able to find their way home without help. There were literally millions of mirrors scattered across the silvery globe. How would an image know which was the right one without entering each in turn? By the time the problem sorted itself out on its own, the original owners of the reflections would be dead and future citizens would have to endure, on their walls and in their bathrooms, an interminable frolic of tenacious ghosts. Naturally they would refuse to put up with this and, in protest, neglect to pay their taxes. Our comfortable regime would rot at the seams, the springs of the judiciary no longer able to support the cushion of the executive.

But what was the best way of reuniting populace and reflections? Although I credit most of my best ideas to Dr Celery, it is Lola Halogen who is the intellectual heavyweight of my Department. She suggested we collect every mirror in existence and fuse them into one single gargantuan specimen. The images would be able to mingle freely and arrange themselves in alphabetical order; the real citizens could then be called upon, one at a time, to claim back their prodigal twins in a glittering identity-parade.

There was one problem. Such a mirror would shatter under its own weight. At this juncture, Lola widened her eyes in disappointment. As I started to drown in her cobalt gaze, I grasped a straw of inspiration and hauled myself, spluttering, onto the shores of wisdom. "The ocean!" I cried. In response to Dr Celery's puzzled frown—the man is a veritable allotment of expressions—I merely trawled through the synonyms, wriggling my fingers like the tentacles of a squid. "The briny deeps, the damp abyss, the watery locale! The snowy heights!" (I must apologise here; somehow an antonym has slithered in).

I stood up and pirouetted on my toes. I elaborated on my sodden utterances. The ocean is the greatest mirror in existence. Instead of trying to join together a multitude of looking-glasses, we simply had to cast them back into the melting-pot of all reflections. Then the lost images would be able to float out of their geometric prisons and beach themselves at the very feet of their concerned owners. Enthused with my vision, my secretary and the Police Surgeon Specific joined me in a swift tango.

The following weeks were spent in a wash of activity. With the President's grumpy blessing—he refused to entertain me, but not to collaborate—the laws regarding bounced photons were changed. Any item that did not absorb light, but cast it back whole, was deemed illegal, possession of which became punishable by death. Immediately after this legal reform, an amnesty was issued: the owners of these items would be able to dispose of them, no questions asked, in the official dumping site, namely the Sea.

Soon the cliffs of our shoreline were crowded with citizens throwing their mirrors, shiny cutlery and polished boots into the foaming surf. Some were more reluctant than others—generally the owners of fancy mirrors, heirlooms and antiques. I aided these with my sherbet voice, sunny and cringing, and my truncheon. I struck out in all directions until my weapon was no longer recognisable as an adjunct to my rank, but merely a twisted length of wood.

Once we were satisfied that every mirror in the world had been given to the ocean, the arduous process of joining owner and image began. Floating out of their silvered cells, the reflections were washed up against the wharves of our major ports. Down at the crystal piers of the Capital, I organised fishing contests. With a jar suspended on a line, the entrants had to catch their own reflections, sealing the jars when successful and taking them home.

Within a year, everything was back to normal. The President, having imprisoned his recalcitrant image in a Champagne bottle, sent me a touching letter. He would consent to being my friend again if I would apologise and help him decorate his emerald tower. Of all the citizens of all the lands, I alone was miserable. My reflection had still not returned. Every morning I fished in vain, hooking peculiar mythical beings (or archetypes from the unlit trenches of my subconscious) but nothing that resembled a Prefect of Police. Back at the station I discussed this with Dr Celery and he descended into the archives again and returned with the same ancient volume.

"Mythical beings?" he cried, throwing open the book at a dog-eared page. "I anticipated this. We didn't read the footnotes." And adjusting the treble of his voice, he recited: *"The ocean is indeed the biggest mirror in existence. But there is more sea than land. Thus the ocean can reflect the whole of human life with plenty to spare . . . In these gaps are to be found the beings of humanity's imagination. Here, in these uncharted regions, glitter the heroes, monsters and demons of legend. For example, Moozsgyrrgtlk, the tawny god of elks . . . "*

"Enough!" I shuddered. I scowled at the book. "Rubbish, pure stuffing and nonsense! I refuse to listen to a chronicle penned in the time of the Spectrum Republics!" I stormed out and returned to the crystal piers. I continued to fish until midnight. When I caught Neptune and was promptly swallowed by him, I had to concede that Dr Celery had a point. The god was real enough; his stomach was full of sunken galleons and triremes from semi-legendary sea-battles. In the phosphorescent light of nameless molluscs and half-digested seaweed, I glimpsed tattered banners of the Yellow President.

The god of the sea dived down into the deepest trench. I escaped by climbing back into his throat and tickling his epiglottis with my truncheon. He sneezed me out and now I am trapped in an air bubble, speeding towards the surface. My truncheon more nearly resembles a piece of driftwood and makes an uncomfortable perch. Which reminds me, you fish have been a wonderful audience, the very best I've had, and I'd like to thank you from the throbbing heart of my submarine bottom.

CRAWLING KING PRAWN

The sun rose like a fishwife and I jumped out of bed with the enthusiasm of a limpet. It is cold in my house, the heating is inadequate. I refuse to pay my fire bills: the idiots insist on spelling my name incorrectly. I am not, nor ever will be, Titan Grubby! The titans were tall, ugly and devoid of friends, whereas I am short, beautiful and the President is my friend, except in winter, when he never visits because of the chilliness of my rooms. He says the real reason is that he hates me, but I think he is just being polite. Anyway, Titian is what I insist on being called; a single vowel, especially one as malnourished as 'i', might not seem much to you, but it is the difference between myth and art. Remember that, my trustworthy readers, and write letters of protest to the Fire Company on my behalf! I shall not even comment on their libellous use of my surname. I enjoy a bath (cold) once a month.

Having abandoned the comfort of sheets and pillow, I dressed in the uniform of the Prefect of Police, which took an hour or so, thanks to an epaulette which would not stand to attention without a stiffening of oil and flour. Then I descended for breakfast, whistling a Django melody, as if some hot jazz might warm up the kitchen. A bowl of icy museli, washed down, or glaciated along, with a pot of frosty coffee, completed my dour repast and invested me with just enough energy to wrap myself in a scarf for the bleak journey along the Fimbul-corridor to my front door. I have fitted a new knocker, in the shape of a rune, a nordic design which is a brutal warning to casual callers of the nature of the interior. Possibly an extravagant touch—it cost more than my unpaid bills—but who shall deny my sense of irony? Nobody, I fear, as I never have callers, but all the same, the principle is sublime.

I have ventured along the corridor many times, but familiarity with the terrain has its own perils. One must guard against overconfidence. A sudden shift in the direction of the draughts can scupper the most stoic explorer. Often I have been forced to set up emergency camp in the small room under the stairs, warming my fingers on a spare candle. Today I was more fortunate: I reached the hatstand without much trouble, rushing the front door with a frenzied twanging of tendons. Fumbling with the catch, I opened it and stepped out into the balmy morning. My limbs unfroze and expanded; I stretched in the slanting rays. The planet, unlike my house, is adequately heated, and the sun has not yet demanded payment. Climbing into the threadbare sky, Sol cast beams like hooks. Removing my scarf, I skipped the whole way to my office.

The Police Station is a nine-sided building, each side representing one of the major excuses of the modern criminal. The ground floor of the 'Absent Father' wing has been knocked into one room. Here I work, curing the realm, purging society of its ills, aided by my colleagues, the most trustworthy professionals in the business. Behind my balsa desk, I watch over all citizens, wagging my finger at the naughty ones, arresting them and throwing them into the dungeons to await trial. The courtyard at the centre of the complex is filled with statues of my predecessors. Soon an addition will be made: I observe the empty plinth from my window. Quartz and topaz, my likeness will sparkle brightest of all. How I long for the time when I stand over the sculptor with a mallet, ensuring he spells my name correctly! It cannot be long now.

Anyway, as I approached the main gate, I was shocked to find my way barred by a guard, musket at the ready.

"What is the meaning of this, Percy?"

"Sorry, Mr Grundy, orders from the top. Mustn't let you in for love or oranges. Told to use necessary force."

"Absurd fellow! How am I to go to work? Do you want recidivists and rogues running free, violating your daughters and bookshelves? Come now, good man, let me through, before I cry."

"Can't do that, sir. Loaded gun this is!"

The fool was torn between conflicting loyalties. I saw I was in for a long argument: Percy Flamethrower is a stubborn old soak, which is why I employed him as security. I sighed and tapped my foot, opened my mouth and inhaled enough oxygen for a lengthy monologue, when a figure came up behind him, waving at me. It was Dr Celery, the Police Surgeon Specific, my most competent colleague. Fixing him with a charming smile, I lightly inquired as to the nature of the problem.

He was very grave. "You've been sacked."

"Nonsense! I have recently achieved a 99.9% success rate at solving crime. The President is my friend!"

"No longer, it seems. Listen, Titian, we've worked together for two decades now, so I think we can speak frankly. Age has numbed your senses and wrinkled your reflexes. You're getting rusty round the gills, losing your hair. Your platinum judgment is suffering from metal fatigue! There was no option but to replace you."

I tried to imagine an usurper sitting on my chair, feet on my desk, smoking my cigars, kissing my beekeeper, scuffing my rug. Would he steal my plinth? I wept sour tears. "Who is it?"

Dr Celery lowered his eyes and muttered: "Raphael Perkins, returned from exile yesterday. The President issued a full pardon for his part in the Jumble-Sale Uprising, the Coup d'Tat."

Collapsing to my knees, I sought to control my quivering lips. "The President must be mad. Perkins is a known agitator. He puts cider in his jelly! How can you obey any of his orders?"

Dr Celery shifted uncomfortably. "Satsuma Ffroyde, Lola Halogen and myself petitioned the President in an attempt to change his mind. No-one was indispensable, he told us. Indeed, he went on to say he had lined up replacements for us, if we wanted to be awkward. For Satsuma Ffroyde was a zestful upstart called Clementine Jungg, and Lola Halogen was shadowed by some hussy known as Mina Argon."

I swallowed. "I remember her! I once rejected her application for a secretarial job. She doesn't even know how to form salts by direct union with metals! This is a disaster: with that lot in charge of policing our cities, criminals will proliferate like profiteroles! Yes, it was better to betray me than the nation! I forgive you!"

This cheered Dr Celery a little, but he still had some wallowing to complete. Leaning closer, pushing his lips through the bars of the gate, he said: "My replacement would have been Professor Fennel, a downy quack of the aniseed order. My dismissal would have taken place in public—my epaulettes would be lashed from my shoulders with a liquorice whip and a symbolic celery stick snapped over my knee!"

I stepped back and walked away. At my retreat, Percy grew confident and cocked his musket. "That's it, sir! Nice and easy, can't have public servants acting like valets! Move off, lad!"

Dr Celery was still mumbling to himself. "Hold the fort, that's the idea, in the circumstances, can't blame us . . . "

I shook my head sadly. "No, I don't blame you."

"Come on now, Mr Grundy, don't try anything foolish. Blow your nose clean off into the shrubbery, I will."

"Thank you, Percy. Take care of yourself!"

When I was out of sight, the tears flooded my ducts. All that work, all those years of toil, of hopes and fears and dreams and cheese! So it was to be in vain! I could scarcely believe it, even when I went back to the gate for a second opinion. Percy was even more violent this time and fired a warning shot which smashed the headstone of Sir Charlton Radish, founder of our order. I guessed a mistake of some kind had been made and that the President would put things right if I met him in person. So now I headed for his jasper tower, which had been moved to the marketsquare, a locale giving him ample opportunity to slip from official business and purchase ugli-fruit fresh from the stalls.

When I reached the tower, I did not even bother to knock. There was a sign pasted on his door which told me what I needed to know. It denied a lifetime of friendship and cracked my remaining pride. It was a simple sign. It said: *No Admittance To Titan Grubby!* I wiped my eyes and walked out of the market, the traders pointing at me and throwing rotting fruit at my departing form. One pineapple struck my on the head, making my ear burn like a spiced heretic. Women mocked me.

From the market, I made my solitary way back to my house, taking an oblique short-cut through the park. The ducks laughed at me as I skirted the water; the fish mouthed silent obscenities. I tore off my epaulettes and cast them into the pond, which turned oily and brackish. I was in no hurry to return to my cold rooms, but meandering could not be maintained indefinitely. At some point, I would have to pass my door, place the key in the lock and enter my refrigerated domesticity. When I took the fatal step, the knocker glared like a lobster.

Inside, I performed a stately dance to warm my innards. Between the steps, I set words on paper with a quill made from an icicle. My letters to the President were generally formal; this one implored him to give me the reason why he had forsaken me. As soon as it was finished, I sent it by carrier-snail and waited for an answer. The days passed in sub-Arctic gloom. The aurora borealis licked the paint above my staircase. Penguins emerged from my taps and filled the bath with their executive antics. At last, during a blizzard in the lounge, I received a reply. Snatching the epistle from the carrier-snail, I devoured it as hungrily as polar-bears devour grandfather clocks (one was busy with the pendulum right now.) My eyes scanned the words and I howled.

"Dear Titian," it said, *"I know this must be hard for you, being an arrogant so-and-so, but really it's quite the most sensible thing to do. Think about it, old chum, and think about what sort of future our people want for their children. Your detection rate is 99.9% and some officials might think that pretty neat, but what about those dead mothers and lost dogs who make up that 0.1%? How can I look them in the face and say that they're just throwaway statistics? No, it's time for a change. Even I've made sacrifices, giving up juggling for bagatelle. Well, I'm sure we can rely on Raphael Perkins to get to grips with that missing percentage. He has the drive you've lost, the sheer fanaticism and gutsy determination. We're on the threshold of a new era, friend, and some of us have to move over to make room for fresh growth. That's how it goes. No hard feelings and chins aloft!*

Signed: *the President*.

Before I could fully digest this news, I noticed there was a second letter on the snail. Easing it from the antennae, I tore it open, seeing at once it was a final demand from the Fire Company. If I did not settle my debts in one week, it warned, I would be taken to court. In the exact centre of my kitchen, I made a little fire with the letters, just enough to boil a cup of mocha. As I sipped and mulled on my future, an upstairs wardrobe suddenly burst in the cold, sending frozen shirts tumbling down the steps. This avalanche swept aside the bannister, continuing into the lounge and completely demolishing the interior. Had I been sitting there rather than in the kitchen, my life would be as smeared as my career. It was a decisive moment. I would call this hollow iceberg 'home' no longer! I would relive one of my earliest dreams, travelling the world in simple splendour, flowery rucksack on my back.

In the room under the stairs, I found the bag, unused since student days. With a rag I polished my thumb. I turned my uniform inside-out and threaded coloured laces into my boots. Then, with no more than a cursory glance back, I hopped off into the noon, down to the wharf and the magic shimmer of the crystal piers. Already I felt stubble pushing through the smooth skin of my establishment chin.

The balloon port was thronged with aeronauts of many nationalities, some of them covered from head to foot in tattoos. Dirigibles from every corner of the scalene world were landing and taking off, bearing cargoes and passengers over the cobalt sea. It was a marvellous sight, a fulcrum of activity, with hopes lifting and falling in tandem with the balloons. I saw fat foremen and skinny accountants chasing captains and navigators to berate them for delays; I watched quayside prostitutes accept payment in helium from seasoned clients; I listened to meteorologists predicting cyclones and typhoons at lazy latitudes.

I was generally ignored as I wandered the balustrades: my petitions for lifts were met with a shrug or a frown. At last, one aeronaut paused in his task of waxing a silk canopy, and explained that commercial craft were no longer allowed to pick up casual passengers, as it violated some insurance rule. He suggested I leave the city on foot and try to hitch a ride from balloons in transit, where crews could operate without company officials breathing down their napes.

Taking his advice, I headed out of the metropolis, a more difficult journey than I had anticipated. When the final suburb receded behind me, I stopped on the side of a country lane and gazed upward. Balloons threw off ballast and rose like … pears in absinthe? Light-bulbs in gravy? Or perhaps like jellyfish in a boundless ocean? Yes, this simple simile was the truest: they were creatures of the deep and I was a sea-slug peering up at this rich harvest. In a daze, I lifted my thumb and beckoned in an elevated direction. To my surprise, a sporting dirigible released helium and dropped a rope-ladder at my feet. I clutched the bottom rung and was lifted, rotating in terror, into the basket, where an auburn-haired girl greeted me with a hearty slap on the back and a bottle of rum. I laughed at this magnificent change in my fortunes.

We sped over the Pallid Colonnades and skimmed the Aracknid Islands and hovered over the sunken city of Amberzar to pick up supplies of damp cotton. It was better than I had imagined as a daydreaming youth. So the years of relentless ambition, of clawing my way to the top: that was the real waste! This was living as it should be, free of petty concerns. Now I was happy for the first time! My hair grew long, my knees grew scuffed and my shoes fell apart. I did not care! Up, up and away, was my cry! It rained, but the rain tasted sweet; it snowed, but the snow was like milk poured over chocolate; it hailed, but hail on the balloon's canopy was a percussion orchestra playing aphrodisiac songs from the figging-oases of Khyor. Grundy was finally gratified!

The auburn-haired girl dropped me off in a mountainous town deep in the Uneven Lands. I took a job here as a waiter and earned enough to buy a mandolin. Then I was back in the basket, with a new crew, heading into the caverns of Doyléu, to barter with the gnoles. Out through the crater of an extinct volcano in Grokkland, I found myself strumming melodies on my instrument, as if my thumbs had been born to the art. The captain and mates danced so wildly the gondola nearly tipped up. I blanched and kept silent for the rest of the day, but the following morning, my insatiable fingers sought out new insidious chords. I began to develop a repertoire of songs, wistful ballads and sarabands.

Frequently, in towns and cities, I met other hitchers, most of whom carried around musical instruments like myself. In Djiwondro, nine of us got together and busked ourselves stupid in the casbah, earning a gallon of scented tea and three days in jail for our trouble. Our relationships were cordial but casual; I picked up the lingo from them, passed tips on how to evade the local police, and shared suppers and scales. There were bouts of love too, both with female travellers and native girls, creases of passion in my previously ironed life. Yet I was chomped by wanderlust and could not settle anywhere. Always I had to ride the next balloon out of town, seeking adventures as fresh as seaweed. Like a barnacle, I felt compelled to attach myself to those bulbous forms. I visited Amana, Cus, Yam-Yam, Xopué, the jungles of Paraparapara.

In was over Qtiztowf that I first noticed the speck on the horizon. For months I felt I was being followed, a sensation which persisted even though I frequently changed balloons and direction, sometimes recrossing my original flight-path. I realised this speck had been with me from the beginning, right on the edge of my vision. In my fevered mind, it became the point of a needle, sewing buttons of restraint onto my freedom. Like a full-stop threatening to end the sentence of my joy, it punctured warm sunsets over the lakes of Ojidra or spotted the parchment empyrean which curved over the steppes of Rholl. Loathing human grammar, I fled nemesis like a crab fleeing an amoeba—sideways, scuttling, eyes popping. Smack in the centre of the Loverlei Prairies, I managed to hitch a lift aboard a military balloon, a spherical dirigible bristling with steel spikes. I was reminded more acutely than ever of a sub-aquatic scene, as the giant urchin released gas and dropped its ladder.

The captain was an old sugar with a beard big enough to hide flying fish, of which many skimmed past, on their migrations to the wadis of Al Datum. He had a heart problem and this was his last mission—to observe troop movements in the forests of Jabboo. He passed me a telescope and I was able to resolve the true character of my pursuer. The speck became a balloon of curious design, with reticulated legs which helped it to swim in the air. I confided my worries to the captain and he seemed delighted at the prospect of adventure. "We'll outfly the blighter!" he exclaimed, gunning his engine to maximum speed. The propellers lashed the clouds to ribbons and they fell to giftwrap the landscape below. The spot vanished for a brief period, but then it returned: through the eyeglass I saw its legs were flapping wildly and that the canopy was red in the face. Never before had I seen prawn and urchin play cat and mouse. The rival balloon seemed to be armed with a harpoon-proboscis.

For many days we lurched over countries and seas, the captain happy and flustered, steering between mountain ranges and under waterfalls. We even ventured into the orchards of Lubbalouana, impaling limes and plums on our spines. But the prawn dirigible would not be shaken off: so right out into the foggy Glib Ocean we headed, where navigation was impossible and only eels could easily find their way home. With the mist choking an engine, we were becalmed while we sought to pull strands of steam out of the ducts. The captain climbed over the rim of the gondola and used only his fingertips to lean over to the engine. It was a precarious business. He was sweating profusely, so to calm him down I took up my mandolin and struck up a graceful tune. Clogged by the fog, the melody warped into an atonal wail which startled the captain. His heart jumped: his visage was contorted with pain. As the blood rushed to his cheeks, his fingers grew slack on the rail and he tumbled down.

I did not hear the splash. I was so distraught I threw the mandolin after him. The reduction in weight caused the balloon to rise: within an hour it was above the fog and in open, very dark blue, sky. The arrogant winds of the stratosphere clutched me and we raced along at a horizontal angle, in conditions as chill and rarefied as those of my bedroom. I was too terrified and upset to look back to see if the speck was still on my ribboned tail. I must have swooned away, but not before I secured my arm to a loose end of rigging. When I recovered, I was over dry land and the balloon had righted itself. I turned the valve to let out some helium; a gentle hiss accompanied my descent into more favourable altitudes. Below lay a bank of cumulus cloud, as fluffy as sea-foam, in which I thought I might glimpse dolphins leaping. My imagination was still watery: holding my nose as I plummeted into the cloud, I strained my eyes to see exactly where I was going. Without a working engine, I was helpless, like a clam sinking into the depths of yeasty beer . . .

The glider came from nowhere, turning at the last moment and fixing itself neatly onto my spikes. With the extra weight I started to fall at a greater rate than expected. The glider pilot made ineffectual attempts to disengage his fuselage, waggling his elevators and rudder like a duck seeking a mate. As we bottomed out of the cloud, I studied the occupants of the craft more carefully. At the controls sat a man and a woman, with a bemused dog lapping the windscreen; behind them another man was trying to force another woman out of an open door. This second woman had a blue apron tied around her waist and her hands were white with flour. She was obviously a mother. One of my spikes had pierced the cockpit and speared up between the legs of the bawling pilot.

Far below, a magnificent city spread its arms to welcome us. In all my months of travelling, I had never seen such a lovely urban landscape. The red-tiled houses, the alabaster towers and aquamarine pools appeared like a vision of a forgotten childhood story, one of those illustrations in a book whose title can never be remembered. The balloon landed in the greenest park and I jumped out of the gondola, eager to apologise to the glider passengers. But I found myself surrounded by a cheering crowd. An army of police officers hurried up to the glider and seized three of the occupants. The mother and the dog were set free. To my amazement, it was my friend, the President, who stepped close to shake my hand. My juggled mind could take no more of this. Holding onto him for support, I managed to blurt: "What are you doing here, sir?"

He laughed. "This is where I live! Come now, Titian, old pal, don't try any of this deadpan nonsense with me! You're a hero again, just like in the days of plenty, when ugli-fruit grew on bushes. What say we drive to my tower in my tortoise-chariot and I'll present you with your award? Not to mention giving back your old job!"

It then occurred to me, as doubtless it already has to my cleverest readers, that I had circumnavigated the planet (no mean feat considering it is triangular) and returned to the capital, where I started from! Let me also provide the solution to the mystery of my renewed popularity. In the glider, so neatly impaled on my balloon, were the chief conspirators of a plot to overthrow the government and replace it with a dictatorsub, which is a deeper version of a dictatorship and far more repressive. The names of these arch-intriguers were Clementine Jungg, Mina Argon and the maverick academic, Professor Fennel . . .

For years, apparently, they had been kidnapping mothers and dogs in a solar-powered glider, hurling the former to their doom and setting the latter free in strange nations to wander in a lost daze. In other words, they were responsible for that 0.1% of unsolved crime! The scheme was to incite mothers and dogs to rebellion: in the chaos, the putschists would drape wet seaweed over the Presidential tower. Tearing off their plastic costumes, they would reveal themselves as mutant prawns, eager to make a cocktail of human politics and philosophy.

I went with the President and we arrived at the marketsquare, where he ushered me into the suite of rooms at the apex of his tower. Words of encouragement were not all: a large sum of gold was also presented. With this, I knew, I could afford to commission my quartz and topaz statue at the Police Station. But first I had to check my old job really was being re-offered. It was: it seems Raphael Perkins had made a useless Prefect, messing up his very first case. He had personally set off to hunt down a felon who owed money to the Fire Company for unpaid bills. Having sailed away in an airship made to his specifications, nobody had heard from him since. There were rumours he had been sighted in the Glib Ocean, hanging in the fog as if he had nothing better to do. If he ever returned to the capital, the President vowed, he would order him to be body-searched. He had a crawling suspicion

'Raphael Perkins' was also a secret crustacean, perhaps even the mythic King Prawn, predicted by the Insufferable Oracle of Tosh. A false and wriggly redeemer.

Well, I took back my job. But I did not spend the gold on statuary; that is a task for posterity. It was just enough to pay off all my debts to the Fire Company, but I have principles. I refuse to pander to stupid bureaucrats; I have enough problems instilling the qualities into my own staff. Yet I did not relish sitting in that cold house; my eyebrows were so weighed down with ice that I walked with a perpetual stoop, beautiful forehead trailing in the frost. A solution came to me while I was giving a lecture to the Order of Pirate Housewives, who knit with cutlasses. As I am so dashing, they were pleased to accept a commission from me, which cost no more nor less than my reward. Now my house wears a woolly jumper and hat, with a scarf wound five times round its gables. The temperature is going up and I am as happy as a squid in a glove. The sun still rises like a fishwife, but now it sets like a lady.

PYRAMIDS OF THE PURPLE ATOM

———— ·◆· ————

I have arrested many large objects in my time. The moon and the grue-some elk-god, Moozsgyrrgtlk, are two of the biggest. The President's nose has still not been outlawed, therefore that suggestion can be disregarded. I am quite an expert at bringing unwieldy, grandiose or overbearing felons to justice. Indeed, Titian Grundy, Prefect of Police, has been witnessed tackling illegal mountains and even tectonic plates with no weapon other than his innate smugness and a hive of trained bees. Because I am him, I must enjoy his credit and acknowledge his admirers, who are numerous but too modest to show themselves. They know my reputation is founded on all things ample, save the bosoms of maidens.

Thus my disquiet when ordered to apprehend the smallest particle in the universe was considerable. Previously, my anxiety had neatly matched the dimensions of each culprit, fitting inside the skin like a righteous skeleton. I argued with the President, but he was more obstinate than an ugli-fruit pip. He had been studying physics in nightschool, in a futile attempt to make friends, and he was having problems with his homework. A question had been set concerning the basic building-blocks of all matter and rather than study boring theory, he decided on a practical approach, enlisting my talents to ac-tually capture it. I had to bring it to him in chains by Monday or else suffer demotion.

"Interrogate it without solicitors present," he barked. "I want the particle to sing like a canape. We'll find out what it thinks it's up to at the sub-atomic level. Quantum rascal!"

"What if it has an alibi?" I hissed.

"Don't fall for that nonsense, Titian. You know the world's not the place it should be. Obviously the fundamental bits which make it up must take the blame. I'm desperately unhappy: nothing is right. Something has got to be responsible for this—it's what women, music and fruit can be finally reduced to. That's the blighter!"

With heavy spleen and cynical lip, I returned to the Police Station in my butterfly-powered rickshaw. The nine-sided building loomed like an obsidional inselberg (simile courtesy of Satsuma Ffroyde, who refuses to reveal what it means.) I stabled my moths with Percy Flamethrower at the gate and entered my office. I called for the Police Surgeon Specific, Dr Celery, and spent the minutes prior to his arrival by dismissing from my mind scenes of nuclear fusion suggested by the frontage of Lola Halogen. Clashing protons, colliding planets: they seemed identical to my fevered but rather comely olive-hued imagination.

Dr Celery was inexcusably late. His white coat was marked with tiny stains, lending him an unfocussed appearance, as if the man had sent his portrait to see me—one painted by a metaleptic pointillist (another of Satsuma's recondite metaphors; I really must sack him.) First I outlined the President's demands and then I berated him for his tardiness. "While I worry about extending, or shrinking, my jurisdiction into the realm of leptons, you conduct empirical research!"

He apologised and named a remarkable coincidence as his defence. He had been working on a chemical which could shrink objects to zero or its existential equivalent. Some of this powder had spilled over my voice as it passed under his door, reducing its importance. Thus his tarrying was without malice. I accepted his grovelling, hoisted him up from his knees by his stringy beard and expressed pleasure that his invention so neatly anticipated a solution to my predicament.

"Well it was your idea in the first place," he sighed. "You told me to end overcrowding in our prisons. I realised that by miniaturising our detainees we could fit more in one cell."

"My idea? Ah yes, I am very clever!"

"I tried the chemical first on inanimate objects. It worked and now geography's not the subject it once was."

As he spoke, the stains on his coat rapidly dwindled to nothing. He beckoned for me to observe them through a magnifying-glass. There was no such instrument in the entire Department. Satsuma Ffroyde had once built a primitive microscope by drilling in a disc of uranium a small hole, in which a drop of pure wine was sustained by capillary attraction. But the sterile and tipsy images presented by so simple an apparatus were hardly appropriate to verify Dr Celery's claims.

Finally, Lola Halogen improvised a device by moulding on her facade two sandwich-wrappers of clear plastic. When combined into a convex lens of rare power, they opened up a fantastic vista of micro-jinks conducted over threads of cheap cotton. The stains were giant lakes, of sulphurous and chloric liquids, which drained rapidly away into buttonhole craters. These exotic dips had been obtained at reasonable cost from the populace of Xopué, which has a surplus of lagoons.

"You were the one who authorised the trade. The lakes came one at a time in buckets suspended from balloons."

"Did I? I thought there was a fishy smell lately."

"I've been experimenting on the pools for the past month. Today the work has paid dividends. My chemical is fully tested and is ready to use on convicts. But I don't advise it, sir."

"Why? Do you think they'll slip through the bars?"

"There's no way of halting the process. Any miscreants subjected to my powder will continue to shrivel until they fall through the molecules of the dungeon floor. They'll keep contracting until they reach whatever is the smallest size possible in our universe. Also, I don't know if the substance is deadly or not to organisms."

"It might kill the user? We'd better test it on a volunteer. Before I select Percy for the task, answer this question: why doesn't the stuff diminish its own atoms out of existence?"

Dr Celery looked uncomfortable. His suggestion that each item has a natural tendency to shrink, and that his powder was a catalyst to unlock this inherent urge, struck me as ludicrous. He theorised that everything wants to be a humble version of itself but is forced by negative gravity to assume macroscopic dimensions—the chemical and the President's nose included. Only when acting upon something else could the powder liberate the elemental compressibleness of matter.

Lola Halogen, our real intellectual, sneered at this, but as we had no alternative explanation, I snorted at her derision, sent her to fetch our trustworthy guard, Percy Flamethrower, and rewarded Dr Celery with a medal fabricated from a shard of crystal pier. When Percy entered, maple musket at the ready, he saluted stiffly and allowed his jaw to be opened with the point of my truncheon. Dr Celery hastened to his laboratory and returned with a phial of powder, while Lola brewed blue-green tea. A cup was offered to our hapless victim, adulterated with a magical pinch, and he drank it down in a single, sweet gulp.

At once he began to shrink. His eyes bulged—though they were soon no bigger than the eggs of a Paraparapara toucan—and he requested in a squeaky tone the meaning of the experience. Percy is always polite, even when the radius of his head is that of a simurgh's oubliette (curse your pitted rind, Satsuma Ffroyde!) Rather than watch him vanish without work to be getting on with, I announced that because of cuts in our budget we downsizing the staff. This did not mean I expected less devotion from him, but his duties were bound to change.

"We've got a new job for you, Percy," I explained. "You must ensure no germs pass this way into the Station."

He saluted again and raised his miniscule musket. "Fill this with a handful of viruses, shall I? Rely on me!"

I hid my grin in a sleeve and picked him up with a pair of tweezers which Lola kept handy for eyebrow emergencies. Then I deposited him on a glass slide, which I placed on the office threshold. I ordered Dr Celery to fetch a dose for myself. However, I wanted to go better prepared than our simple guard. I filled a suitcase with all manner of equipment, some of it official, most personal. The dandrum identikit, for example, was a waste of space. They have agents nowhere.

When the Police Surgeon Specific returned, Lola threw herself about my waist. If I was going to irreversibly diminish, she cried, I might as well do it over her. This raised the question of what substance I should stand on as I vanished into the sub-atomic cosmos. Decorum precluded the use of Lola as a base. Dr Celery proclaimed the whiskers of a cat as the most suitable location to surf the short-wave depths of inner space, but I felt he was being facetious. My poet's cat still lurked in the Station cellar, guarding my collection of cheese.

After careful consideration, I decided to ask the President for the use of the miniature village in the corner of his overgrown roof-garden. Accordingly, I took the second phial from Dr Celery, kissed Lola goodbye and steered my butterfly-rickshaw out of the City to the mighty Cliff of Puff, where the carnelian tower of our ruler stood at a precarious angle on the actual summit. On the difficult ascent, my mounts were eaten by a basilisk and I had to climb the remainder of the distance on my feet. It was a lengthy haul, but there was no alternative. The caterpillars in my groin-pouch were too feeble to saddle up.

The President received me cordially, without diluting to taste, and agreed to rent me his village. It was a cruel joke, of course, for rains had long since pounded it to charming fragments and in its place stood a perfect replica of the Capital. From the roof of the tower I could study the filth and beauty of the real thing, the alabaster houses and verdant parks stretching to the jaded horizon, and then glance down and perceive the same details as if from a vast height. Indeed, the simalacrum seemed nicer than the original. I chose the Temple of Drigg in the model as the starting point for my hypo-spatial jaunt.

Squeezing in by the altar, upon which gleamed a scale of the Cosmic Serpent, I broke the phial and swallowed its contents. Percy had come to no harm as he shrunk, but I was still nervous as my stomach digested the powder. I felt only a muted discomfort and the sensation of contraction, which I assumed would be violent, was entirely absent. Instead, external objects began to shift and change, growing blurred, pushing outwards, in a hitherto unsuspected display of ambition. The whole world, I realised, was growing, leaving me behind, like a fat child excluded from a game of leaptoad. The walls receded like females.

Soon, the Temple of Drigg had assumed its correct dimensions, and I was astonished at the craftsmanship which had gone into its manufacture. Everything in the imitation was rendered with superb precision. Even the grumpy icons were plated in bronze and neptunium. I had entered, without a visa, a city within a city, but I was afraid. My descent was too quick to acclimatise my sense: I needed time to fully absorb my predicament. I had picked the best place to extinguish my fears, where the horror of my condition might be assuaged by illusion. Leaving the Temple, I convinced myself this was the genuine Capital, a fraud possible to sustain so long as I did not look up at the enormous sky.

Risking excommunication, I broached the adjacent outhouse where the mouse-sleighs sacred to the denizens of the Heavenly Realm are kept, and borrowed one. In my city, sixty rodents drag each vehicle; here a single mouse was enough. I cracked the reins and directed it towards the second Cliff of Puff, up the slippery slope. The sides of the sleigh rose above me. At the base of the President's tower, I disembarked and hastened up the steps, which grew wider as I ascended. Once more in the roof-garden, surrounded by buildings smaller than me, I breathed a sigh of outrageous relief and wriggled into the Temple of Drigg, observing that yet another scale of the Cosmic Serpent glowed there.

Again the walls and ceiling parted from my body. Once more precious icons expanded to satisfy my aesthetic longing. These were less artistic than the first set, executed more clumsily, as was to be expected. After a few minutes of rest, it was time to leave. There were no mouse-sleighs in the outhouse of this Temple, but one powered by an aphid was adequate for my needs. We rattled down cobbled back-streets, under the lengthening eaves of restaurants patronised only by spiders. Indeed, I was forced to arrest one which refused to pay its bill. For a horrid moment, I thought I might not have enough handcuffs to restrain the arachnid, but Lola had slipped a spare pair into my groin-pouch.

Praying I would not meet a criminal millipede, I continued my slide to the third Cliff of Puff and up to the President's tower. The model in this roof-garden was far clumsier than its predecessors. Houses leant at wrong angles, warped bubbles of glass serving for windows. Petty reality was adopting an alien aspect, but at a pace I could accept. This was the gentle introduction to the microcosmos I needed. I entered the Temple of Drigg, noted the scale of the Cosmic Serpent, and waited. Sure enough, I fell to the size of a regular worshipper.

It was at this point that a low rumble became audible to my hirsute ears. What did it signify? Perhaps the volcano on the City outskirts had erupted again? If so, there was no hope for me. How can a man whose legs are becoming shorter outrun a river of flame? Then I realised this was a fallacious worry. Bodies are burned by heat which surrounds them, not by heat which exists elsewhere. As I continued to dwindle, the greater part of any lava flow which covered me would always be receding, bearing away most of its calefaction. The only fire which could now engulf me was one smaller than the spark of two glowworms rubbed together, a somewhat meek singe in the temperature scheme of things.

This fact was reassuring. But my confidence was boosted yet further when I left my sanctuary to confront boulders of dust tumbling along the pavements like marbles in a renegade gutter. So the rumble came not from geology but acoustics! Vibrations in the air from insectile movement was responsible. I looked up and beheld monster fleas bounding like sundered moons over my comprehension. My voyage to the fourth Cliff of Puff, in a sleigh drawn by an amoeba, was intriguing. Up the tower and into another roof-garden, where a more debased Capital and Temple awaited. The Cosmic Serpent had shed even on this altar, a scale from the tip of its tail, a rainbow disc as subtle as a jaguar's itch.

I repeated my flight from tower to tower seventeen times. My mounts grew increasingly bizarre and feisty—radiolaria, bacterium, virus. The model became distorted beyond recognition, mere lumps of corundum acting as civic buildings and bandstands. Only the bright scale remained itself and I eventually decided to cease my exertions here and permit myself to be sucked down into quarkland without the mirage of theatre. I was ready for anything. When I was small enough to mount the altar and crouch over the flake, it suddenly occurred to me I had no way of returning. Even if I managed to arrest the recidivist particle, it would evade justice on a technicality. Oh, the law is an asymptote!

No matter: the President had issued a warrant and I am loyal enough to be imprudent. The scale widened beneath me, knocking away my feet and accepting my body as I fell onto its surface. I stood and gasped as blue and orange tints swirled and grew in its translucent depths. Within five minutes, I was in the centre of a vast reptilian plateau covered in tiny cracks which opened up like famished mouths. I skipped between them, but whenever I found a solid place to rest, it soon became riddled with more fissures, yawning one within the other, like an old man locked in an old woman who is herself locked in a tortoise.

I stumbled on the edge of a crevice which expanded into a valley. I found myself stuck on an isolated fibrous outcrop, unable to move in any direction. As my island became a continent, my malady challenged it to a duel, scarring its puffy cheeks with fresh chinks. I tripped and bridged a cranny, blinking in horror as its edges receded beyond the reach of my hands and feet, sending me plummeting into the velveteen dusk. Down went I, tumbling like an electrified voltigeur, into nanospace, screeching in a myriad accents as my tongue changed shape under my voice. Long strings of globes rattled close: sticks of bells for an angstrom jester. With an astounded shout, I understood these to be chains of complex molecules in their Sunday best, preparing for reactions.

Since the beginning of the expedition, my breathing had become more laboured as I contracted. The oxygen which passed into my lungs was much coarser than my usual brand. Now its atoms lodged in my throat, swelling rapidly and causing me to choke. I doubled up in pain and spat them out, clamping my mouth until they became too large to enter. At this level, I no longer needed to suspire—the rules of nature were twisted. Below my aching frame, a cluster of smooth spheres winked in rotation, drawing me into orbit around it. Vivid as a bunch of purple eyeballs, it was an odd but edifying sight, a jewelled knot among the bland nuclei which hurried past my ears. I struggled to identify the element. Ruthenium? Nobody has ever analysed the Cosmic Serpent's varnish.

All relevant speculation was terminated by a projectile which smote my knee, exploding into visible waves of energy which burned my face and ungloved hands. One of the electrons which looped the lilac nucleus like warrior elks around a convoy of chuck-kayaks had broken my concentration and bruised my bone. The fissionable surge caught me up and cast me into the electromagnetic field of a central proton which ballooned to receive me. I landed heavily on its glossy surface and lay for many minutes in a ridiculous position, arms flung over my eyes. When I lifted them, I felt a delight hitherto only available to those devotees of the Supreme Roger who own private bannisters. I had stopped shrinking. My ordeal was over. I had attained the smallest possible girth.

Exploring my environment, I tried to whistle appreciatively through my teeth, not an easy task when there is no air. This was no boring atom with inadequate facilities. On every side I beheld inorganic forms which presented the appearance of foliated clouds of the highest rarity—they undulated and broke into vegetable shapes, tinged with maroon splendours compared with which the amethyst glaciers of Grokkland are mere baubles. Far away into the interminable distance stretched broad avenues of these gaseous forests, dimly transparent, behind which lurked anthropoid forms like silhouettes in a shadow-play illuminated by sparkling wine, flaming brandy and hot chillies. But what was this nearest me? A shade which had the semblance of a woman! Miniature humans?

She swept out from between the rainbow-curtains of the cloud-trees, her charms beyond any attempt at inventory, save perhaps her mystic eyes of emerald and lustrous auburn hair, and my unpasteurised heart curdled. What a pale, vapid ghost of woman-loveliness! I fell in love as promptly as citizens should pay their fines. I decided to call her Animula, which seemed an appropriately erudite name for an impossible beauty. Caught in an unbearable passion, I boldly hailed her.

"Animula! What a gorgeous divinity you are! Such sleek and romantic limbs protruding from an impeccable torso!"

She responded with a fierce scowl: "My name is Mandy."

Even her frown was exquisite. I felt an urge to abase myself before her ankles. She was quick to stall my intention by slapping my mouth and stamping her perfect heel. I was entranced.

"You speak my language? Really, Animula, this is astonishing! Where did you learn it? Shall we spend all our honeymoon in bed or must we try mature pastimes as well? Come close and let me mumble a hastily composed sonnet! I am Titian, a poet from paradise."

"I rarely speak to ugly men, but you're plainly a foreigner so I'll make an exception today. This is the nature reserve of Semaj-Ztif on the proton known as Neirb'O. It is not I who speak your language but you who converse in mine. Your tongue is too small to pronounce any words larger than those which are used in Esperatto, the lingua franca of most atoms. Only the denizens of posh nuclei prefer not to use it. For instance, the helium people judge it too common and generally rely on anticipation and telepathy. Does that answer your question?"

I was forced to admit it did. What other knowledge was to be gained from my beloved Animula? I took her in my arms, but she was too powerful to hold, and I clutched my bleeding nose in dismay and adoration. If all my words were uttered in her bijoux dialect, it was best I kept my poems to myself—they might not translate well. She retreated and I followed. I chased her among the violet drooping silken pennons, which I theorised were wisps of raw energy rather than peeled matter. At regular intervals she turned to deliver a forceful kick in my direction and only my padded groin-pouch saved me from excessive injury.

While we gambolled in the rituals of courtship, a shrill noise from above made us pause. A thrilling aerial sight greeted my vision. Figures with plumage and extended feet were surfing the proton's electromagnetic field, diving to hurl pyramidal objects before veering away. These weird apparitions were not as grotesque as mutated brutes ought to be—if you wish to visualise them, imagine the descendants of a race forced to mate with ostriches. But they propelled Animula into a fit of acute trembling and sobbing. The surfboards were part of their anatomy, but the pyramids most certainly were not. The size of milking stools, each connected with the ground and dented it with a dull clang.

Spying us, one of the eldritch surfers dipped closer and loosed his geometric shape directly over my head. It screeched down and I whimpered in anticipation of death. The nape of my neck seemed to burst and I knew my attacker had achieved a direct hit. I walked away, surprisingly calm, but instead of advancing in a linear direction, as one expects when feet are operated in traditional fashion, I vanished and reappeared at a fair distance behind Animula. I tried again and now a zoetrope must have been spun backwards—events reversed themselves until once more I was in the crepuscular void with a damaged knee, hurtling towards my target proton. Is any genre of love worth such affliction?

My landing was even heavier on this second occasion. I staggered up to regard my beloved. The raid was over: pyramids lay tumbled across the terrain, half-concealed by cirrus drapes. High above, the marauders were returning to a neighbouring sphere, possibly to indulge in a barbecue of truly insignificant proportions. Who were they? How did they alter space and time with their bombs? What beer would they choose to complement the feast? I enquired and Animula was obliging.

"They are the inhabitants of Yar, a militant kingdom on the neutron known as Sgnimmuc. Centuries ago they declared war on Neirb'O and sought to destroy our culture. They failed and have turned instead to politics, declaring independence from the purple atom. They want to split it apart by shelling us with quarks. They wrench them up from their own world and deposit them on ours. Any imbalance in the quantum structure of the atom will eventually cause the nucleus to detonate with massive loss of life. Their ruler, Nosliw Nairb, is totally mad."

I stooped and raised a pyramid. "This is a quark?"

"Yes, the tiniest known particle. The building-block of all matter. You should have ducked when it struck you."

"But how did it propel me through time and space?"

"Not my concern. That's your problem."

Because I am fiendishly cunning, once winning an award for decoding the prismatic runes of Achromia, I understood at once what had happened. For quarks, overlooked by the general laws of physics, improbable events were normal. Their behaviour did not always correspond to my prejudices, which assumed particles must have regular habits. Quarks were frequently indeterminate in their lifestyles and also in their influence over other objects. Thus the one which landed on my neck had temporarily pitched me into a reality where crazy rules applied. This was fascinating, but duty beckoned—I had found the renegade at last. I slipped the shape into my suitcase and bent my knees in satisfaction.

Before I could wonder how I might get it back to the President, the ground shifted and I started to expand. Obviously Dr Celery's potion was wearing off! This was extremely convenient, as are many of the incidents which make up my life, though others may dismiss them as coincidence and the dictates of chance. I know differently. I sow my own luck, nurturing it in a pot with pear compost and optimism.

"Animula, listen to me! Your atom is doomed. The people of Sgnimmuc must surely triumph over those of Neirb'O. But I can offer you an escape from the madness. Come with me back to the big universe and be my bride! You know it makes sense. Why perish here when there is a greater destiny awaiting you in heaven? Give me an answer!"

Her lips quivered. Her nod was almost imperceptible. She climbed in my suitcase, curled up next to the pyramid and I shut the lid. I was not sorry to be leaving the proton. My sojourn had been brief but productive and it appeared I would not have to indulge in any more adventures. Just for a moment, observing the surfers of Yar aligning their mental dipoles to thoughts of destruction and chaos, I thought I might be in for months of Lucianic satire, involving heroic fights in ruined cities and decayed mansions, violent encounters with beasts, alien cheeses, tulwar-wielding gruntbugglies and embalmed gods with carious fangs. Instead I had a pair of gratifications: a quark and a girl-friend. There is a twist to my tale but first I must reclaim my original state.

Molecules fell away around me. I reappeared on the Cosmic Serpent's smallest scale. My growth was much quicker than my de-scent and there was no time to leave the Temple. I burst it asunder like a heretic, swelling over model after model until I finally reached my authentic cosmos. Here I stretched my limbs, left the roof-garden and carried the suitcase down to the President. It was Monday, the deadline for my mission. He smirked with childlike glee when I threw back the lid and hoisted Animula to her feet. Wrapping her in chains, I presented her to him, bowed elaborately, planted a farewell kiss on her brow and absorbed his praise. She did not take kindly to captivity, protesting vigorously but to no avail. In this reality, her language was incomprehensible.

Why had I delivered my sweetheart to the President? Never let it be declared that Titian Grundy's emotions choke his reason. My apprecia-tive study of Animula when I first encountered her in the glade enabled me to calculate her volume. It was plain she was a single particle rather than a being constructed from individual units, else such units would have to be smaller than quarks, which according to modern science is impossible. I also visually calculated the volume of the pyramids which were dropped from above (one-third the height multiplied by the area of the base) and reckoned that although shorter, they took up more room in total than did Animula. Thus she was the illegal particle.

I left the President to his homework and hastened down the Cliff of

Puff. But a terrible shock greeted me at the Station. It was flooded and most of my colleagues had drowned. Dr Celery's lakes had swelled to full size again on his coat. I arranged for them to be returned to Xopué with a demand for compensation. My cheese collection is ruined, but my poet's cat escaped by commandeering an experimental submarine. The macroscopic, bloated cadaver of Percy Flamethrower was never recovered—it drifts in mysterious currents around the building, occasionally appearing to knock on a window and give a mordant salute. Satsuma Ffroyde is also listed as missing, but I suspect he has survived and is evolving into an amphibian in one of the obscure offices in the attic.

In the comfort of my own home I experiment with the pyramid. All it will take for me to have more power than anyone before me is to work out how to operate its quantum properties. I perch on the apex and shake the reins I have looped about it. Mouse and hattock away! One evening I will ride back into the distant past to arrest my very first ancestor. I hold him responsible for all my subsequent troubles, the misery of my life. In the end I will be avenged on myself. Women—you too have betrayed me! I want nothing more to do with any of you, nothing more to do with beauty. Leave me now, you cruel soft-bodied devils! Oh, Animula! If only you had acted your slipper-size instead of your age!

THE SUPPERTIME STING

Titian Grundy here, long chin of the law, reporting direct from the swirling mists of the chronoflow. My mission: to seek out and arrest my first ancestor. Balanced precariously on a green pyramid, a time machine which is a tomb for centuries—watch how it gobbles up the past as my heels scrape a hold on its smooth sides! I can't say this is a pleasant mode of transport; I much prefer my winged chariot launched by monkeys. But nothing in my career is ever comfortable, save the ample charms of Lola Halogen, which are inert and noble, and therefore beyond the reach of *this* chin.

In a pocket of my waistcoat I keep a watch captive. It once solicited an hour in an alleyway, and employed many cogs to do so, some of them underage, with copper teeth instead of bronze. I hesitated less than a single tick before taking it in. "We'll see how you like to tock in the cooler!" cried I, as I sealed it in ice. But friction from the unrepentant escapement melted it free. There was only one place secure enough for a nefarious timepiece: inside a vest woven from the sound of closing doors. "Into the slammer with you!" roared I, and that's where it has resided ever since, in solitary refinement, without visitors: a terrible fate for a neighbourhood watch.

Now as I raced to the source of the chronoflow, I felt the hour hand spinning backward like a dish of cats on the stick of an ailurophobic juggler. The dial stimulated my left nipple as it did so, and I blushed with shame at this betrayal of my true love, my micro-darling, Animula. The minute hand, of course, was travelling so rapidly that it was a stationary wheel and did not inflame my amours, which is just as well, because I don't like sixty lovers in an hour, or a lover who asks for sixty seconds to be complete.

The problem with this asymmetrical nipple caress was that it tended to pull me to one side of the chronoflow, rather than keep me steady in the middle of the stream. The currents of time flow truest in the centre; near the banks of the present they are disrupted by shoals of amnesia and eddies of *what if?* It is easy to drift off course and become grounded in alternative history. I realised this was happening and sought to rebalance my craft by manually pleasuring my other nipple. Unfortunately I love myself too much—now I lurched to the right, violently, like the President when confronted with the results of a plebiscite. No slur on the lovable autocrat!

Without warning, my pyramid struck an analogy reef and capsized. I closed my eyes and plugged my ears with my toes as I tumbled—my position was unnatural and indefensible. Liquid time washed over me, tasting like an immature yesterday—a combination of scrambled eggs and abbey pepper. Then I was on the very edge of the chronoflow, on the verge of re-entering conventional time. I grasped the current with my large hands, but to no avail; off I slipped and landed on wood. What happened to the pyramid I cannot say: perhaps it continued without me back to the singularity which birthed the cosmos. Or maybe it veered off at some other antique location; a desert land whose architects would borrow inspiration from its tapering sides.

Who knows? And *whoa nose!* For my proboscis seemed intent on burrowing into roughly-hewn planks like a navvy worm. My fingers, which due to my desperate scrabble at the chronoflow had been last to depart the stream, and were therefore older and wiser than the rest of me, came together to extract the organ from a knothole of its own sneezing, and to lend my dripping nostrils their sleeves. Then they scratched my brow, but the mind behind was still young enough to absolve, rather than solve, all riddles—forgiving them for being cryptic, provided they left town and didn't return until the statue of limitations was up, and that's one statue I've never seen up, or down, because it hasn't yet been sculpted by Rodin Guignol, our greatest chiseller, who has *no* limitations, though he made a hash of two of my renowned predecessors—Charlton Radish and Nitrogen Parsley—when he should have made a crumble.

Anyway, I had no idea where I was. But slowly I began to learn, which is always the way, isn't it? Weird coincidence, that: how *every* time you arrive in a new place, provided you don't already know, you instantly start working out where it is! I was in a room without a carpet. A cold hearth did not blaze in merry cheer to one side; this was no Festive Season. The wall was festooned with ultra-modern contrivances—flintlock pistols, chamberpots, thumbscrews. There was a window overlooking a mountainous vista, and between the serrated peaks, a sea. Above my head swung an iron chandelier. See how acute my powers of undue suspicion are? Evening all.

I stood slowly and blinked. "Well Titian, here's a sherry affair, for a rum business would be darker. Anybody at home?"

A door opened and a melancholy figure entered the room. He was a sartorial glum, all done up in satin and velvet, with a drooping flower on a wide cap tickling his cheek. In one hand he clutched a bottle of Oloroso, and he bared his teeth on seeing me, crying in an incomprehensible stutter: *"Bishy, bashy, jibber, jabber!"*

"I think not, ancient felon," returned I, "nor do I approve of your eyelids, which are heavy and suggest a life spent toiling in basements with forger's apparatus. Hold still and desist from gesturing at sundry ornaments scattered about the place."

"Hexas hoxas, hijy abago bijy hago?"

"This is your last warning. Speakish properly or you will be held in tongue-irons under Section 2æ of the Diphthong & Grammar Act. Ignorance and past ages are no defence—the law is retroactive, like a fever in reverse!"

The fellow came closer and took my arm, as if we were old friends, or confederates in a failed plot. Then he poured two glasses of Oloroso and we sat by the dead fire, sipping the liquid and murmuring appre-

ciatively. Strangely, I also felt that I knew him. Later, when the sky grew
dark, he stood and guided me into a room, before stomping off down
a draughty passage. I entered and found a bed, which greeted me like
a sprung simile. The pillow smelled of pterosaur sweat. Had I travelled
back to the Cretaceous era? Best to sleep on it. No: under it, so that the
moisture evaporated away from my nose toward the cracked plaster of
the lofty ceiling.

The following morning I was woken by a pounding on the door.
My host opened it and thrust in a silver tray of cakes. They were unsweetened and I scowled. When I had finished, I rejoined him by the
fireplace. *"Combo oostead?"* Although his language was still illegal,
I felt it was making some effort to reform—the vowels, I could tell,
genuinely wanted to be law-abiding sounds. I turned a deaf ear, still
rank with toe-cheese, to his vocal misdemeanours. We would see how
his mouth morals developed; at the first hint of recidivism, I would
lock up his consonants behind the bars of his teeth, drilling a lock in
one of his incisors and fashioning a key from *my* tongue. Because I am
not an actor, tailor or poet, the fitting of key into tumblers would thus
be a remote possibility.

I made for the seat by the hearth, where I had drunk his wine the
previous day, but he gripped my elbow and made plain by a combination of smiles, frowns and grimaces that I was expected to work. He
was engaged in tying together various items from his shelves and mantelpiece—figurines, jugs, a globe with too many continents, a rusty
gauntlet, a curved dagger, lanterns, a book with undulating covers,
powder horns, a telescope and tripod. Although I had no clue as to
what I was doing, my older, wiser fingers seemed relaxed enough. They
helped fix the objects one to another, with bootlaces and liquorice.

We paused for lunch and I stood at the window and peered down
into the chasm. It was evident I was in a castle on an exceedingly rugged island. Before I could fully digest the view, my host tapped my
shoulder impatiently and we returned to our labour. He was satisfied
with my progress, although I could not say whether I was working ef-
ficiently or not, for I still was ignorant of the point and dimensions of

whatever it was we were constructing. Occasionally, my new colleague would look up and make a comment in what I assumed was an approving tone. *"Boowhen, grassy is!"*

Shortly before dusk—it was difficult to be sure of the precise time because the only hourglass in the room lay at the base of our bizarre contraption—he stretched and yawned and clapped his palms. I understood this to indicate the end of the working day. Again we sat by the chilly hearth and drank Oloroso. And then we retired to our respective beds. As he departed down the corridor, little bells hidden in the walls chimed softly. I had not noticed these the night before, being too overwhelmed by the total swish of my environment.

I slept badly, dreaming of leathery wings and drooling beak. Breakfast consisted of the same unsweetened cakes, and the rest of the day of the same peculiar work. I found myself growing accustomed to his language, as if I was remembering something I had already learned but forgotten. It became possible to communicate after a fashion—a rather ungainly fashion, I must admit, with starched ruff and slashed doublet, not to mention three places to wear a sock: left foot, right foot, codpiece. This time we connected candles, tablecloths, paintings in oil, cutlery, pokers, creaking greaves, spittoons, mandolins and amber jewellery. Then digestion of Oloroso, and bed.

This routine continued for a week. At the end of this span, the room was empty of all furnishings, save a pistol above the hearth which my host seemed to regard with a special fondness. By now, his words had completely reformed and made legal, as well as syntactic, sense.

"Look here, fellow," said I, at the close of this seventh day. "Much as I value your Oloroso and cheese, I really must protest—now I am able to do so and be understood—at this tying together of your possessions. They have been connected with no thought as to the niceties of aesthetics. Why, here is a rotten old scissors adjoined to a cousin-of-pearl snuff box! What is the exact meaning of such seemingly revolutionary juxtaposition? And hurry with the answer, because I am from the future and mustn't wait too long for the past to justify itself—every second approaches my jurisdiction and the feasibility of me summoning reinforcements to club you senseless!"

"It's ready, of course," he responded, pointing at the pile of inter-laced junk which covered the floor. "Now hand me your watch!"

"Ah, so you seek to liberate a fellow criminal and conceal him in a selection of other intricate objects d'art? Clever indeed, Mr Antique, but futile. I have been known to find a single stalk of hay in a stack of needles. The famous detectives of the past—your future—are as noth-ing compared to me! Dupin was a lupin; Holmes was a hovel! Thus your dastardly scheme is foiled even before it is implemented!"

Taking the pistol from the wall, priming it and aiming the barrel at my head, he sighed and added: "Don't mess around, Señor Grundy. Give it to me!"

I pretended to be frightened and complied with his demands. "But how do you know my name? Am I famous before my birth?"

"Don't be foolish," he replied, as he took the watch. "We are col-leagues and this is our great invention—the time machine!"

I gazed dubiously at the pyramid of knick-knacks. "But who are you?"

"Humberto von Gibbon, of course, at your service. Or rather, re-ceiving your service. As I have already explained, I am a prisoner in this castle. There is no way down onto the rest of the island. For years I have attempted to escape, but all my efforts came to naught. The scoundrel who trapped me here—Ugolino Cadiz—was very careful to ensure none of the furnishings could be used to flee my confines."

"Well I am sorry for you, but I fail to see how my watch might be of help."

Rolling his eyes, Humberto beckoned for me to climb on top of the mound of ornaments. I had no wish to die, so I did. Barometers crunched underfoot as I scrambled to the miscellaneous summit. To my surprise, my host scaled the other side, until we were perched face to face near the fragmented ceiling. Then he flipped open the lid of the watch and sprinkled the contents over the assorted junk.

These contents proved not to be cogs, as I had expected, but drops of the chronoflow! I held on tightly as the entire mass suddenly shifted from orthogonal time into the chaotic currents which made a delta of futures, presents, pasts and elsewheres. Unlike my green pyramid, this structure was ponderous and unstable. Humberto noted my nervous expression and sought to distract me with an improbable yarn.

"I was on the point of believing I would never escape when you appeared from nowhere and broke a floorboard with your nose. Were you an agent working for Ugolino? No, it was plain you were too ugly and silly for that. And you did not speak Spanish. As the days went by, we began to learn a little of each other's language. You informed me that you had arrived in my time on a green pyramid, or rather had been cast off from it. I wondered if it might be possible to reconstruct such a device here, but although you knew the shape of the contraption, you had no idea how it was powered."

"And that fact remains true," I grumbled.

"Certainly. But droplets of the chronoflow had leaked into the workings of your watch. When you were hurled into normal time, the watch stopped and trapped the liquid between the teeth of the cogs. With a little shaking I was able to dislodge them. There should be just enough to send me back to a point in time before Ugolino built this castle and trapped me here. I intend to kill him first."

He gestured with his pistol and grinned.

"What do you want with me?" I stammered.

"Extra weight, to keep the pyramid in the middle of the chronoflow. Also as a decoy to distract Ugolino. He is a powerful sorcerer. While he is busy turning you into a curtain rail, I will have ample opportunity to finish him."

While he spoke, I was aware of a deficiency in my foothold. The hatstand which had supported my heel was no longer there! Indeed pieces of the junk ziggurat were vanishing at astonishing speed. Humberto had not noticed; nor did I feel it strictly necessary to inform him of the phenomenon. He would find out for himself in due course. Gradually, I realised that the component pieces of our machine were making themselves absent in the reverse order in which they had been assembled. Thus the pyramid was gnawed away from the top down—coins, armour, vases, all blinked out of existence. Then the tripod, telescope, dagger and globe.

Finally we were left with a single spoon. As we fought with each other for the best grip, this too shimmered away. We landed with a bump back in the chamber, and it was full again. All the ornaments had returned to their original places!

"Of course!" I cried, snapping my sagacious fingers. "No time machine can go back to a point *before* it was built! As we travelled back through the past week, our work undid itself, because the ornaments existed at different locations at those instants! It is only possible to travel far back on a time machine which already exists!"

Humberto shrugged. "I will fetch a bottle of Oloroso from the cellar and we shall toast our failure."

When he was gone, I pondered the futility of all our toil. I also worried about the integrity of the green pyramid. Would it not also come apart as it raced to the source of the chronoflow? But no, it was a quark enlarged, and as such was indivisible. I was so engrossed in my metaphysical speculations that the bells announcing Humberto's return along the passage startled me. I jumped and fell on the boards, my nose spearing a knothole. I stood quickly, not wishing to belittle myself in front of my host. He bared his teeth on seeing me.

My ears heard, *"Bishy, bashy, jibber, jabber!"* but I understood these words to mean, "Let us drink away our sorrows!"

He took my arm and led me to the hearth. We sat and sipped.

"We can always try again," I said. "Build another. Not to travel back into the past but to send me into the future. I am the Prefect of Police and can requisition a hot-air balloon. I will be able to return with it here and you will be able to escape this castle in a more conventional manner."

He was delighted. "Excellent. We shall resume work tomorrow!"

As good as his word, Humberto helped me to recreate the junk pyramid. Because they had not yet been sprinkled in orthogonal time, the drops of the chronoflow were still trapped in my watch. At the end of the week, I mounted the device and bade my antique friend farewell.

"Bat and haddock away!"

Were there enough drops to carry me upward to my own time? Assuredly, for once on the forward currents of time, which run parallel to the backward ones, the component pieces might drink their fill. And though they might turn rusty and worm-eaten, perhaps even crumble to dust under the weight of dying centuries, they would not traitorously fly back to shelves and mantelpiece without so much as a by-your-leave! And so I was confident enough as I hurtled forward, using my watch as a guide as to where to get off. At the appropriate hour of the correct century, I deliberately steered for the shallows and grounded myself in my own office.

I called for my assistant, Satsuma Ffroyde. He arrived with his customary glower and citric attitude. But as my deputy, he was bound to follow my orders.

"Contact my wife!" I roared, "and ask her to come to the station with her largest hive."

I sat back and waited for the object in question to arrive. My wife, who by my orders is allowed no further than the lobby, came quickly; her perfume wafted down the corridors, preceding the hive, which was carried at arm's length by a disgruntled Satsuma—he will never make a mandarin in *this* Force.

"Now, Satsuma," I clipped. "There is a terrible felon existing in the past who refuses to speak a law-abiding language. At first I thought his vowels were reforming; now I realise it was a trick, a case of my ears acclimatising. I want you to mount this time machine and arrest him. You'll know at which date to disembark, or rather the date will disembark you. When this pyramid of junk falls to nothing and leaves you stranded in a room, consider that your destination. The fellow who enters with a bottle of Oloroso is your target!"

Satsuma sulked. "What if he's armed?"

"Throw this hive at him. The bees within are suitably vicious and will despise the drooping flower on his cap. Freeze the felon with this canister of sub-zero vanilla and find a way of moving him to a location which will eventually become the site of our underground dungeons.

225

Freeze yourself in the same place. The moment you depart, I'll go down and check the dungeons. I'll throw you both out and release you both—you because you are innocent, and he because he will have served his sentence."

Satsuma grumbled and moaned, but his options were severely hampered. He mounted the pyramid and I sprinkled the contents of the watch—which I had refilled on route to the present—over the junk, neglecting to give him the timepiece, to prevent him returning prematurely, or indeed returning at all, save orthogonally, sealed in ice.

He shimmered away and I skipped out of my office, down the spiral stairs to the dungeons. I checked each one in turn, but Humberto and Satsuma were not there. Plenty of other dastards and desperadoes—elks, cabbages, moondwellers, wasps, glider pilots, clockwork prawns—but no pair of nonsense babblers. Would I have to petition the President for a repeal of the Diphthong & Grammar Act?

I was fearful that I might, and mentally prepared myself for the harrowing voyage to his insulated tower in the crater of the smoking volcano on the outskirts of the city, but then as I returned along Death Row and up Poorly Passage, I noted something on the stone floor of the first cell, which I had assumed was empty. Scowling in the dim light of the moondwellers' luminous antennae, I unlocked the gate and went in. Peculiar sort of captive! I didn't remember arresting this suspect. A plate of cakes.

Stooping, I crammed one into my mouth. Sweetened . . .

I frowned.

THE MISCHIEF TOWERS

———•◆•———

(i)

The President is a man with perfect timing, but all of it is bad. On the last occasion he summoned me, I was in the middle of tricky negotiations with an official from Amnesty Interstellar. A miserable lot, those Civil Rights people, raving about Justice and Equality, as if I don't take the issues as seriously as they do! In fact, I devote most of my working day to keeping the former as far away from the latter as possible. It's very difficult, even with a pulley, a bronze rope and a crowbar cast from the titanium shin of the Supreme Roger. Once I stretched both ideals so much that something snapped, probably my conscience. I awarded myself a medal and strutted up and down my shadow.

For some reason, this official had the notion I was mistreating the prisoners in my charge. Our dungeons were full of natural disasters, not just winds but mudslides and avalanches and earthquakes, and we had been forced to stuff them a dozen to a cell, because the asteroid impacts had ruined one whole wing of the prison, and would have continued to destroy the world had we not granted each crater a job in the kitchen as a dish, a position from which a meteoric rise to sink looked feasible. Certainly the narrow space meant that some of the weaker catastrophes were bullied by the larger. Glenda the Monsoon, for instance, kept putting down Myron the Sandstorm, mushing his aridity.

But this was hardly to be avoided in any system of confinement.

The forest fires and tidal waves were bound to cluster together in clans and pick on each other, however gently or roughly we dealt with them. So the fault was not ours. It was the intractability of the universe and I felt sour at taking the blame for its behaviour. While I boiled, my tormentor took shrill notes on a foolscap parrot, hurling the occasional glower at me and clucking his liberal tongue.

"Mister Grundy, here is a breach of regulations!" he finally cried, as he peered into the tiniest cell.

I scratched my chin. "Ah, the tornadoes."

"They are underage, perhaps only dust-devils. I will have to report you for minor climatic harassment."

"A horrible slander," I replied, "for I run a tolerant regime. None of my men have ever broken a wind."

"You must understand more, condemn less!"

"The principles of rehabilitation are familiar to me, I assure you. This morning I argued for the early release of Myron. I concluded he had already paid his dunes to society."

"Locking up a desert seems such a waste!"

"Sometimes it's necessary. They get agitated, fluffed, stardrunk. I blame it all on bad precipitation."

"You are a callous idiot, Mister Grundy!"

While the official scolded me, a dozen workmen entered the corridor and began attaching pulleys to the ceiling. I grimaced, for I recognised them as the same labourers who had constructed a suspension bridge above the President's bath. Had they come to help me pull Justice and Equality even further apart? No, for these wheels were relatively fragile, unable to bear the mass of a Scruple-Fission Reaction. They sparkled in the icy light of the recidivist Aurora Borealis thrown in with the tornadoes. In a minute the workmen had finished, threading platinum string through the pulleys, leaving without even a request for a mug of sugary wolf-whistle tea or a hobnailed nob for dunking.

Instantly the wheels began turning and I forgot the presence of the official as I watched the strings move. He was blabbering and preaching, but his voice faded into a hum as another sound entered the prison. Slow and stiff, it grew louder, until the metal wall and floor were vibrating and chiming in harmony. Then I saw it coming down the corridor: a puppet with iron shoes, done in the exact image of the President, dangling from the strings on the regularly spaced wheels! It jerked closer and stopped only when it stood face to face with me. For a moment it swung awkwardly on its supports, head and arms and feet swivelling in random directions. Then it offered me its wooden hand.

I took it and the marionette turned and led me along the passage to the outside. But the Amnesty Interstellar official wasn't keen to see me escape his attentions, so he clutched the hem of my jacket and the three of us stumbled into the sunshine. I was astounded to witness a series of posts newly hammered into the soil, extending to the horizon and beyond. Each one held a pulley and was a predetermined course for my guide. Such a peculiar method for the President to communicate his desire! He mostly relied on carrier-partridge or gibbon-sleigh. When we reached the slopes of the Carbuncle Hills, the puppet steered us with precision through the hazardous verruca fields. No sweat.

And all this while, the official was distending my jacket, shouting in my ear or flipping the feathers of his parrot, ranting on about Truth and Mercy and other exotic notions.

"Mister Grundy! You really must answer me!"

We were within sighing distance of the President's tower and I felt my burden had grown excessive. I tried to knock his hand off with my own but he was tenacious. The puppet dragged us through the open door in the building and deposited us before the man himself, who was standing below the last pulley, working the cords.

"Titian! Why are you so late?"

I grovelled, but with a sneer. "Your servant was tardy." I gestured at the marionette and the official.

"Freeloading passenger, eh? What audacity!"

I nodded. "He increased the net mass and hampered my righteousness. He works for Amnesty Interstellar."

The President shrugged. "In that case I'll make him illegal. Arrest this miscreant, Titian! Hurry now!"

The official protested vigorously as I twisted his arms and secured them with my belt. There was nowhere in the tower to lock him up, so the President gave me his permission to take the puppet apart and reassemble it around the body of the criminal. I placed the key of a dungeon in the wooden fingers and we sent it back to the prison. The marionette rotated on a polished heel with a nasty leer and stalked off, footprints exactly fitting those of its first journey. The official inside begged to be let out and pounded the chest of his captor. When it reached its destination it would open a cell, incarcerate itself, lock the door and wait for him to starve. But not swallow the key.

The President pouted. "Come upstairs with me."

(ii)

My powered unicycle was reaching its maximum speed on the marble streets under the Pallid Colonnades when a line of Talking Plaques began jumping from the parapets into my path. I swerved to avoid the bodies and nearly tumbled into oblivion myself, but I didn't reduce my speed. I was trying to impress Beatrix Trifle, the President's wife, who witnessed my antics from her sofa at the top of her Ironic Column. This was the right way to woo her, which is why her husband never succeeded in showing her his own pillar. Her lips were a century of yards above my own, and her mouth was even more inaccessible. I can't say I adored her, or even liked her, but she knew how to prevent a puncture.

Being one of my best ideas, the Talking Plaques were a truly horrid feature of the landscape. They cropped up almost everywhere, chanting in careful disharmony, reciting the details of any crime that had ever been committed on that spot. They drowned out the sound of my engine, hurting my sense more than a bee trained as a bailiff. Each time I trundled past on my circuit of passion, I heard the same dismal lists: "Dolores Spleen ruptured a cashew here on 67th October 3624," or "Martin Mocker raped a rope on 3rd April 1951," or "Andy Fairclough hid an owl in a mandolin on 12th January 2001." It was more than I could bear, so I daringly plugged my ears with honey while in motion.

But that bear (which was more than I could) must have licked it out quickly, for the voices were still audible and awful. Even Beatrix, high in the glowering sky, wrinkled up her face, which actually made her look pretty, in the same way that a small accident can improve a teapot which lacks a spout. My underwear experienced a desire to be torn from my rump and projected to her. It was risky to oblige but underleg adventures are my buttock and butter, so I sat sidesaddle and worked them down. As more Talking Plaques cascaded, my unicycle left its own remarkable skidmarks. I loaded the garment into my catapult, aimed and struck my target with a Parthian shot—not a misspelling.

Her nose hooked the item and my bowels fluttered with joy. Then she blew one nostril in my embroidered initials and it was all I could do to keep my balance. But now the Talking Plaques were leaking red liquid all over the surface of the road, spoiling the pallid glimmer and bathing my wheel like a tired mushroom. I changed gear, slowed down and finally the real reason for the mass jumping became clear. They were being shot by a sniper from afar! Somebody was deliberately inserting bullets into their spines, causing them to fall forward over the edge of the walkways. Such precision had an executive smell about it. I suspended my affections for Beatrix and considered the victims.

Now I understood they were being killed in a particular order. When a Talking Plaque reached a certain letter in his statement, a shot would ring out and he would plummet before me with the solitary sound still on his tongue. The force of my passing would pluck it out and my ears would drink it like mulled whine. The result was a bloody message for me, made out of the last sighs of thirty souls. Because the text had already been repeated a dozen times, the death toll was a number even higher than the circumference of my lesser ego expressed in cubits. My innate arrogance, you see, has a satellite—a moon which waxes at home with my hive, but wanes in the presence of free elks.

Anyway, I decided to concentrate on the content of the message when it was broadcast again. As feared, it was from the President. The fellow who had to intone the crime of Dolores Spleen only managed to get as far as "cashew" before he was shot, and this letter "c" formed the beginning of the bulletin. So too, the accuser of Martin Mocker reached "rope" and expired on the "o", whereas the one with Andy Fairclough's reputation to dilute gave up his own life on the "m" of "mandolin." And so on, until I had decrypted the following demand:

"Come to my tower immediately, Titian!"

I trembled and waved farewell to Beatrix, who was inserting my gift into a tube embedded in her column. Peculiar place to store underwear! I thought no more of it and steered for the President's edifice, which was located in a field between a sock and a soft place. The previous week he had swallowed eight cushions for a bet and was rushed to hospital, where his condition was described as comfortable. Now he was back and unstable and juggling his heart out, like many a lovable tyrant. Blast! Just as I was getting somewhere special and vertical with his wife! I sped through a door of his tower and dismounted.

"Hello! Any lunatic autocrats at home?"

But he wasn't sitting on his throne and his chamber was in complete chaos, with breakfast-pianolas snapping, cracking and popping, and not a few inverted bowls of fruit defending the carpet like bosom armour. Then a gruff voice hailed me from above:

"Hasten upstairs, my trusty Prefect . . . "

I bounded up the steps. "Here, sir! Good shooting, by the way! What can I do for you? Strum your chin?"

"No time for that, my friend, more's the pity! Take a look at this, would you? What do you make of it?"

He was standing on the balcony which rings the summit of the tower, holding a telescope to his eye, using his nose as a support in lieu of a tripod. A high-powered rifle stood propped against a table on which were spread charts and diagrams. These revealed the location of every Talking Plaque in the land and the texts they had to recite. An accurate sundial also stood on the surface. It was clear he had been timing the sentences of the chattering men in order to murder them at the correct letters for his summons. In the distance, the Pallid Colonnades bleached the horizon like filthy cream, and I could just make out Beatrix with my nude eye. I oozed a bead of sweat from my brow.

The President whipped out a handkerchief from his pocket. "Not over there, clever chum! Peer this way!"

I accepted this cloth and was about to mop myself when I recognised my initials and the inconstant mucus. The handkerchief was my underwear! So the President knew about my attachment to his spouse! How grotesquely would he punish me? By declaring my groin illegal? By setting a reformed dandrum on my bugaboo? Forgetting my birthday? But no, I'd misjudged his devotion to duty, his love of work.

He gripped my shoulder. "Yes, I'm aware of your attempted affair. I may not visit Beatrix very often, for aesthetic reasons, but we exchange the evidence of our sins via pneumatic tube. I do plan to get very angry and have already smashed up the contents of my abode in preparation, but until then I require your talents."

He raised the spyglass to my eye and I allowed him to focus it at a dark glade in tangled Jester Woods.

Blinking thrice, I gasped: "Heavens!"

(iii)

I was sitting on my favourite cloud, the young female nimbostratus, when the inverse smoke-signal reached me. I yawned and stretched and squinted at the blankets which rose past my gaze. Unwelcome but tightly woven. Up into outer space they continued, until the blue of each pattern formed a miniature sky in the airless void. They lifted in a particular sequence, easily readable as a command. The President wanted me back on Earth. The smoke which pushed the blankets up was solid and jagged. A refrigerative machine of some kind must have been setting it firm as it coughed from a fire in one of his hotline grates.

Grumbling to myself, for I was enjoying my vacation in the Heavenly Realm, I opened my sack of meteorites and selected a nickel-iron sphere. While my soul cavorted in the aether, my body lay in suspended animation in Dr Celery's sub-zero vanilla crypts. He was due to thaw me out in two weeks and to prevent this occurrence I had been slinging cosmic rocks at his skull, wholly without success. Now I had to arrange the opposite and compel him to re-animate me early. I leaned over the edge of my cloud and aimed for the water-clock which controlled the calender of Police events from the courtyard of the Station.

My first attempt was a catastrophe, striking the eighth side of the nonagonal building, the 'Genetic Disorder' wing, and demolishing it. The surviving prisoners would have to be rescued and levered into full cells elsewhere, just before an expected visit from Amnesty Interstellar! Poor timing, but it couldn't be helped. My second shot was better, landing in the barrel of the water-clock and hurrying on the date by fourteen days. Dr Celery and his stringy beard came out to investigate the noise, noted the reading on the dial and went off to the crypt to melt the vanilla. I sighed and waited to become flesh.

Before I could kiss goodbye to the cloud, a tunnel opened up in the aether and I was sucked toward a brown light—the light is blue in the other direction. I floated down reluctantly, my stomach heaving. Then my senses were jangled and I found myself stuck inside my torso. A terrible disappointment, I must confess, for a soul to be knotted to tendons in a cage of bones. Dr Celery slapped my cheeks, also my face, not because it was strictly necessary but as revenge for my assassination attempts. And I roused fitfully, shivered and called for my uniform. He shook his head at this, his mind still unbrained.

"Wiser for you to rest," he declared.

"The President must not be defied. Fetch my medals and chin. Oil my tickshaw. Dress my lettuce cloak!"

A minute later and I was respectable, at least for a buffoon. But I was still unsteady as I mounted my transport and sprayed the formic acid over the aphids and mites. The tickshaw jerked forward and I curled deep in the wicker seat as gravity drew my thoughts to my heels. The tower of the President loomed sharp, like a nagging finger, and the spokes of its giant wheels glittered in the dusk. The fire and frozen smoke were being dismantled by workmen, having served their purpose. I braked the vehicle with a honey spray and lurched out. The President was on the roof of the edifice and I staggered up to him.

"Thanks for coming, Prefect. Look at this!"

I accepted the heavy telescope. "Another tower! And there's another Titian Grundy staring back at me!"

"Now point the lens a little to the right."

"A third tower, with a third Grundy! What's the meaning of this? Do I have an obsessive club of fans?"

"No, your only fan is the silk one passed down from Charlton Radish for ritualistic purposes. These other towers and its inhabitants are not simulacra. Eight in total, including this one. I first noticed them this morning, mere dots on the horizon. Since then they have trundled closer. It appears we are all converging."

"Oh dear, so an accident seems inevitable."

"My fears exactly. What are we to do? Where have they come from? No odder event has transpired in my remarkable career. I'm fond of my tower and do not wish to see it smashed. Although it is shielded by a field of negatively-charged emotions, I don't think they're sufficient to protect this structure from annihilation."

"We must instantly divert your trajectory."

"Impossible, Titian! My tower is designed to move of its own accord under an Unfathomable Synthetic Will. I rarely know from one hour to the next where it might decide to go. Hidden springs in the walls click into motion and the wheels start moving and my building crosses the landscape to a new location. It is a good way of avoiding assassination, but now I regret the cunning of the scheme."

"Are there no ways of braking it manually?"

"None. I am a prisoner of its whims. The alternative Presidents and Titians on the balconies of the other towers look as worried as we do. I conclude we must perish together."

"Woe! My prepared tomb is not wide enough!"

"By the gods, Titian, I'm scared."

"I don't think the gods exist, sir. At least I saw no evidence of a metaphysical order of beings during my stay in the Heavenly Realm. After you declared them illegal, maybe they willed themselves to nothing? Some felons go to vast lengths to evade Justice. I would like to discuss this situation with Dr Celery or Lola Halogen, even Satsuma Ffroyde, but I am fed up with the way they always mock my cerebral ineptitude. So I won't. I'll unravel this problem myself."

"A promotion if you're successful, Titian!"

"I am already at the summit of my profession, sir. If I am promoted again, I may trip over the top of the career-ladder and plummet down the far side and become a shoe-clerk."

"Just save my dwelling from demolition!"

I bowed deeply, not out of respect, but because I was so weary from acclimatising to the higher stresses of flesh life that I needed to rest my head on the floor. It lay there for long minutes. The President found this a charming gesture and he was mollified a little, a very little, so small a little that he grew angry at the modesty of it and raved against serenity, declaring it illegal. But still I couldn't lift my skull. Then he lashed out with his boot and kicked me straight. Because I am not yet a shoe-clerk I can't say what make of boot. But it doesn't matter. Eight towers were coming together to kick harder than this. And they were shod in silver and stepmother-of-pearl.

(iv)

"He's glaring back at me!" I hissed.

"An abominable situation," agreed the President, "but I have to put up with your face from much closer."

"You are my friend and therefore immune."

"Not so. Ugliness does not function in the same way as bacteria. My stomach still heaves at your smile."

I had recently arrived from the moon, and my knees were aching. The President had summoned me while I was collecting blackness from the Dark Side for use as eyeliner for my beekeeper wife. There were no flowers to pick, so beauty products were the only romantic gifts I could offer her. Trying to serenade in low gravity is a fine way of making other husbands furious. Songs tend to spin past the window of choice and into the wrong bedroom. Makeup remains the only secure option. Not that she appreciated my efforts. In fact I hadn't spoken to her since the last Lunar Eclipse, an occasion she used as cover for her escape. I fumbled in the dim rooms of my dwelling but she had vanished.

While I was crouching on the edge of a crater, scooping up the best blackness with a spade, a selenite with a hose attached to its head came up behind me and jumped into the hollow. I sighed and turned and saw how the hose ran off the horizon into the void, the other end originating on the Earth. The President's tower hadn't enjoyed standing on the moon and had returned to the mother planet. He had taken a menagerie of selenites with him, partly because he liked strumming airs on their antennae. This creature was one from his collection and it had a careworn look, bloated from rich oxygen mixtures and callow cheese. It squatted on its heels in the dust, mouths agape, arms folded.

A few hours later, the first trickle spilled from the hose, licking the parched moon soil and swirling in unprecedented eddies. The selenite paddled fitfully, as I waited for the message. The President has a large tap in his bathroom, and optimum pressure, but this crater was very deep and required a lot of filling. I passed the selenite a handkerchief from my pocket and instructed it on how to knot it into a hat. The liquid was now up to its lower shoulders and it seemed unhappy. None of my business how an extraterrestrial entity chooses to waste its leisure! But no, the President had probably forced it to comply on pain of sanity, which is a dreadful fate for a lunatic citizen.

Eventually the sorry creature was wholly immersed and had to detach its head to save itself from drowning. The throat bolts slid out and its skull bobbed to the surface of the new pond, flared nostrils sucking the airless atmosphere in soundless undulations, purely for pleasure, as its lungs were still at the base of the crater. The last drop spluttered out of the hose and I peered closer in anticipation of the official message. It came at last in the shape of a bulge in the hose which worked its way very slowly between worlds, like astral digestion, and finally disgorged itself in the centre of the lake. A sealed bottle containing a letter. I hooked it with my spade and read it.

In old-fashioned zincplate script, the President formally requested the pleasure of my presence in his elongated domicile as soon as rapidly convenient. I turned and bounced back to my lunar cottage, preparing the seat of my Shanks' Pony. The porcelain hybrid was uncomfortable but very efficient, provided the chain didn't break. I aimed it for the peninsula which connected Earth and Luna and flushed it a dozen times. It frothed, grumbled and slushed as the cistern refilled, projecting me in wide arcs across dry seas and jagged peaks. Once I landed hard and cracked the lid but the main functions remained unimpaired. Down the thirty-nine million steps into the hygienic ozone layer!

The continents lay spread before me like a half-eaten banquet, with spilt-ale oceans and bagel atolls. The President's tower had moved to an isolated forest where clowns practised seriousness privately. My Shanks' Pony weaved between trees and I switched off the afterburners. My bowels were grateful for that. Coasting through blackberries, I stained my chin and reputation with juice. I parked my transport outside the President's gate, a childhood touch recalling the era when every latrine was located outdoors, and hoofed it under the portals. He was upstairs with a single spyglass and eight resentments, so I joined him and shook at the phallic creepiness of the additional towers.

I studied one Grundy after another. "Ugh!"

"My sentiments exactly, Prefect. But they are getting closer by the blink. What do you think they want?"

"To go in a different direction, by the look of it. They don't care to meet us any more than we wish to meet them. By the way, don't you try to weed your roof-garden sometimes?"

"It's only a cheesewort, Titian! Ignore it and it'll probably leave you alone. It's a mature perennial."

I sat on one of the houses in his miniature village and eased spiky tendrils from under my toes. "I could accuse the scene of impossibility, but it won't stand up in Court. The other towers are overgrown too. They can't be used as concrete evidence."

"Shall I summon Professors Warp and Woof?"

"The University quacks? No, I'll resolve this on my own. They would only make matters worse. One might suggest burning the towers down while his rival advocated freezing them up, and in tandem no progress would be made at all. Give me a little time."

"You have five grey seconds and one pink!"

"Not enough! Wait, an idea has birthed. Instead of trying to fathom the physics involved in this crisis, we should act first and then obtain the facts during interrogation. For instance, by declaring all the other Presidents illegal, you will sanction me to arrest them. They might have more insight into the event. If not, we can keep them locked up, because ignorance of the law—any law, including those used in science—does not constitute a plausible defence."

"The identity parade will be bewildering."

"I will ensure you don't accidentally pick yourself. And if you do, I'll get you a very good solicitor."

"My legal insurance has run out. It escaped from the stocks a month ago. I hope this anomaly truly is scientific in character, not artistic. Otherwise there'll be no laws to be ignorant of, and we will have to let the other Presidents walk free. But I trust you, Titian, even though you once attempted to fondle my cheese."

"Fondue, not fondle, sir! A charity jape. No, I can't lie to you! I admit the deed. It had auburn rind."

He raised an imperious thumb and pointed. "Go thither and apprehend the extra Presidents, to the tune of seven, for I now declare refraction of identities to be bent behaviour."

The tune in question he played on an ugli-fruit balalaika. I prefer the melody of pi myself, or any irrational number other than the root of 2, which is for squares. Seven is a ditty for hepcats and much too young for officials. But the President is a mean ugli plucker, as few citizens will deny, and he ushered me vibrantly on my way, down the steps, though not vibrantly enough, for he followed me closely, humming the words with the panache of a sour belch locked in a radiator. But a surprise greeted us when we attained the main hall at ground level. Another Titian Grundy glided through the door on centipede-skates, each tiny leg fitted with a castor, shaking his truncheon at us.

"What are you doing down there, you fool?"

"No, sir, that's an alternative me, from a parallel dimension. He's obeying the orders of an analogous President to arrest you! At least one of your variations has had the same idea first! You've declared yourself illegal from a different direction."

The impostor roared: "Evening all. Enjoying ourselves, are we? Best come down to the prison for a chat."

"What sort of chat, you myriapod mounter?"

He winked. "Just a little one."

"Beware, sir! That's the most dangerous form of chat. His breath is reminiscent of teapot vapours. Plus he is me. I advise total mistrust of all his banter. Use me as a shield."

The President ducked down behind my rump, but I skipped aside. "Not this me! The other me! Him! Hide behind him, so that he can't seize you. Crouch behind my own me and he'll guess where you are as precisely as if he had eyes in the back of my head!"

"If I hide behind him, you'll have eyes in the back of his head and may strike a deal to scrutinise me."

"How can you question my loyalty, sir? I protected your wife's nose from a demented Savoy, picking the former, pickling the latter, when the cabbages spouted against the kings."

"Beatrix is still retroussé about that. But this is stupid prattle, serving no purpose in the greater narrative. No, the point is that I can do as I please. I refuse to be disgraced in front of my Prefect(s) in my own tower and thus am disinclined to hide. Instead I will declare Titian Grundy illegal. Arrest him quickly!"

I flicked out my handcuffs and approached the impostor, but while

I was walking toward him, I somehow managed to secure my own wrists in the hoops of brass. Because I was now illegal, I had instinctively fulfilled my duties, apprehending the nearest version of myself, which was me. The President stamped a foot as I held up my chained wrists and coaxed a sad guilty rattle from the yellow links.

"Shall I knock myself about a touch, sir?"

"Police brutality is against the spirit of the age, though still in accordance with the wine of the aeon. Set yourself free, Titian. Ah, the key has snapped! Weaving them from chives has disadvantages. By Hopp and Drigg, I declare handcuffs illegal!"

The moment this pronouncement struck his ears, my impostor leapt to snap his own handcuffs around mine. This released me, because mine hoped to make it easier on themselves by offering no resistance. But now there was a paradox in the room, for the handcuffs which had arrested mine had no alibi, and the other Titian Grundy was forced to let the first lot go to secure the second. And then he had to let the second go to secure the first. And so on. Until the President wearied of this display, acrobatic though it was, and suddenly shouted:

"I decree an exclusion zone on confusion!"

The limit was set at one mile, and the impostor was forced to skate out of the building, the way he'd come, to avoid trespassing. I was very happy to see the back of him, because I had always wondered what my nape looked like. Horrid. I won't cut my own hair again. No time to regret my style, for doubts were also growing askew. You can imagine our sorrow as we watched him race into the haze. If we didn't understand the phenomena of copied towers soon, and understand it like logicians, with a cool nod at each strange twist, we would have to join him in exile. The exclusion zone is relevant to every confusion.

(v)

Because I am Titian Grundy's reflection, my good looks are mostly on the wrong side. But it doesn't matter, because they're all ugly anyway.

When I went missing from his mirror I didn't expect to be gone for good. Just a holiday is what I had planned, a fortnight at the bottom of a saucepan or possibly a month in a cat's eye. But the President wanted me before I was able to pick. He caught me in transit, passing through a chrome axle under his tower and easing me off with a hatchet. He said nothing to the real me, preferring him to think I had deliberately absconded forever to a realm beyond identity. My owner searched for me in the corner of every myth and so was swallowed by Neptune.

The President riveted my image to a shiny panel and lifted me up to the roof of his home. Seven different towers pulsed in the distance with matching occupants and gilding. I peered at each through a telescope and saw they were watching me, some of them actually shaving by my features. The rival Grundys were unappealing, as I already knew from reflecting my individual model, but I never imagined that a multiplication of Prefects would increase the distaste geometrically, rather than arithmetically. I beheld an octagon of repugnance. I knocked on the surface of my panel to attract the President's attention and he took me down from the telescope and held my flat lips to his fat ear.

"It must be a crease in the cosmic fabric."

He shuffled. "I was told the cosmos was made of starched vacuum and couldn't be crinkled. My tutor lied!"

"The staff at Dictators' School always deceive their pupils. That's why you have had such a brilliant career in politics. Somehow this tower has duplicated itself, or has been duplicated by an outside agency. Laws of common sense have been infringed."

"An outside agency? Amnesty Interstellar?!"

"Eight Presidents are the last thing they'd want. No, it's far more likely to be a haphazard anomaly in the weave of space-time. I wonder if these other towers are past and future echoes of our reality? A temporal mirage of some kind. It is feasible."

"I don't think so. The Titian Grundy on that tower is making rather rude gestures at you in real-time. His tongue is poked at this moment. I suspect a more serious perturbation."

"If they were just echoes, a collision would present no problem. We will merely pass through each other. But if they're as solid and real as this one a tragedy is on the agenda."

"Why do you think I summoned you, Prefect?"

He hadn't actually, but I kept quiet, because his patience had worn so thin it could be used as a noose to hang a virus. I tugged at my chin and fretted. What if there was more than one dimension? What if a number of alternative universes existed side by side? They might have their own histories, similar but not exactly the same, with variations of culture, geography and fruit. They would be unaware of each other's presence in a continuum which extended sideways through the body of creation. Yes, the scenario was likely. A mandala of potentials. They should be detached by lateral space-time but at this point they had overlapped. I communicated this numbing hypothesis in a whisper.

The President was very unhappy. "You mean to say those other towers are as valid as mine? That they have equal status in objective life? And does this also apply to my variants?"

"I'm afraid so, sir. None of you can really be considered the model for the others. There is no archetype as such. You evolved independently in eight parallel, but not identical, realities. These rival rulers have prolapsed into the fulcrum around which they revolved. Do not treat them as impostors, or you curse yourself!"

"So humane evasive action must be taken . . . "

"I can think of nothing, sir. Nets might be cast over them, but few fishermen are willing to work for you these days, not since you declared boredom and escaping the wife illegal. Somehow we must divert the towers around each other so that they miss."

"Dig curved trenches to guide the wheels? My towers would then pass harmlessly in a kind of giant waltz."

"There might be trouble where the trenches met. Remember that these structures are converging from eight different directions. Also it would take too long to excavate that amount of soil. No, we need to propel the towers into the air over each other."

The President steamed up my surface with his desperate breath.

Then he inhaled sharply, almost sucking me through the glass, an idea burning one eye like naphthol on a jellyfish.

"Atomic trampolines! We'll set them up in front of the other towers and bounce them into an exchange of position. Then they will all trundle their own way, on divergent courses."

"That will also be quite amusing to watch."

"I'll order every gymnasium to hand over their fast-breeder springs while you beat your guard, Percy Flamethrower, about the kidneys with an iron rod to produce the heavy water."

"What if the Presidents in the other towers also decide to lay down atomic trampolines? Could get nasty."

"With so many minor details at variance in the parallel dimensions, it's unlikely more than one reality has invented such equipment. No need to panic, Titian. Let's get to work."

"Wait! I've just remembered that we're one of the realities without atomic trampolines! Cancel the plan!"

"Blister it, you're right! We don't even have radioactivity in this universe. Better think of something else! What if we stand large mirrors in front of every other tower? That should bring forward the date of the collision to a time when we aren't there. Then we will just proceed over the ruins like a capricious obelisk."

"Reflections have fled their mirrors in our world, remember? Titian is searching for me at this instant."

The President sighed. "I wish I was a puppet!"

(vi)

In a military balloon bristling with steel spikes, the sole passenger of an old sugar on his last adventure. That's where I was. I never expected the President to reach me out there, particularly as he'd terminated our friendship numerous months previously. But he knows which side his uglis are juiced and is capable of suspending all grudges for profit. And he's capable of suspending a whole wardrobe of jackets from his nose.

But I'm bragging for him now and that's his job. Anyway, I had become a rover of the sky, a mandolinist and romantic, with teeth so rotten the plaque had decayed, leaving them shiny and dazed. The wonders I had seen! Amana and Cus, Hogsbrud and Yam-Yam, Nouth and Niggle, Paraparapara and Djiwondro, rubber garters up a damsel's skirt!

Not that I'm in the habit of admiring such items of lingerie when I try to peer up skirts, but this is the modern age and boundaries keep on sliding. Can't be halted or reversed. Fly with the times, is what I say, at least now—when I was Prefect of Police I'd rather say arrest them! Clobber those upstart times! Lock them in a clock! That is because I was basically unhappy, a fretful cog in the diseased machine of society. The story of my life was a novel whose missing chapters included empathy and kindness and tolerance. Quite a blank tale really. Won't say I've caught up with my humanity, or made up for lost time, by voyaging this world in baskets, but some of the frustration has flaked away. O! the hot zephyrs of Khyor! Plus its perfumed cheese!

Just let me roll this smoke, finest Qtiztowf resin, don't you know, and I will proceed with my yarn. That's better. Light it from the engine above my head. The old sugar doesn't mind my drug habits, partly because his nostrils deserted in the trenches of the second Garlic Offensive and he can't smell the pungent dream, so he doesn't know what I'm doing. Not that he's an intolerant sort anyway. The nicest military man I've met in a long while. The Top Zincs in the offices are the unimaginative idiots, not the soldiers in (or above) the field. Consider the zoetrope reels of the Liliaceous Wars. They're all puffing parsley, grooving to Psychopomp Rock, mostly Jammy Cockrix and Joe Henner. No need to worry. Mauve haze, whole in my shoe, voodoo chilblain.

Guess I'm rambling, mind as well as body. Listen up then: it was in the orchards of Lubbalouana that the President came back into my life. I had almost forgotten him, but I still recalled his parting insult before I left the Capital. So I could visualise the words but not his nose. The strings on my mandolin were sighing softly. My socks were maturing, hole and rind, perfect for grating. Everything was mellow ochre, as bald coat singer Pegg Donzelcart might say. Not that he ever did. Too busy cooking green kebabs on his 13-string catarrh—traitor! Anyway, those orchards are the main source of the planet's plums and limes, which is heavy news for twigs, and it was impossible not to impale a thousand or more on our spikes as we pushed gently through.

However, once clear of Lubbalouana I realised the way the fruit was aligned on our armoured canopy wasn't random. Reading them from the top, a message was apparent. Each plum represented a dot, each lime a dash (a dash of lime is also good in overproof rum) in Morose Code, the glummest genre of encryption known to telegraphites. It was obvious the trees had been planted in a deliberate sequence to ensure this communication. Only the President has enough free time to bother with something so elaborate and unnecessary. Leaning out of the basket and craning my neck upward to read, I understood he was summoning me back to his tower. That is all he ever writes to me for, even on my birthday. The plums and limes demanded my instant return without a please.

"The blasted arrogance of the man!" I grumbled.

My impulse was to ignore this message. Though I couldn't tear it up and cast it away, I might drink the juice of its individual letters. But a second reason for ignoring it was that it was impractical to obey. The realm of Lubbalouana is half a triangular globe away from the Capital on the Isle of Chrome, and a balloon must travel at the mercy of the winds, even powered examples such as ours.

Smug musings on this fact were interrupted by a deep hum, the sound of another engine, hidden in the clouds. It wasn't a balloon, for it was travelling too quickly. Then it emerged—a biplane made of stiff card, with pictures on its wings. A propeller whisked the mists. And seated in the front cockpit was Satsuma Ffroyde, my acidic deputy, with his pitted forehead and eyes peeled for facts.

He sneered at me: "Pipped at the post, Titian!"

"Segmented lackey! What are you doing here? Nobody from the Station may pick me up except Lola Halogen, who never does. The Code of Leverage prohibits it, page 78, fulcrum 43."

"President's whim. Jump over."

"I might fall and become destructed far below."

"The wings predict you won't."

Something in his voice convinced me, for I gripped the old sugar in a farewell hug and said: "I'll be back as soon as I can to continue this adventure. Consider my absence a parenthesis to my wanderlust. I plummet down to establishment values in order to return to their converse with a fresh vigour. It has been so long since I was a stooge of the government I've forgotten what I'm rebelling against. My memory and rage need to be flexed again to keep them healthy."

"A diet of figs," he croaked in unfathomable reply. He didn't truly care about my companionship, so I balanced on the edge of the basket and flung myself into the rumbling sky.

I span as I fell and Satsuma piloted his biplane under me. I landed in the rear cockpit, bruises hatching on my legs. Then my deputy giggled and banked his machine to the west.

"Full speed for the Capital!" he announced.

"Exactly what sort of aircraft is this? Why is there a picture of a *monk* on the upper left wing, that of the *sun* on the upper right, and *two coins* on the lower left, not to mention *eight swords* on the lower right? A rather elaborate set of designs."

"It's a Tarotplane. The pictures change to predict engine problems, adverse weather and other trouble."

"Did you invent it, you scurvy antithesis?"

"It was unearthed during recent excavations of the tomb of Nitrogen Parsley. At this moment the wings prophesy that we'll land safely in ten hours or so, although we can expect reproaches and arguments on the way. I suggest we get them over with now, you vile subhuman, to save time. Do you use vole-oil to fry your chin?"

"Never! Sheathe your frugiferous slanders."

"They are fated, not willed. See! Now the lower right wing has been shuffled into the *four of sticks*. You are going to be invited to a meal. There is a pickle under your seat."

I retrieved the gherkin and chewed it moodily. Arcane turbulence is the enemy of the stomach, as obtuse stomachs are the enemy of the heart. When it was all gone, apart from one green crumb, which I flicked at the back of Satsuma's head, because it clashed with the orange, I turned all my attention to the wings, hoping to catch them in the act of shuffling. But they were waiting for me to blink, changing in that fraction of dark between lid and eye. Now the upper left wing depicted a man dangled from a tree by his feet, a drawing which my deputy insisted meant "downfall". Turbulence over the Aracknids fulfilled this, and we dipped to less than a sacrifice's length over the tallest temple, wherein a crabby, seasoned Sideways Priest nipped a holy mass.

I hissed to myself: "Villain!"

Satsuma turned to face me. "Ah, you sound more like the old Titian! Has the mellowness truly worn off?"

It had. I retorted: "Keep your eyes on the altimeter, or I'll strip you of the Order of Grand Marnier."

That medal was Satsuma's favourite possession and the juice drained from his face in distress. The wings remained optimistic for the rest of the flight and the Tarotplane cruised above the Capital. The President's tower had left the market square, rumbling through the highest city gate into the open country. Oddly, there were seven other towers collected in the same location, and Presidents and Prefects on each of them, pointing up at our aircraft and attempting to tell their fortunes without seeming to appear too gullible. We circled the converging structures like a moth around an array of unlighted candles, not at our wick's end, nor theirs, but certainly waxing wroth. A guttering soul, mine. The soot is internal and unavailable for making pigment.

"Which is the genuine tower?" I bellowed.

"For you, the one without a Titian Grundy on the summit. You're the last to arrive, by the look of things. Undo your seatbelt and prepare to disembark. Note the upper left wing! It has now become the *House of God*, which often suggests a fallen man."

And so saying, he inverted the Tarotplane with a jerk. I disengaged from my seat with a slurp and fell again, cursing my deputy's morals and stalk, but unable to arrest him, because there can't be extradition from the sky, not until the Courts sport wings instead of wigs, and even then the flapping will probably have an adjournment. So I continued to hurtle down, like a bag of disappointment in a vertical laundry-chute, toward a doctored meeting with a cushion of nettles. The stings broke my doom and the President broke my ears, shouting at me to mind his weeds, which was poor advice for my brow, already studded with nodules of agony. I jumped up and saluted him and his idiotic precepts, most of which were mine. He smiled askew but grimaced straight.

"Titan Grubby! This is the latest you have ever been early! So what kept you? A social conscience, eh?"

I licked my blistered lips. "I left that behind in Lubbalouana. Now I'm keen to serve whimsical autocracy. Who do you require me to oppress? My truncheon was lost in far climes, but when it is done beating them it is bound to make its own way back."

"You can't frighten a cosmic flaw with a piece of wood, Prefect. We are in dire straits here, because our enemies are no longer the ordinary people, but an elite—ourselves!"

Then he told me the awful story. Back among establishment hypocrisy my past felt relieved, but my present felt betrayed. Those other towers, he pointed out, were simultaneously equal and lesser versions of his own abode, and their occupants both trespassers and rightful owners of their properties. He juggled the contradictions nicely, dropping a dozen or so but making it look part of the act, except when they rolled over the rim of the balcony and were lost forever. I listened with a face so grave it used my chin for a mossy headstone.

"Parallel dimensions, you say? That's a severe blow to our sense of uniqueness, if not our sense of smell. But the resins of Qtiztowf, which I've recently imbibed (and fined myself seven coughs for so doing), have expanded my consciousness and given me a very original idea. We must act before the towers move any closer."

"Speak your plan, gross chum. No dawdling."

"You must declare all the other towers illegal. Then I'll lock them up inside this one, the same way a recalcitrant amoeba (a single cell of crime) is cooped in a dungeon (a larger cell of punishment). Then at the trial, we'll exile them back to their own dimensions, one at a time. Our cosmos shall be uncluttered again."

"Silly Prefect! Those towers are identical in size to mine. How can you possibly fit them inside this one? Do you mean to grind them to dust and pour them in through the roof?"

I leaned on the railings. "No, that would take too long. Tell me if visually they are a matching size."

"From this distance they obviously look smaller, but that's not the point. It's a trick of perspective. Because they're still a league or so apart, they appear smaller than we do. They'll be within breathing range before another day is out, with violent contact the day after that. Then you'll see them as they truly are."

"Best not to let matters come to that, sir. It occurs to me that if you declare the rules of perspective illegal, I might stride over to the towers and pull them up, carrying them back under one arm. I suggest you implement this decision immediately, as every minute which passes brings them closer, thus increasing their size and weight. As things stand, the process will only take one sortie."

"Outlaw perspective? Why not? I hereby do so!"

I stretched my muscles, ready to bound over the rural vista, fields and meadows and dales, like a fairytale giant, when a shadow loomed from high above. It wasn't Satsuma in the Tarotplane, nor a Tsunami from deep Aracknid seas, nor Beatrix Trifle on her Baluchitheriumobile, but me, an amplified version thereof, with all the wrinkles, pimples and blemishes, repugnant enough in the original, here swollen to nightmare proportions, such as might cause geology to shudder. A gargantuan Titian Grundy, blue in the cheeks from the frosts of high altitude, bones cracking under the density of his own frame, eyes forming holiday skies for geese, stooping painfully down and taking hold of our tower between finger and thumb, to pluck us from the earth like a peg.

The President wept. "You've stolen your idea!"

(vii)

It should have been the happiest day of my life, which is why I expected to be mournful. I'd always wanted to be married in white, and ghosts had scared me thoroughly the night before, on the orders of my best man, the President, so I was still pale enough to dispense with fabric to achieve the desired colour. Those phantoms had been phoney, made from sheets and springs and pasteboard, as I afterwards learned. But far from reassuring me, this revelation was even more appalling because it implied that real ghosts didn't assume I was worth spooking! What a blow to my reputation! And a callous trick on the part of our endearing leader, who had damaged my residence by hollowing the walls to insert the puppets! Next to haunt me would be the bill for repairs.

After ten hours of shuddering, I was exhausted when the hearse came to pick me up. I slumped in the back while the chauffeur jerked the silk reins on the Black Widows. A traumatic voyage past crowds of ill-wishers and dung-hurlers, terminating at the Temple of Drigg, packed with all my relatives. Of course, having no family, this ensured there was plenty of space for the other guests. None of my staff had showed up yet, with the exception of Lola Halogen, who was all hat. Indeed I suspected there was nothing under the brim and that she too had let me down. The tall priest had to stoop under the low arches to sprinkle cheap wine over the altar. The scale of the Cosmic Serpent seemed to wink as rogue sunbeams impaled the moisture. Romantic and nasty.

The President slapped my back as I arrived and whispered a dozen or so friendly insults into my ear. He had hired the Supreme Roger to be my chief witness—not the genuine Supreme Roger, for it was felt that the pelvic attributes of such a fabled worthy would draw unwelcome attention to my own untested nuptial endurance, but a lesser Supreme Roger. A Vice Roger, in a sense. There were other Rogers in the pews: acolyte, rookie, fledgling Rogers. They held dishes of glands. I'd hoped for confetti but the President insisted on glands. In one corner, the disharmonium hissed a rendition of Mendeleev's *Periodic Wedding Concerto*. My bride was here! I resisted the impulse to glance over my shoulder. I heard her cries and complaints as she was wheeled in.

The locked chest came to a halt next to the altar and the President was kind enough to remove the chains and throw back the lid. My gorgeous Animula struggled in her shroud. To think that once she had been the sad inhabitant of a subatomic particle! But I had rescued her from the realm of the microscopic, dragged her into the bigger picture, for the sake of a sweet love (and because I'd been ordered to) which was now about to be sealed according to our religious code. The beauty of the notion was too much for her. She writhed and kicked, impatient to become my wife! I was already married, but my beekeeper spouse had stung me too often by proxy to expect loyalty from me, so the President had repealed the bigamy laws within the ellipse of my embrace.

The disharmonium finished its work, having jarred all our nerves in a truly undelightful fashion. I'd waited for this moment since my return from the proton Neirb'O, where Animula had pranced in the energy-forests of the Semaj-Ztif nature reserve. Now the Aracknid priest sprinkled more wine over the Cosmic Serpent's scale. But something went wrong here, for there was a tiny explosion within the mystic facets of the relic, and it jumped off the altar. A bad omen?

Not really. It was the proton Neirb'O detonating under the virulent onslaught of the quantum-surfers of the neutron Sgnimmuc. For years they had been bombarding Neirb'O with quarks, in an attempt to destabilise it and destroy the atomic bond between the two worlds. Finally they'd added enough quarks to attain their subdastardly stratagem. Animula's home had been destroyed! A more symbolic marriage smash than the breaking of dish or plate! But she wasn't pleased.

I removed her gag. "Animula! What's wrong?"

"My name is Mandy and all my friends and family have just perished. Apart from that, cramp in a leg."

"Superb! That will keep you static in bed."

"I spit on you! Let me out!"

"Ah, she is so eager to satisfy my desire! For twelve years she has languished in a dungeon, serving time for daring to be the very small-est thing in the cosmos, dreaming of nothing but the date of her release and her subsequent marriage! She is drooling so heavily with impa-tience that her saliva is spurting across the considerable gap dividing us with such force and accuracy that my blushing cheeks are plashed! Animula! Tonight I must take your maidenhead. I've no idea where I'll take it but you can come along as well, if you like."

She grimaced in gratitude. "Swine monster!"

Before I continue, permit me to point out that this Temple of Drigg was the miniature one in the model village in the roof-garden at the top of the President's tower. It was cheaper to book than the bigger temples in the real city, and more likely to be filled with my meagre companions to a level just above embarrassment. This was the place where I'd shrunk on my jaunt to Neirb'O, anticipating all sorts of ad-ventures, other than those of love—which hurt more!

Now the priest swayed from side to side and the President groped in his pocket for the ring. It was a diamond solitaire-confinement, but the gem had escaped by tunnelling through the platinum band. No mat-ter: kiss and tickle require no tokens other than themselves. Animula and I had no need of ostentatious signs of our mutual affection. While the Vice Roger lifted her out of the box, holding her in a firm embrace, the priest and his congregation shuffled and cleared sundry throats. Another minute and I'd be the happiest husband ever!

Then the President dropped the ring and it rolled out of the Temple into the garden. He hopped after and brought it back. The priest scowled and routinely asked if anyone present had just cause for pre-venting this union between Animula and myself.

This question is pure tradition and nobody ever expects a person to actually raise an objection. Indeed the priest scarcely paused to listen for a reply before launching into the next part of the service, which is outdated drivel about obedience and honour (I certainly didn't in-tend to obey Animula!) and similar nonsense. But it was too soon to congratulate my fortune, for the President suddenly lifted his arm and cried out that he had an objection, a large one.

"Cancel the wedding! Replace the wife!"

The priest rubbed his mandibles. "What is the nature of your qualm? Does it consist of moral doubts?"

"Not at all. It is strictly practical."

"Pray reveal its character."

While I wept in frustration and betrayal, the President dipped into his other pocket and removed a portable-semaphore. It was a cube on legs with moving arms, a fine example of the signallers' apparatus. He walked forward and rested it on the priest's shoulder, so that it was angled at the window at the rear of the altar. Then my (misnamed) best man twisted a knob to work the arms. Because he had his back to the congregation, it was impossible to read what message he was relaying. The priest remained ignorant of the content of the missive too, for the device prevented him from turning his head. When the President had finished, he stepped back, lowered the semaphore and yawned.

We waited. Through this rear window, far away across the landscape, to the Carbuncle Hills, the President's message had danced, to be caught up by a semaphore tower on the highest peak. In turn, this tower relayed the message yet further over the horizon, where it was plucked from thin air by a second tower, and passed to a third, and so on, until the words of the dispatch were hastening to the ends of the planet. Eventually, it would reach the corner of Groof and Lyg, the most remote place of all. I failed to see what connection that distant clime had with my marriage. A hopeless rage filled me, a desire to be free of the President, who seems always destined to cancel my joy.

He sat down in one of the spare pews. After an hour, the priest and the Vice Roger followed his example. So did I, finally, and even Animula sat back in her case. There was no sense questioning the President as to the substance of his bulletin. It was obvious from the nonchalant way in which he sprawled that he was confident the matter would resolve itself. The congregation fidgeted, the minor Rogers started playing a game which involved constructing anagrams of the word 'bannister'. I was paying for the delay. With the Fire Companies still chasing me for unpaid bills, my solvency was rapidly coming unstuck. I swallowed my impatience and grief and counted the indolent minutes.

Late in the evening, when all our thumbs were so twiddled they were bloated but floppy, like the nuptial lance in my trousers, the President jumped up to rouse the priest. He pointed to the entrance of the Temple. The open door looked out over the other side of the realm, and the giant semaphore tower on the opposing hill began to turn. Then I comprehended. The message had circumnavigated the entire planet, travelling beyond the corner of Groof and Lyg and returning on the dark side, until it arrived back at its point of origin. The priest blinked at the moving arms. Here was the objection to my marriage!

By the time I had craned my neck to study the news, the message was finished. Short and bitter, like my childhood! The priest nodded, called to the congregation to depart, and they all left in single file, with my bride pushed in the care of the Vice Roger, until only the President and myself remained. Then I demanded:

"What did the message say? What do you want?"

"It was a command for you to drop everything and hurry to my tower. I'm glad to see that you obeyed."

I was outraged and flabbergasted. "How can you possibly order me to your tower? We are already here!"

"But a summons is a state of mind, as well as a physical condition. Although I couldn't ask you to arrive here, if you already were, I could convert your presence into an entrance by removing the others. When they departed, it made up for the fact that you didn't move. The final result was identical, in the same way that fruit can be juggled by leaving them immobile in the air and manipulating the man who throws them. I summoned you by changing the environment."

"I grudgingly accept your logic. But why exactly am I here? It must be very urgent to spoil my life."

"Follow me." The President led me out of the Temple of Drigg and to the edge of his garden. I looked over the panorama. Far away, but not so far as the nearest semaphore, stood seven other towers. Rivals from some mysterious republic, interlopers.

"Your abode has committed structural polygamy!"

He sighed heavily. "I first noticed them when I ran out to retrieve your ring. We are obviously on collision-course. They are too monumental to be cheap imitations. So I conclude they are just as real as mine, and staffed with genuine Presidents."

"I suggest they have collapsed into our universe from a sequence of dimensions parallel to this one."

"Lateral timelines don't usually overlap."

I snapped my fingers. "The annihilation of Neirb'O! That detonation must have disrupted the space-time continuum, causing eight realities to prolapse into just one location."

"What can we do, Titian, dear friend?"

"Arresting the other Presidents or towers won't help. But you might consider banning all rival realities. Then I'll lock them up inside each other, move them out of the way."

"I agree. Best to keep elsewheres off the streets! But how will you manage to do that? Dimensions are enormous, stretching the entire length of the universe. I know you've arrested many big things in your time. My nose, however, remains at large."

"And so do the rival realities! But not for long! What is a dungeon other than an enclosed space with a lock turned by a key? Each dimension already has a bounded limit. They are, in a sense, potential dungeons. I merely require something to lock them with. If I can create a key of the correct size, we'll be able to secure them inside themselves. Naturally, there'll be no chance of parole."

"Can you really fabricate such a key?"

"I've already got one! Remember the green pyramid I gathered on the purple atom? It's an expanded quark, with power over the chronoflow. The rival dimensions are extensions in time and space. That's all a universe really is anyway. My pyramid is a building block of both time and space. It can seal the other realities."

"Quick, Titian! Carve it into a key shape!"

I shook my head. "It is a minimal particle and can't be subdivided. Its shape just can't be altered."

Before I could fret further over this problem, the President called to me in considerable anxiety: "Look at that! A giant version of you has stepped out from that tower and is striding over to that other tower and is trying to uproot it from the ground! Luckily it has failed and is now returning to its own building . . . "

I blinked. "He'd make a wondrous best man!"

(viii)

Sitting on the apex of my green pyramid, shaking the reins, hoping to be hurled into the past. Feeling like a bad actor, a salted ham, especially as the sweat on my mouth had dried in the breeze of my flapping, leaving pale sodium deposits on my lip. Reminded me of days with Beatrix Trifle, can't say why. The quark seemed disinclined to go anywhere, past, future or home, but I felt it could be encouraged. I was off to arrest my first ancestor, in the primal slime, for committing a genetic felony which had eventually led to my doleful existence. I would remove him from the game of evolution and thus stall myself.

Just before tripping out of the present, there was a rap on my door and a hunched figure entered my room. He wore a diseased pelt, carried a gnarled club and was so hairy that his shadow consisted of nine thousand monkey outlines knotted together. His brows were huge, also his toes. He dragged the yellow knuckles of his free hand on the bare boards and gave his name as Ug. I was familiar with the appellation, for it had belonged to a Palaeolithic thief, whose horrible crime was related by the Talking Plaque wedged up the chimney. Was this the same villain? It could hardly be, unless Time was playing a joke.

With many obscene gestures, mostly directed at his groin, he led me to the conclusion that he was precisely what I was looking for. But what had brought him to his future? The power of my imagination? No, for that has exerted precious little control over ladies. Perhaps he'd decided to turn himself in? A likely solution.

"So you are my very first ancestor? Ug!"

I was expressing disgust, not calling him, but he nodded and struck the floor with his club. "Ug! Ug! Hrungh!"

"Ah! I get it! I have already travelled into the past on my pyramid but the journey was so smooth I didn't realise it! So this is the age of the early hominids, eh? Funny how my room looks exactly the same! Was it carried back with me? Yes, that makes sense, in the same way that moulds are carried forwards in time with their host cheese. Well now, I suggest we step out to explore the jungle."

He helped me dismount from the quark with several well-aimed blows. But he ensured that I took the pyramid with me, balanced on my shoulder. Then he clubbed me out of the door, down the stairs and outside. I shall confess to feelings of disappointment at this juncture. I'd expected all sorts of extinct beasts, mammoths and smilodons and readers, but nothing much was different. There were streets and buildings and people, and the President's tower in the distance, outside the city. It was identical to the present! What a pity! I turned to my new companion to comment on the coincidence, but he replied with a savage blow to my neck. I tripped and winced. Clearly the entire world had travelled back with me, overlapping the past, so that prehistory was now no different from my own era. Maybe this was the reason for his temper?

"Ug! Ug! Ug! Hrungh! Ughsagh!"

"I'm going as quick as I can! Patience, you autochthonic bully! The President will have much to say about this, when I complain to him. Just wait to see whose side he'll take!"

This statement caused Ug to snigger.

It soon became apparent that we were travelling to the tower of our absolute leader. As we passed under the main gates of the city, out into the barren countryside, Ug started hitting me with regular strokes and I dropped the quark. He roared in fury at this, beating my knees until the pyramid was restored to its place on my shoulder. I leaped the remainder of the distance, thanks to the club's propellant power and we gained the bright cylinder within an hour. The door was open and I entered. But the President was not at home. I called for him, but there was no reply. Was he visiting his wife at the Pallid Colonnades? Almost certainly not! The only option was that he was hiding.

This was true, but not as I had imagined it. With a cruel laugh, Ug stood up straight, dropped his weapon, cast off his mask and wig, ripped open his pelt and angled his nose to reveal—the President himself! He had been in disguise all the while!

"Are you really my first ancestor?" I groaned.

"Don't be silly, Titian. It was a ruse to summon you here. I didn't want you escaping into the chronoflow yet. Something else has come up. I need you to solve a serious crime."

He led me up to the roof-garden and showed me the other towers. The sight was overwhelming and I lurched, though this might have been due to my wounds. I grasped the President.

"They are buildings from a number of parallel dimensions which have collapsed into one point," he said.

"Obviously so. You must declare them illegal!"

"No, I suggest that the actual dimensions be outlawed. They must be locked inside each other. But we need a key able to turn the tumblers of time and space. That's why I insisted you bring the pyramid with you. It is a quark and thus will serve to fasten the rogue space-time continuums which have tumbled open into ours."

"But it can't be shaped into a key!"

"In that case the lock must be made to fit it, instead of the other way round. When these rival realities are all safely incarcerated within themselves, the key can be swallowed. No that's impossible. It's too big and won't be chewed or digested . . . "

"Maybe the lock can be eaten!" I responded.

"Yes, if made of some edible substance. Here's a block of cheese. I was keeping it for a special occasion. Carve a lock out of it which will be an exact fit for the pyramid! Then insert the quark and turn it seven times. Each time you turn it, one of the dimensions will be locked up in the one in front of it. The final turn will fasten those rival realities inside ours. All to serve the law."

"Best with a tawny port and olives."

But it was worth a try. I took the cheese, scooped a pyramidal hole and sprinkled the resultant crumbs over the few carnivorous blooms which still gossiped at our heels. They had dined on rare flies and so were in a grand mood for dessert. Feathery tongues licked ultraviolet lips. When the lock was finished, I positioned it on the railings and pointed it at the furthest tower. Then I inserted the green quark and rotated it once. The fit was perfect and I heard the tumblers of a whole universe clatter in response, and a cosmic bolt slide into place somewhere in space-time, a sound pithier than wedding-peals.

The effect was instantaneous and amazing. The target tower, and the dimension to which it belonged, grew darker, as if a door was closing on it, and vanished! It had been locked up in the dimension in front of it. Then I pointed the cheese at this dimension and rotated the quark again. This universe also disappeared, secured inside the one in front. Another turn, another captive! Justice on a macroscopic scale! A fourth, a fifth and a sixth! Now there was a solitary illegal reality to contend with. I resisted the temptation to regard it as the ringleader (the rogue towers hadn't converged symmetrically, or they would have formed an octagon and troublemaker nodes from my position may have existed next to each other, not in front or behind). I dabbed my forehead with a sleeve, feeling the heat of a pasteurised responsibility.

The President gritted his molars. "One more turn! Let them have it, Titian! The soft-cheese-softly approach is maturing! Get those elsewhere cheats off our teleological patch."

I rotated the quark a final time. The seven deviant dimensions were now in jail, locked within the walls of our own. Best place for them! No need for a trial, because you can't prosecute the undetectable, and even cosmic rays won't hop between alternative presents which are sealed. The rascals only existed in theory now, which is the way it ought to be, and when we got round to arresting their textbook sympathisers, in libraries and colleges, even that luxury would be denied them. No geometry volume, however crisp, was going to keep a Non-Euclidian vigil for this pack, if I had my way, or even if it had me.

Now it was time to destroy the lock, to prevent any mischief-makers from releasing them. I removed the pyramid and elevated the cheese to my mouth, but it was too big to be consumed by just one man, even an unjust one. The President refused to help me. He'd already had lunch. There was enough for eight gourmets, without crackers, and I resigned myself to an evening of pure greed, something to compare with the legendary feasts of the Unbearable Supper Wars, when an entire continent was devoured by the state which sat on it (an event often held to mark the end of the Yellow Dynasty and rise of the Green, but rarely held in any other sense due to shortages of spare edible geology.) Try bolting food when it has already bolted seven of your extra bellies!

As if this notion had called for assistance, I heard a clatter from the ground floor and hurried down the stairs to see what the matter was. The President stayed on the balcony, enjoying his triumph. To my relief, I found a table spread for a party, with seven occupants in eight chairs surrounding it, waiting for me to appear. They cheered and rattled their knives against their plates. I laid the lock in the centre of the table, took the empty chair and helped to carve the cheese into equal wedges. A glad snack followed, washed down with hare's-breath wine, a vintage ear. When finished, I dabbed at my lips and belched. It was during the moment of mild awkwardness which comes in the wake of most communal feasts that I appreciated my mistake. My dining-companions were me! The other Titian Grundys from the rival towers! Why had I not noticed? Possibly because I am so *proud* that anything I do is tainted with this quality. Thus I look at the obvious in *vain*, missing it.

Now one of the Grundys spoke: "A fitting start to our negotiations, for we have decided to act in a curdled, I mean mature, fashion, and the cheese was a witty symbol of that."

"Negotiations?" I cried. "What do you mean?"

Another Grundy explained: "Instead of trying to devise malignant or traitorous methods of outwitting each other, we conclude it is better to band together to cure our problem. After all, we're in the same trouble. It was Titian here, that one, not him, who had the courage to depart his tower and visit Titian there, on your right, to suggest a truce. So they called on Titian, opposite you, and the three of them raced on to try to persuade Titian, at the far end, to join up. It worked and he aided them to win over Titian, on your left, plus Titian. Then they set off to work on the seventh Titian, who was me."

"I see their labours were productive. Now you've come round to talk me into also shelving hostilities?"

"We don't preach peace, but redirected brutality. We have assembled here to plan a rebellion, for it's the President who has always been the major source of bother for us, the sharpest thorn in our joy's sideshow. No longer! We intend to kick him out of government and take over! That's what this conference is about. Each of us has contributed one facet of a geminous putsch and when they're combined, a fresh era will dawn, though probably not in the east, unless we go there on vacation, for it will be wherever we are. The first Titian brought the napkins, the second hurled in the knives, the third the wine, fourth and fifth added the plates and table. The sixth donated the chairs. Successful insurrections are always plotted over lunch. Otherwise they never come to pass. You have provided the location—this actual tower!"

"No, I supplied the meal. Incredibly, it wasn't a simple cheese but a transdimensional lock. You don't know what you've done! You're trapped in my dimension forever, beyond your own presents! More to the point, we now outnumber the President, who is upstairs alone, and so can usurp him without excessive risk. Follow me!"

I stood as fast as my digestion permitted and prepared to scurry up to the balcony, keen to storm the doldrums of my human condition, namely the ruler who had wounded me as only a friend might. I was suffused with a weird delight, a brute, raw, peeled exultation that had been festering under my stable exterior for the greater part of my whole life. To crush the President and his whimsical decrees! To inaugurate a new republic, a Dynasty of Prefects, an octagonal oligarchy! But before my happiness had a chance to familiarise itself with my mind, testing all the corners and lobes, raiding the larder for subconscious impulses, the eloquent Grundy who had last spoken rose and cried:

"Wait! I'm the seventh Titian and you haven't yet heard what I have contributed to the coup! I didn't realise the other dimensions were shut away and I presumed we had to have something tangible to scheme against, so I brought the other Presidents!"

I paused with my foot on the bottom stair. Just then the President, my version, came bounding down, excited and frothing. He had leaned over the rail of his balcony and observed seven alternative hims loitering at his gate, juggling all sorts of inconsequential stuff to waste the time, including ridiculous plot devices and strained effects. He asked if they had escaped from jail already, and I nodded, too apprehensive to explain that they'd never even been incarcerated. He went out to learn the truth and it was patent the rebellion was over before it had begun. Presidents and Prefects to the tune, spume, fume of eight apiece, but only a single dimension! I was back where I'd started, in a multiple singularity, with one last chance to rescue the coup.

"Do we slay tyranny or not, comrades?"

Seven Grundys shuffled uneasily. The collective nerve had gone. The fault was my own, for I had framed the question poorly, making it appear like a call to suicide. Before I could amend my meaning, the eight rival Presidents entered the tower, led by mine, each finding the Grundy which belonged to him and setting about his head and body with whatever hadn't been dropped in the juggling display. I received a fistful of air on the chin, and the increase in atmospheric pressure around that projection, a cataclysmic event in facial history, spattered the surface with dimples. The entire collapse of my face seemed imminent, for these craters joined together, dropped to the bone and commenced to drag me in after them. To be sucked inside-out by one's own compressed jut! Then I grasped why the various Presidents were so furious.

For a dungeon in a prison is any locked volume. That's the official definition and it has naught to do with size. A cell's *dimensions* can be those of an entire *dimension*, in parallel, and still be an enclosure for captives. And what enters a prison other than felons and their visitors? Precious little, I can tell you! The President was quicker to comprehend the facts than I. When he saw his doubles, he realised he was within the slammer, not outside it, for they had stood in single file to greet him, and it is files which are generally smuggled into jails, often in cakes, sometimes in postures. I had locked our existence inside the others, and our sentence was interminable, unlike this one, which now staggers to an end at the same time that my consciousness slips under the will of boots and knuckles. Soon I hope to be lost in the bowels of the system, nearer the old days end of my span. There was purpose and sense then. It roamed free at times. Else I may take the less noble, shoelace route out of the frustrations of this confined hole.

Because this universe simply isn't big enough for both, both, both, both, both, both, both, both of us!

Printed in the United Kingdom
by Lightning Source UK Ltd.
118915UK00001B/58